SONGBIRDS OF SEDONA

LISE GOLD

The beautiful journey of today can only begin when we learn to let go of yesterday.

— STEVE MARABOLI

1

GEMMA

I deserve to be here. That's what I keep telling myself when things get tough, and today is a tough day. *I took a life. I deserve this.*

I'm reading the card that arrived in the mail this morning, fighting the wave of emotions that always comes with any contact from the outside world.

"Happy Birthday, honey," the card reads. *"I wish you would let me visit today. Just know that I'm thinking of you. Hang in there. Not long to go now. Love always, Mom."*

I feel tears prick at the corners of my eyes, but I blink them away. Crying is a weakness I can't afford to show here, so I've learned to keep my emotions locked away. It's the only way to survive.

I appreciate my mother's words, but they also sting. *Not long to go now.* It's bittersweet. Even a day in this place feels like an eternity, and now another year has passed. Another year wasted.

The buzzer sounds with an ear-piercing screech, jolting me out of my bunk. It's lunchtime at Perryville Prison. I put away the card, rub my eyes, and pull on my navy blue scrubs and white slip-on shoes. The fabric is coarse and worn thin from too many washes. My cellie Tonya is snoring softly on the bottom bunk, and I nudge her awake before I shuffle out into the concrete hallway already swarming with inmates.

I join the throng of women in blue flowing toward the cafeteria, careful to keep my distance and eyes fixed straight ahead. You learn fast in here not to make eye contact unless you're looking for trouble. The noise builds as we march through the double doors into the massive, high-ceilinged dining hall. Fluorescent lights buzz overhead, glinting off the stainless steel tables bolted to the floor in uniform rows.

I grab a red plastic tray from the stack and get in line, inching slowly forward as the kitchen workers, inmates themselves in white aprons and hairnets, slop food onto each tray. Today's lunch is a cold bologna sandwich, potato chips, beans, a bruised apple, and Bug Juice, the overly sweet red drink that claims to be "fruit punch." My stomach protests, but I've learned to choke this stuff down.

Tray in hand, I scan the cafeteria for a safe place to sit. Perryville is worse than Lumley Max where I spent the last six years before being transferred here a year and a half ago. At least in Lumley, I had the protective walls of my private cell twenty-one hours a day. I only had to deal with other inmates during chow time and rec hour in the yard.

Here in Perryville, a medium-security prison, there's a lot more "freedom." Our cells are left unlocked most of the day so we can access the day room with its worn couches and staticky TV. We can sign up for classes and job assignments to earn time off our sentences. But with the additional privileges comes more risk. More time to interact with unpredictable inmates and end up in fights that could send me to the hole or get more time tacked onto my sentence. I've seen it happen and I'm determined to keep my head down. I've got six weeks left on my ninety-two-month sentence and I'm not going to blow it now.

I finally spot an empty table in the corner, far away from the cackling cluster of Norteñas gang members holding court near the cafeteria entrance. I keep my back to the wall as I sit down, always vigilant. My eyes dart from table to table, marking potential threats. You never really relax in prison.

There's the cadre of meth heads with their pockmarked faces and jittery fingers drumming the tables, twitching for their next fix. They're mostly in for drug offenses, burglary, identity theft—the things addicts do to get money for that next hit. I steer clear of them and their drama.

Then there's the OG lifers, mostly in their forties and fifties, in for violent crimes. They look hard, joyless, their faces etched from decades behind bars. But they keep to themselves unless you cross them. I give them a wide berth.

At the next table over is a group of young women, barely eighteen. The detention officers call them "babies." They're pretty, with their long hair and thick eyeliner. They're giggling and throwing food at each other. They haven't been in long enough for this place to grind them down.

A tray clatters down across from me and I nearly jump out of my skin before I register it's just my cellie, Tonya. She grins, flashing the gold front tooth I've never asked about.

"Gemma. Damn, girl, you look more uptight than usual today," Tonya says, digging into her bologna sandwich.

"Just counting down."

"Eyes on the prize," she says. "And then what?"

"I haven't figured that part out yet," I mutter. "I suppose I'll have to move in with Mom until I find a job." The thought alone exhausts me. Not because I don't want to work, but it's no secret how hard it is to find a job with a conviction. Especially one as serious as mine.

"Same," she says. "I'm moving in with my cousin to look after her children while she's at work and I might look for a job in a coffee shop since I'm a certified barista now."

"You finished your training? Congratulations."

"Yeah. Just in time. I figured I'd need something to fall back on." She regards me. "Are you going back into real estate?"

"No chance. No company would hire me, but I'm hoping to find a job as an electrician."

Tonya chuckles. "Oh yeah, I forgot you got your degree."

"Why is that so funny?" I ask, arching a brow at her.

"I don't know. It's just..." Tonya looks me up and down. "You look nothing like an electrician. I'd peg you for a beautician with your long hair and flawless skin."

I shrug. "The course gave me something to do, but again, it's unlikely someone will hire me, so I might start my own business and hope for the best."

"You'll get there," she says. "We both will."

Tonya's been somewhat of a friend to me since I transferred to Perryville, as much as you can have friends in here. More of an ally. Someone to watch your back. We keep each other sane, make sure neither of us catches a disciplinary case that will delay our release. She's short-timing it too and will be out a few weeks after me.

We eat quickly, talking through mouthfuls. In prison, you learn to devour your food before someone bigger and hungrier comes and takes it from you. Mealtimes are when trouble starts, as the chow hall is one of the few places where rival gang members can get within striking distance of each other. The detention officers patrol the aisles, but things happen fast. Trays start flying, and if you're not careful, you can catch a blindside blow to the head and wake up in the infirmary.

I keep my head on a swivel as I force the food down. The trick is to look aware without looking scared. Here, fear is like blood in the water; it draws the sharks. You have to armor yourself in a hardened facade, even if you're quaking inside.

"This is gross," I say, scraping the last of the beans from my tray when a commotion breaks out across the cafeteria. An alarm blares and a swarm of detention officers sprint toward a heap of flailing limbs and guttural screams on the floor.

Tonya looks up. "What's going on?" Two women are ripping into each other, blood spattering the white tiles. I can't make out who they are before the guards wrench them apart and haul them off, still kicking and cursing.

The alarm shuts off and a deafening silence follows. Every eye follows the guards as they march the two prisoners out, each held firmly by an arm. The rest of us keep our eyes down and mechanically continue eating as if nothing happened.

A few minutes later, the guards bark at us to line up and clear out. I bus my tray and take my place in line. I was hopeful when I first got transferred here. I thought things would be better, easier. Now I know there's no such thing as an easy prison bid. You just trade one set of dangers for another.

2

LORI

*T*he tires crunch on the gravel driveway as I pull up to the farmhouse, dust billowing in my wake. I cut the engine and for a moment, I sit in silence, staring at the property that is now mine.

My friend Charlotte gets out of her car behind me and I follow suit.

"It looks just like I remember, only a bit more weathered. And bigger," I say, trying to inject some optimism into my voice. "My new home."

Charlotte peers at the farmhouse through oversize shades, her glossy black ponytail swishing as she cocks her head. "It's got potential, Lor. A little TLC and this place could be gorgeous."

"I'm not so sure about the 'little' part." I bite my lip as I study the peeling white paint and sagging porch. When Aunt Maggie left me her farmhouse and orchard in her will, I had visions of living in a quaint, idyllic hideaway. A place to start fresh after leaving my controlling ex and quitting my soul-sucking corporate job. Confronted with the reality, I feel a swell of doubts. I haven't been here in thirty years, and I've clearly romanticized it in my head.

With a fortifying breath, I head to Rosefield Farm with Charlotte on my heel. We follow the overgrown path to the front porch, and I fumble with the unfamiliar keys before finding the one that fits the rusted lock. The door creaks open, revealing a dim interior that smells of dust and neglect.

"Oh..." Charlotte winces as she peers in. "How long has it been empty?"

"A year," I say. "Aunt Maggie got sick and had to go to a home. She didn't have kids or close family apart from my mother, so no one's been here since. I didn't even know she'd passed away until I got the call a few months ago."

I step inside, my footsteps echoing on the hardwood floors. Faded floral wallpaper peels above the chair rails. A layer of dust coats every surface like a shroud. Charlotte moves past me, her heels clicking decisively as she throws open the heavy brocade curtains, sending dust motes dancing into the sudden flood of light.

"These windows are amazing," she says, gesturing to the ceiling-height casements that overlook the orchards. "You've got a killer view."

I join her at the window, taking in the neat rows of trees across the landscape, the red rocks of Sedona rising behind them in the distance. It looks like a postcard, but all I can think about is how much work those hundreds of trees must need.

"I don't know the first thing about growing fruit," I admit, my voice small. "What if I kill the trees? They're probably dead already. No one's been taking care of them."

Charlotte spins to face me, hands on her hips. "They

don't look dead to me, and you're not going to kill anything. How hard can it be?"

I raise an eyebrow. "Harder than being an attorney, I'm guessing. At least for me."

"You hated that job," Charlotte reminds me. "This is your chance for a totally different life, so just sit back and let nature do its thing."

I wish I had Charlotte's breezy confidence. But then, she's not the one who just staked her entire future on a farm she knows nothing about.

We continue our exploration, moving from room to room. The kitchen looks like a time capsule from the 1970s with its mint-green refrigerator and Formica countertops edged in chrome. I open the oven and a family of mice skitters out, making Charlotte and me yelp and jump back.

"Okay, so it needs some updating," Charlotte says, warily eyeing the dark recess of the oven.

That's an understatement. The linoleum floor is gummy with decades of grime. The sink is stained with rust, and I don't even want to think about what the bathroom looks like.

We drift back into the living room with its hulking stone fireplace. I run my hand along the mantelpiece, raising a layer of dust. Above the mantel, a large painting depicts the farm in its prime—rows of trees heavy with apples, peaches, and pears, and a golden sun hanging low over the hills.

"I was eight last time I visited Aunt Maggie and Uncle Frank. They were so proud of their farm."

"What happened?" Charlotte asks. "Why did you lose contact?"

"My mom had a fight with Aunt Maggie. It must have been a serious one because she broke off all contact, and with that, I lost contact with them too. I could have visited later, when I was older, but by then, I felt so far removed from them that I never did." I sigh. "I feel guilty about that now."

"But they didn't try to contact you either, right?" Charlotte squeezes my shoulder. "Whatever happened. Maggie wanted you to have the farm, so you must have had a special place in her heart."

"She didn't have much choice," I mumble. "Apart from Mom, she didn't have any other living family members." I blow out my cheeks as I tally the repairs—the outdated electrical work, the stained walls, the chipped paint around the windows. Not to mention all the work the orchards likely need. New trees planted, old ones pruned. And what about irrigation? Pest control? Harvesting? My head spins with all the unknowns.

I sink onto the sofa, sending up a puff of mustiness. "I'm in over my head, Char. I thought I'd have enough savings to fix the place up, but this is beyond a cosmetic update. The plumbing, the electric...it's too much."

Charlotte plops down beside me, nudging me with her shoulder. "Hey. You're doing something really brave, you know that?" She looks me square in the eye, her expression earnest. "And you're not alone in this. I'm here. I'll help however I can. We'll rally the troops and throw a painting party. We'll hit up yard sales for furniture. Poco a poco, right? You've got this. And it's clear you can't sleep here tonight. Not until we've done a thorough clean, so you can stay with me until it's a little more livable."

"Thanks, Char. I honestly don't know what I'd do without you."

"Let's hope you never have to find out," she says, flashing me a cheeky grin. She hops to her feet, offering me her hands. "Now, let's see what kind of treasures Aunt Maggie left upstairs. I'm feeling vintage chic decor vibes."

Laughing despite myself, I let her pull me up. She threads her arm through mine as we climb the creaky stairs. The whole house seems to exhale, as if it's been holding its breath for a long time. I know the feeling.

As I open the curtains in the master bedroom, dust swirls in the slants of light from the grimy dormer windows. The bed is made up and a hairbrush lies on a dressing table. The sight makes me sad, so I turn my attention to the wardrobe where I find Aunt Maggie's clothes. "It looks like most of her stuff is still here. I think she was expecting to return to the farm."

"Poor Maggie." Charlotte flicks through the garments. "She had some nice clothes. You could definitely sell these online." She puts on a silk dressing gown and strikes a pose. "I'll be your model."

"I might have to take you up on that offer," I say. I sold a ton of stuff when I moved out of my ex's apartment in Prescott. I wanted to start fresh with as little clutter as possible, but now I've inherited ten times more. "Let's check out the other rooms." I pull Charlotte along, and she sneezes explosively as we enter another bedroom, the sound muffled by the insulating press of old clothes, stacked paintings, and shrouded furniture. It's like an antique store exploded in here.

"Looks like Maggie had a hoarding room." She rubs her hands together. "Let's get to rummaging!"

For the next hour, we pick through Aunt Maggie's belongings, unearthing a rusty birdcage, a gilt-edged mirror, a chipped enamel bread box. Charlotte dives into a trunk of clothes, emerging with a faded calico dress and straw sun hat.

"Oh my God, Lor!" She pulls the dress over my tank top and shimmies it over my shorts. "It's straight out of *Little House on the Prairie*! This is so your farm-girl aesthetic!" She plops the sun hat on my head at a jaunty angle before stepping back to assess the effect. "Yep, it's official. Farmer Lori is in the house! Those chickens won't know what hit 'em!"

"There are no chickens," I remind her, laughing as I straighten the hat. "It's a fruit farm, remember? And I think you're more farm-girl chic than I am."

She purses her lips. "You know what? I could totally rock the gingham and clogs."

We dissolve into giggles just as her phone chimes from her back pocket. She wrestles it out and glances at the screen, her grin fading.

"It's work. Some emergency with the Barton account." She heaves a sigh. "I'm sorry, Lor. I have to deal with this."

A pang of guilt twists in my stomach. Here I am, running off to play farmer while Charlotte picks up my slack at the office.

"Hey," she says, reading my expression. "I'm thrilled to cover for you, and a new guy is starting next week so things should calm down." She pulls me into a hug that smells of L'Occitane. "You've got this," she murmurs in my ear. "Poco a poco, remember?"

We head back downstairs and out into the afternoon sun. The orchard shimmers in the heat, the leaves on the apple and peach trees trembling like a mirage. Cicadas drone in the brush, and the air smells of baked earth and the slightly fermenting tang of fallen fruit.

Charlotte pauses beside her sleek Audi parked behind my sensible Corolla. Her oversize sunglasses are back in place, but I can still see the concern pinching her brow.

"You sure you're going to be okay out here today?"

"Yeah. I'll be fine," I say, glancing at my car that's packed to the brim. "I'll unload and drive back and forth to the storage a few times. I want to get that out of the way first."

"Sure. Well, you have my key, so just let yourself in," Charlotte chimes before waving me off. "I'll see you later."

She drives off and then it's just me. Just me and rows upon rows of trees and a ramshackle house full of ghosts and dust. I take a deep breath, the hot, dry air searing my lungs. I have no idea what I'm doing. No idea if I can actually pull this off. I left a successful career for an unknown life, and I don't even know where to start. *Poco a poco*, I remind myself, and open the trunk to my car.

3
_____

GEMMA

*T*he sun beats down mercilessly as Tonya and I walk slow laps around the yard. The recreation area is a stretch of flagstones hemmed in by towering razor-wire fences that glint menacingly in the harsh Arizona light. There's a handful of metal picnic tables bolted to the ground, their surfaces hot enough to blister skin, and a few withered patches of grass that crunch beneath our feet.

Despite the oppressive heat and the watchful eyes of the guards, I cherish this small slice of outdoor time. After so many years, the bleak yard feels like a gift, a tiny taste of freedom.

Tonya fans herself with her hand, her dark skin gleaming with sweat. "Girl, it's hotter than Satan's armpit out here."

I nod in agreement, wiping my brow with the back of my hand. It's rare to have a heatwave so early on in the year, and the air shimmers, distorting the figures of the other inmates trudging around the yard.

We keep walking, hugging the perimeter. Yard time is when all the prison politics play out, when scores get settled, deals get done, and pecking orders get reinforced. I've seen fights break out in a blink, and although Tonya and I do our best to steer clear, sometimes trouble finds you whether you're looking for it or not.

Case in point—the new girl, a beefy redhead with sleeve tattoos and a hardened stare, is headed straight for us. She's been throwing her weight around since she got here last week, trying to assert herself as top dog.

I tense as she approaches, my footsteps faltering. Tonya shoots me a warning look. "Eyes forward. Keep walking."

But the new girl has other ideas. She veers into our path at the last second, her shoulder slamming into mine with enough force to bruise. I stumble, biting back a yelp of pain.

Tonya catches my arm, steadying me. She glares at the new girl's retreating back. "Bitch," she mutters under her breath.

I rub my throbbing shoulder, my heart hammering against my ribs. A part of me wants to whirl around and confront her, to show her I'm not some pushover, but I force myself to keep walking. I can't afford to catch a case, not now when I'm so close to the door.

"Just ignore her," I mutter. "We'll be out soon. She's not worth it."

Tonya shakes her head. "Damn straight. I can't wait to walk freely without bitches like her making me look over my shoulder twenty-four seven." She sighs. "What's the first thing you're going to do when you get out?"

"Hmm..." I smile. "You first."

A slow grin spreads across Tonya's face. "Fried chicken," she says matter-of-factly. "A whole bucket, extra crispy. And then I'm going to find me a man and ride him like a buckin' bronco."

I snort with laughter, picturing Tonya tearing into a

drumstick, grease dripping down her chin while ogling men. "Food and sex, huh? You've thought about this."

"Of course. Haven't you?" She waggles her eyebrows. "Hey, a girl's got needs! Two years is a long time."

I can't argue with that. My time inside has felt like an eternity, and the ache of loneliness is a constant companion, as familiar as the scratchy sheets on my bunk.

Tonya nudges me with her elbow. "Your turn. What's top of your list?"

I tilt my face toward the cloudless sky, squinting against the brutal glare of the sun. "Being outdoors. Like really outdoors, not just this cage. Feeling grass under my bare feet. Watching a sunset."

"Mm-hmm. And what else?"

"A long, hot shower in a bathroom with a door that locks and my favorite shampoo and shower gel. And no one timing me or yelling at me to hurry up."

Tonya makes a low sound of agreement. "Amen to that. I'm going to soak in a Jacuzzi till I turn into a prune. I've just gotta find me a man who has one," she jokes.

We walk in silence for a bit, both lost in visions of the luxuries we once took for granted.

Then Tonya gives me a sly look. "You didn't mention sex. Or dating."

I keep my eyes fixed on the sky, my jaw tight. "Nah. I think I'm done with all that. Relationships. Love. It's brought me nothing but trouble."

"Men can be dicks," she says.

"So can women."

Tonya frowns. "What? You're gay?"

"Yeah. Is that so surprising?" Now that I'm close to getting out, I don't care if she knows, and I don't think she'll tell anyone.

"Kind of. You look so straight. Like I said, I pegged you for a beautician."

I can feel Tonya's gaze boring into the side of my face, curious and intrigued. I don't talk much about my life before Perryville, about what landed me here. Most people assume it was drugs. I've never corrected them.

I don't tell Tonya how I fell for a woman with a smile like the devil and a temper like a volcano. How she could make me feel like the center of the universe one minute and a worthless piece of shit the next. How I thought I could fix her, change her, how I kept forgiving and forgetting, just like my mother used to. Until I became a ticking time bomb of anxiety. I don't tell her about my mother's abusive boyfriend, that last night when my anxiety got the better of me and my world blacked out. When I caught him attacking my mother, when I hit him over the head with the first thing in sight. When the world turned red and wet and my future shattered in a single, irrevocable instant. I don't tell her what I'm capable of.

"I miss pizza too," I say instead, changing the subject. "And wine."

"I'm with you on the pizza," Tonya says. "But I'm done with drinking. Like women for you, alcohol has done me no favors, and I'm going to be a better person. Third time lucky."

"Third time?" Her comment makes me realize how little we know about each other. I always assumed it was her first time in prison; our conversations have never been that personal until now, until the end was in sight. "I didn't know."

"Yeah, there's a lot we don't know about each other. I've been around. Done bad stuff. Not bad-bad though," she corrects herself. "It's not like I killed anyone." I flinch, but she doesn't notice. "Do you think we'll see each other when we're out?"

"I hope so," I say honestly, because Tonya is the closest thing I've had to a friend in the past seven years and six months. Before I did what I did, I—a squeaky-clean realtor —would never have exchanged a word with someone like Tonya—a streetwise serial offender. But in here, in the confines of these concrete walls, we're all the same. Names reduced to numbers etched on uniforms. The lives we once led, the identities we claimed, stripped away like layers of weathered paint.

I always believed I was different. I navigated a world of manicured lawns and polite chitchat, my growing pain and anxiety hidden beneath a smile. I looked at the faces of the condemned on the evening news and thought, *That could never be me.*

But I'm no different. Prison has a way of distilling us down to our rawest elements. Here, there is no pretense, no artifice. The labels that defined us on the outside—mother, daughter, wife, criminal—fade away, leaving only the essential truth of our humanity.

"How about ice cream?" Tonya asks, unaware of my mental reflection. "We could meet up and get ice cream together. What's your favorite flavor?"

Before I can respond, a sharp whistle cuts through the shimmering air. "Yard time's over, ladies! Line up for count!"

Tonya and I exchange a rueful look before falling into line with the other inmates. As we wait to be ushered back into the bowels of Perryville, I stare out at the sky over the razor wire.

I'll walk out of here soon. I'll step into the blinding Arizona sun a free woman. But a part of me will always be imprisoned by the choices that brought me here. By the things I've done that I can never undo.

The heavy metal door clangs shut behind us as we shuffle back inside, and the AC hits my sweat-slicked skin, raising goose bumps on my arms. My armpits and back are sweaty, and my shrubs will smell as soon as the synthetic fabric dries. I'm dying for a shower but I have to wait another four hours to scrub off the remnants of the day so I can feel clean again. A deeper part of me knows better, though. Knows that some stains never come out, no matter how hard you scrub.

4

LORI

I set down the rag I've been using to wipe down the ancient Formica countertops and peer out the window when I hear a car pulling up. It's Charlotte, which is no surprise, but I see she's not alone.

Wiping my hands on my jeans, I head out to the porch, the screen door slamming behind me. Charlotte unfolds herself from the driver's seat, all long legs and drama while a woman with close-cropped hair, jeans, and a navy T-shirt emerges from the passenger side, her sharp gaze taking in the surroundings.

"Lori!" Charlotte yells, waving enthusiastically. "You won't believe this. I've got the solution to all your problems!"

I raise a brow, glancing between her and the mystery woman. "I'm pretty sure I've heard that before," I joke, referring to the countless times she got me in trouble with all the best intentions.

Charlotte laughs, bounding up the porch steps to engulf me in a hug. "Always the skeptic. But hear me out, okay?" She steps back, gesturing to the woman, who has followed her at a more sedate pace. "This is Miranda Alvarez. She's a parole officer and she runs this amazing program that pairs ex-cons with small businesses for rehabilitation and job training."

I feel my guard go up instantly. *Ex-cons? On my farm?* But I paste on a polite smile as Miranda reaches the top step, extending a hand for me to shake.

"It's a pleasure to meet you, Lori," she says, her voice warm but businesslike. "Charlotte's told me about your situation out here."

I shoot Charlotte a look, but she shrugs innocently. I turn back to Miranda, trying to keep the wariness out of my voice. "It's nice to meet you too. Can I get you a drink? Coffee? Tea? A beer?"

"Oh, I'd love a beer," Charlotte says, and Miranda nods too.

I lead them over to the now-clean wicker chairs I've arranged on the porch, trying not to wince as they creak under their weight. I've spent the better part of the week cleaning the house from top to bottom, airing out the musty rooms and scouring away decades of grime. But there's only so much I can do with the mismatched, outdated furniture that came with the place.

"I like what you've done here," Charlotte says, raising her voice as I slip inside to get us beers. "It's got a kind of retro charm, now that it's not buried under inches of dust."

I snort as I hand them a beer and a glass. "Retro. That's a kind word for it." I nod toward the shiny new laptop perched on the rickety card table I've set up as a temporary desk outside. "My new Wi-Fi router looks completely out of place amid all this seventies decor."

"At least you've got your priorities straight," Charlotte says. "Netflix is a necessity."

I roll my eyes and laugh. Trust Charlotte to find the silver lining. "So how do you guys know each other?"

"Miranda and I dated," Charlotte says, raising her bottle in a toast before she takes a long drink. For someone as polished as her, she does drink like a man, and that always amuses me.

"Oh?" My gaze switches between her and Miranda. I don't recall her ever mentioning a Miranda, but then Charlotte dates a lot, and I can't always keep up with her latest conquests. "And you're friends now?"

"Yeah. Something like that," Miranda says, shooting Charlotte a wink. "We still meet up on a more intimate level from time to time. We get along." She clears her throat and leans in, steadying her elbows on her thighs. "Anyway, Charlotte and I met up last night, and after she told me about your farm, I think I have a proposition that might be of interest to you."

I can see what's happened here. I stayed with Charlotte for two weeks until I moved in here last night. She was obviously desperate for some action and called on one of her "special friends" the moment I left. But I appreciate that she's trying to help, so I shoot Miranda a wide smile. "I'm all ears."

"Great. So, about the program," she begins, regarding me. "We work with nonviolent offenders who we carefully screen nearing the end of their sentences. They have to meet strict criteria to be eligible for placement. It's difficult to find work with a record, so we help them by matching them up with small businesses who can house them and help them get their feet back on the ground. In return, they temporarily work for a low fee, so everyone wins."

I chew my lip, considering. "But how can you be sure they're rehabilitated? That they're not a danger?"

23

"Look, I'll be completely honest with you. We can never be one hundred percent certain, of course. But these individuals have undergone extensive counseling, job training, and behavioral assessments. They're highly motivated to succeed and build new lives for themselves." She pauses while I let that sink in. "I understand your hesitation. It's a big decision to invite someone into your home, especially someone with a criminal record. But I truly believe this program can be a win-win. You'll have the help you need to get the farm up and running, and they get a chance to gain valuable work experience and a supportive living environment."

"Okay...do you have anyone in the program who knows about fruit farming?" I ask.

Miranda shrugs. "That's unlikely, but we have hard workers who aren't afraid to get their hands dirty. And you can select them on the skill sets they've either acquired during their time in prison or before. We have certified plumbers, electricians, builders, hairdressers, beauticians, baristas—you name it."

"I know it sounds a little out there, Lor," Charlotte says, her expression uncharacteristically serious. "But this program has a really impressive track record. The recidivism rate for participants is way lower than the national average."

I absorb this, turning it over in my mind. Having an extra set of hands, even inexperienced ones, could make a world of difference, but an ex-convict? "What about liability? What if they get injured on the job or...or steal from me?"

Miranda nods, unfazed. "All participants are covered under the program's insurance policy for work-related injuries. And theft is grounds for immediate removal from the program and re-incarceration. It's a risk, but a calculated one. If it makes you more comfortable, we can limit your options to female participants. Some female hosts find that preferential, especially in a live-in situation." She smiles. "Anyway, I'm not here to pressure you. I just wanted to leave you with our information pack so you can take your time to read it through and think about it."

I nod as I take the file she hands me. My gaze drifts out over the orchard, the vast stretch of trees. I'm close to panicking every time I look at them.

Charlotte reaches over and squeezes my hand. "You've got such a big heart, Lori. I know it's scary, but think of the difference you could make in someone's life. The difference they could make in yours."

I turn back to Miranda, meeting her patient gaze. "Okay," I say. "Tell me more about how this would work and I'll think about it."

A smile spreads across Miranda's face as she leans back in her chair, crossing her legs at the ankle. "Absolutely. Let's talk details."

5

GEMMA

The guard's hand is firm on my elbow as she steers me down the echoing corridor, the rubber soles of our shoes squeaking against the polished concrete. My heart hammers in a dizzying mix of anticipation and anxiety. A visitor. I rack my brain, trying to imagine who it could be. My mother? I told her not to come anymore, and the thought of seeing her makes my stomach clench.

We reach the visitation room and the guard ushers me inside with a nod. The room is large and rectangular, with rows of tables, each flanked by two plastic chairs. Vending machines hum along one wall, offering a meager selection of snacks and soft drinks. The air is heavy with the mingled scents of industrial cleaner and stale sweat.

I scan the room, taking in the clusters of inmates and their visitors, hunched over the tables in tense conversation. Mothers bouncing fussy babies on their knees. Girlfriends twirling their hair and laughing too loudly. Lawyers in ill-fitting suits, shuffling papers and checking their watches.

And then I see her. A woman in a crisp pantsuit, her dark hair cropped short, sitting alone at a table in the corner. She looks up as I approach, her gaze sharp and assessing. Not my mother. A stranger.

The guard gestures for me to sit, and the woman extends her hand across the table.

"Gemma? I'm Miranda Alvarez. I'll be your parole officer."

I shake her hand warily, my palm clammy against her cool, dry skin. "Nice to meet you," I say, my voice rusty from disuse. "Is this about my release?"

"Yes." Miranda smiles, her teeth very white against her tanned skin. "I wanted to have a chat with you to see where you're at. Do you have plans regarding your release? Do you have somewhere to go? Any potential job prospects? Do you know anyone who could help you get a job?"

"I can stay with my mother," I say. "It's not ideal. I haven't seen her in years and we're not close anymore, but I've spoken to her and she says I can stay on her couch for as long as I need." I shrug. "And work...I want to work, of course, but no, I don't know anyone who could help me with that. My friends distanced themselves from me after my conviction, and I only have my mother, so I don't expect it to be easy."

"I understand," Miranda says. "Well, if you need a little help once you get out, I have some good news. According to your file, you've been an exemplary inmate. There's no mention of trouble whatsoever, and with a new qualification in electrics and seven years of voluntary group therapy, you've been selected for a rehabilitation program. A work placement."

I blink, stunned. "A job? On the outside?"

She nods. "That's right. It's a fairly new initiative we've been running for a few years. We're placing eligible inmates in supportive work environments to help with the transition back into society. If you're interested, I'd love to tell you more about it."

I lean forward, my heart suddenly thrumming with a wild, desperate hope. "What kind of job?"

Miranda consults a file in front of her, her finger skimming down the page. "It's a fruit farm, actually. Just outside Sedona. They're looking for help with the harvest, general maintenance, and an overhaul on the electrics in the farmhouse. You seemed like the perfect match."

"I have a degree, but I got it in here," I say. "So I don't have any work experience on that front yet."

"That's okay. We all have to start somewhere."

A fruit farm. For a moment, I imagine it. The whisper of leaves, the sweet scent of ripe fruit, the vast expanse of open sky, no concrete in sight. It sounds like heaven, and I fix my eyes on Miranda with an intent stare. "What's the catch?"

She chuckles, shaking her head. "No catch. It's a legitimate opportunity. Room and board provided, a small stipend. A chance to build some skills and references while you get your feet back on the ground."

I nod slowly, hardly daring to believe it. "And the farm owners...they know about my record?"

Miranda hesitates, her fingers drumming lightly on the file. "The specifics of your case are confidential," she says. "Your employer will know that you're part of a rehabilitation program, but the details of your conviction won't be shared unless you choose to disclose them."

I absorb this, biting my lip. The idea of starting over, of not being defined by my worst mistake...it's dizzying. "What if they look me up? What if they find out what I did?"

Miranda leans forward, her expression softening. "Yes, they can do that, but Gemma, this is a fresh start. A chance to prove that you're more than your past. The employer has agreed to participate in this program because they believe in second chances."

I swallow hard, blinking back the sudden sting of tears. "When would I start?"

"If you like, you can move in on the day of your release. I'll personally help you get settled in. There will be regular check-ins with me, drug tests, and some ongoing counseling. But as long as you stick to the terms of your parole, this could be a real turning point."

"What about my living situation?" I ask. Two weeks. Fourteen days until I walk out of here, until I smell fresh air and feel the sun on my face. It hardly seems real.

Miranda smiles. "The farm has four bedrooms and two bathrooms. You'll have your own private bedroom and bathroom, and you'll share the kitchen and other communal spaces. The owner is a single woman. She's new to farming, and she's just getting to grips with everything herself, so she's super grateful for any help she can get. In return for room, board, and a small monthly stipend, you're required to work five hours a day, five days a week. This is our standard arrangement with employers for the first three months."

"That doesn't seem like much," I say. "Why only five hours a day?"

"It's a calculated contract. You'll find that once you get out, especially after a long sentence like yours, the smallest things can be quite overwhelming. Prison life is highly structured and regulated, which is vastly different from most work environments. Adapting to a new workplace culture, social dynamics, and expectations can be challenging and takes time. Besides that, adjusting to the autonomy and responsibility of managing your own time and making decisions can cause anxiety because you're not used to it anymore."

"Hmm...I hadn't even thought about that." I still find it hard to picture myself living a life without someone looking over my shoulder. "And what are my parole conditions?"

"I'll go over those with you in detail in our next meeting, but we haven't set a curfew or any other conditions that will limit you in any way. Needless to say, you won't be allowed to leave the country for the coming three years and two months—the remainder of your sentence. If you want to leave the state, you'll need my permission."

I feel a rush of relief so strong it makes me dizzy. "I'll do it," I say, my voice steady despite the tremor in my hands. "I want to do it."

Miranda's smile widens. "Excellent. I have a good feeling about you." She stands, extending her hand again. "I'll see you same time next week. In the meantime, stay out of trouble and start thinking about your goals for the future."

I shake her hand, feeling a flicker of something I haven't felt in a long time. Something like hope.

6

LORI

I lead Joseph Delaney, an old friend of Aunt Maggie, into the orchard. He moves slowly but steadily, his weathered hands gripping a gnarled wooden cane. His pale-blue eyes, sharp despite the wrinkles that frame them, scan the trees with a practiced gaze.

"I really appreciate you coming out here, Mr. Delaney," I say, pausing to let him catch up. "I'm feeling a bit over-whelmed by all this, to be honest, so when I found your details in my aunt's accounting books, I thought calling you might be worth a shot."

He chuckles, a dry, rasping sound. "Please, call me Joseph. And it's no trouble at all. I've been tending these trees for decades. It's good to see them again." He walks on, the soft crunch of his footsteps muffled by the dense carpet of grass and fallen leaves. "Your aunt was a remarkable woman," he continues, pausing to inspect a low-hanging branch heavy with peaches. "She poured her heart and soul into this place, especially after your uncle passed. That's when I started working here full-time."

I nod, feeling another pang of guilt. "I haven't been here

since I was a child, and I don't know the first thing about running an orchard. Where do I even start?"

Joseph stalls and lingers, his gaze thoughtful. "Well, the first thing to know is that it's a year-round job. There's always something that needs doing, even in the winter months." He points with his cane to a nearby tree. "Right now, your main concern is the harvest. These beauties won't wait forever. In fact, by the looks of them, you've got about five days."

I follow his gaze. "How do I know when they're ready?"

"You'll learn to tell by the feel," he says, limping over to the tree. He reaches up and cups a peach in his hand. "Here. This one is already ripe. See how it yields, just a bit? That's when you know it's ready for the picking." He twists the fruit gently and it comes away in his hand, rosy and perfect. He hands it to me with a smile. "Have a taste. Nothing like a peach straight off the tree."

I take a bite, my teeth sinking into the flesh. Juice runs down my chin as an explosion of sweetness hits my tongue. "It's incredible," I say, wiping my chin with the back of my hand.

Joseph nods, his eyes crinkling at the corners. "That's because you've never had a peach that wasn't picked green and left to ripen in a warehouse somewhere. There's no substitute for tree-ripened fruit."

"How do I know which fruits to pick first?" I ask, feeling a bit daunted by the sheer scale of the task ahead.

"Start with the stone fruits," Joseph advises. "The peaches, apricots, plums, although there are only a handful of plum trees. They have a shorter window of ripeness. The apples and pears can hang a bit longer." He shows me how to tell when a plum is perfectly ripe—a gentle squeeze near the stem—and how to spot the blushed cheek of a perfect apple. "It's a lot of work," he warns, pausing to catch his breath in the shade of an apple tree. "You'll want to hire some seasonal pickers to help you out, and you need to act fast so you don't lose out on the peach harvest. I can put you in touch with some folks who used to work for your aunt during harvest season."

"Thank you. That would be great. And what do I do with all this fruit once it's picked? Aunt Maggie used to sell at the farmers' market, didn't she?"

Joseph smiles, his eyes distant with memory. "She did indeed. Every Saturday morning, rain or shine. She'd load up that old pickup truck of hers until the springs groaned and haul it all down to the market square." He chuckles, shaking his head. "She'd set up her stall with the most beautiful displays you ever saw. Like something out of a painting. People would line up for a taste of Maggie's fruit and her homemade apricot jam."

"She made jam?"

"Oh yeah. I still have her recipe if you're ever interested."

"Sure. But I don't have her culinary skills or her farmers' market flair, I'm afraid," I joke while I try to picture it—my elegant aunt in her floppy sun hat, bantering with customers.

"I think you'd like the market, being new to the area. It's a great way to meet people..." Joseph stalls again to catch his breath. "But she also sold to wholesalers, of course. That was her main income. She had her regulars. Most of them are local and still operate. Give them a call—I'm sure they'll be delighted to hear that Rosefield Farm is up and running again."

"It's sad that she didn't have anyone but her estranged niece to leave it to," I say.

"She wasn't lonely," Joseph assures me. "She had friends,

her community, and she had me. My wife died too, so we were very close. I was with her when she passed, and I knew she'd leave the farm to you. I was just thinking about stopping by to see how you were doing when you found my number in Maggie's files."

That thought gives me a little comfort, and I'm so glad now that I called Joseph. While we continue to do our round, he regales me with stories of harvests past, of bumper crops and late frosts, of long days in the sun and cool nights under the stars. He almost makes it sound romantic.

"There's nothing quite like it," he says, brushing his fingers through the leaves. "Working the land, watching things grow. It's hard work, backbreaking at times. But it's honest. Satisfying in a way that nothing else is."

I wish I shared his enthusiasm. So far, the farm is giving me more anxiety than satisfaction, but I am where I am, and I'm not giving up until I've tried at least one season.

As we near the end of the last row, Joseph pauses, leaning heavily on his cane. "I meant what I said before," he tells me, his pale-blue eyes intent. "You ever need anything, you just give me a holler. I may not be as spry as I used to be, but I've still got a trick or two up my sleeve. Do you have anyone who can help you with day-to-day stuff? It's not easy to run an orchard alone."

"Yes, I have someone arriving next week. A woman who's not afraid to get her hands dirty. She'll be living with me for a few months while she helps me out," I say and feel a nervous flutter at the thought of having an ex-convict in my home. Even though I've been assured this woman is perfectly safe, I've still had sleepless nights over her arrival. I don't mention her situation. Miranda advised me not to, as it's essential for ex-cons to get a fair start without prejudice, especially when they move into a small community.

"That's good. I'm sure it will be nice to have some company if it's just you. You should probably get a dog too."

"A dog?" I frown at him. "It's never occurred to me to get a dog. I've always lived in the city and worked long days, so it was never an option. Is there a lot of crime in the area?"

"No, it's pretty friendly around here, but you don't have neighbors nearby, so I suppose it will make you feel safer at night." Joseph points to the farmhouse as we step back onto the driveway. "How's it looking?"

"It needs a lot of work." I shrug. "Most of the interior hasn't been updated since the seventies, but I guess you already know that. The roof is in good condition, though. I had it checked last week, so that's a relief."

"Yes, I remember Maggie had it done about five years ago." Joseph looks nostalgic as he gazes at the rickety porch.

"Would you like a cold drink or a coffee?" I ask, realizing it must be uncomfortable for him in the sun.

"A coffee would be nice. But since we're here, let's have a look in the barn first." Joseph points his stick at the small building that looks more like a shack than a barn. "If you're lucky, the harvesting baskets, scales, and yard tools might still be there. I'll talk you through it and show you how it's done."

7

GEMMA

"Gemma, be ready in ten minutes." The guard sounds cheerful as she hands me a canvas bag, like she's genuinely happy for me. It's the first time she's called me by my name, rather than "inmate."

I swing my legs over the side of the narrow bunk where I've been reading after breakfast as usual, my bare feet hitting the cold concrete floor. Today is the day I walk out of here.

Tonya is perched on the edge of the top bunk, her dark eyes fixed on me. "So," she says. "This is it, huh?"

I nod, my throat suddenly tight. "Guess so." I've been preparing for this moment for months, counting down the days, making plans. But now that it's here, I feel strangely unmoored. Like I'm about to step off the edge of a cliff, unsure if I'll fly or fall.

"You're going to be fine. You don't know how lucky you are, landing yourself a job." Tonya jumps down and stretches her arms overhead until her joints pop. "Come on," she says, pointing to the few belongings I have here. "I'll help you pack."

"No. You keep it." I smile. In prison, belongings are currency, and even the silliest little things like a bottle of body lotion or a book are considered a luxury.

"Really?" Her arms fly around my neck. It's the first time she's hugged me, and it brings a lump to my throat. "Even the MP3 player?"

"Yes," I say with a chuckle. "Enjoy my dated music collection in your last month here. I also got you some presents from the commissary. I figured I might as well empty my account." I lift the bedsheets where I've been hiding the surprise, and Tonya slams a hand in front of her mouth at the sight of the chocolate bars and bags of potato chips.

"You're the best!" She shrieks with joy, jumping on the spot. She puts the stash under her sheets, then changes her mind and hides it under her mattress instead. "There. That's better. Let's hope my new cellie isn't a klepto," she says and hooks her arm through mine. "Let's go."

We walk side by side down the long, echoing corridor, past the rows of cells with open doors. Some call out to me as I pass, their voices ranging from envious to encouraging. I didn't tell anyone but Tonya I was getting out, but word gets around, I suppose.

"Lucky bitch!" someone yells. "You take care out there, you hear? Don't come back." We've had a few brief conversations, but I don't even know her name.

I nod and wave, trying to commit their faces to memory. Prison has been my world for so long that leaving feels scary.

At the end of the corridor, a guard is waiting with a clipboard. She checks my name off a list, then nods toward a door on the right. "Through there for processing."

I pause, turning to face Tonya. She's trying to smile, but I can see the shine of tears in her eyes. "Hang in there. I'll see you soon." I know she's afraid. She'll get a new bunk mate and she has no idea what kind of woman she'll be.

"Yeah. I'll see you soon," she says, pulling me into a fierce hug until the guard's voice roars through the corridor.

"Inmates! No touching!"

Still, I cling to her for another beat, breathing in the familiar scent of her—sweat and cheap soap. "I'm going to miss you," I whisper before stepping back. I square my shoulders and walk through the door, into a small, sterile room where another guard is waiting.

"Strip," she commands, nodding toward a pile of clothes on a table. My clothes, the ones I was wearing the day I was arrested. They look foreign to me now, like relics from another life.

I shed my prison blues, the coarse fabric that has been my second skin for so long. I stand naked and shivering as the guard runs her hands over my body, checking for contraband. It's a familiar routine, but today, it feels different. Like I'm shedding more than just clothes.

I dress slowly, my fingers clumsy on the zipper of my palazzo pants. My white shirt is not here. It was covered in blood spatter and used as evidence in my case. Instead, I'm given a plain, white T-shirt that does the job. The blazer is a little tight across the shoulders, the pants a bit loose on my hips. I've been doing press-ups and crunches to kill the time, and my body has changed in here, lean and hard where it used to be soft.

The guard hands me a pair of shoes, black pumps with a high heel. I stare at them for a long moment before slipping them on. The leather feels strange against my feet, the angle of the heel unfamiliar. I take a few tottering steps, feeling like a newborn calf learning to walk.

"You'll get used to them again," the guard says, a hint of amusement in her voice. She hands me a small bag, containing the few possessions I had on me when I was arrested. A purse with a wallet, a lipstick, my phone, a handful of crumpled receipts, a watch, and a pair of gold earrings. It all seems to belong to someone else, a girl I barely remember, but I'm delighted when I spot the fifty-dollar bill in my wallet. It's not much, but it's an emergency buffer.

"This way." She leads me down another corridor, and we pass through a series of locked doors, each one clanging shut behind us with a heavy finality.

And then...we're at the last door. The guard pauses, her hand on the handle. "Good luck out there," she says.

I nod, my throat too tight to speak. She pushes the door open and I step through, blinking in the sudden, blinding light of day.

The sun is high and hot, the air heavy with the scent of asphalt and exhaust. I shade my eyes with my hand, squinting against the glare. The world seems too bright, too loud, too much after the muted grays and hushed sounds of prison.

A car is idling by the curb, a sleek black sedan. As I approach, the driver's door opens and Miranda steps out.

"Gemma," she says, her smile warm. "Right on time."

I nod, clutching my small bag to my chest like a shield. "Thanks for picking me up."

Miranda waves a dismissive hand. "It's part of the job." She looks me over curiously. "That outfit doesn't seem practical for farm life. Do you have any clothes or things you want to pick up on the way? I brought some stuff I found in the charity pile in our office in case you don't. It's not fancy, but it's clean, and I got your shoe size from your file."

"Thank you," I say as I slide into the cool, leather interior, the seat cushioning me like a cloud. I've almost forgotten how it feels to be in a car. "I have some clothes at my mother's house, but I'd rather meet her when I'm a bit more settled. I haven't seen her in years, and I'm nervous enough as it is."

"No problem," Miranda says. "Have you spoken to her? I have her as your emergency contact."

"Yeah. But our relationship is complicated so I need some time."

Miranda nods and doesn't pry. She's read my file, so she probably has an idea. Instead, she hands me a takeout coffee. "Here. I didn't know how you like your coffee so I got you a cappuccino with an extra shot and there's sugar in the side compartment. I figured anything would be better than that prison drab."

"Oh my God. Is that for me?" I'm so grateful I want to hug her. "Thank you. Why are you so nice to me?"

Miranda chuckles. "I'm a parole officer. I have a lot of bad days in my job, but this is a good one. You have no idea how happy it makes me to hand a kind woman her first good coffee in years. Makes me feel like fucking Santa."

I smile and inhale over my cup as we pull away from the curb. The prison recedes in the rearview mirror until it's nothing more than a smudge of gray on the horizon. My eyes shift to the road ahead, the endless miles stretching out before me like a promise. I don't know what tomorrow holds, but for now, this coffee is enough.

8

LORI

She is not what I was expecting. Gemma is tall and slender, with long, dark hair that falls in waves past her shoulders. She's dressed in what looks like office attire—a black suit and heels. As she approaches the house, I notice the way she moves—cautiously, as if she's not quite sure of her footing.

"Gemma?" I call out, descending the porch steps. "I'm Lori. Welcome."

She looks up at me, a tentative smile on her face. "Thank you," she says, her voice soft. "It's nice to meet you."

Miranda joins us, greets me, and hands Gemma a small duffel bag. "Here's your stuff. I've got to rush—I have an appointment—but I'll drop in soon. In the meantime, I hope this works out for you both. Any issues, give me a call. You know how to reach me."

Gemma seems just as nervous as I am. I was kind of hoping Miranda would stick around for a coffee to ease us into the situation, but this is her job and she's not here for chitchat. A silence falls between us when she leaves, and I turn to Gemma.

"Is this all you've got?" I ask, pointing to the duffel bag.

She nods, tucking a strand of hair behind her ear. "For now, yes. The rest is...it's stored elsewhere."

There's a story there, I can tell, but I don't press. "No worries," I say, trying to sound upbeat. "We'll get you settled in and then we can figure out what else you need. I think we're the same size, so I have some clothes you can borrow."

Gemma follows me inside, her heels clicking on the hardwood floors. I lead her down the hall to the spare bedroom, freshly aired out and with clean sheets on the bed. It's not much, but it's the best I could do on short notice.

"I'm sorry it's not more..." I trail off, gesturing vaguely at the sparse furnishings. "Homey."

But Gemma is looking around the room with something like wonder on her face. "It's perfect. Really, it's...it's more than I could have hoped for."

I blink, surprised by the emotion in her voice. I take a closer look at her, noting the fine lines around her eyes, the way she holds herself—like she's trying to take up as little space as possible.

"I'm glad," I say. "I want you to feel at home here."

She looks at me then, really looks at me, and I'm struck by the intensity of her gaze. "Thank you," she says again, and there's a weight to the words that I don't fully understand.

An awkward beat passes and then Gemma clears her throat, glancing down at her feet. "I should probably change," she says, a rueful smile tugging at her lips. "These shoes are killing me. I'm not used to them anymore."

She sits on the edge of the bed and slips off the heels, sighing in relief as she flexes her toes. I try not to stare, but I can't help noticing how delicate her ankles look, how pale her skin is.

"Of course," I say, shaking myself out of my reverie. "Your bathroom is next door. I put fresh towels in there. When you're ready, come find me in the kitchen. We can have some tea and...and talk about how we're going to do this if that's okay with you?"

She smiles and nods, already reaching for the duffel bag. I slip out of the room, pulling the door shut behind me. In the hallway, I lean against the wall for a moment, taking a deep breath. This is going to be interesting.

In the kitchen, I busy myself with making tea, trying to calm my nerves. I've never done anything like this before— opened my home to a stranger, let alone one with a criminal record. But something about Gemma makes me want to really give this a go. Maybe it's the quiet strength I sense in her, the way she seems to be holding herself together despite everything. Or maybe I'm just lonely, rattling around in this big old house by myself.

The sound of footsteps makes me turn. Gemma is standing in the doorway, dressed now in jeans and a T-shirt. Her feet are bare and her hair is pulled back in a ponytail. She looks younger somehow, more vulnerable.

"Hi," she says, hovering uncertainly. "Is it okay if I...?"

"Please, come in," I say, waving her toward the kitchen table. "Have a seat. I made tea. Or do you prefer coffee?"

"Tea is great. I just had my first real coffee in over seven and a half years, and it's made me a bit shaky," she jokes.

"Oh..." I wince. "That long, huh?"

"Yeah. It was a real treat, but the extra shot did me in." She chuckles and holds out her hands to show me they're trembling.

"I'm so sorry. I didn't even think about the fact that

you've missed out on so much. Do you prefer lemonade? Wine? Beer?"

"No, no, I'd love to have tea with you." She takes a seat, her hands awkwardly folded in her lap. I plate cookies, sneaking glances at her out of the corner of my eye. She's looking around the kitchen, taking in the old-fashioned appliances, the faded curtains. "It's a lovely home," she says, and I can tell she genuinely means it. "So peaceful."

I set a mug of tea and a plate of chocolate chip cookies in front of her, sliding into the opposite chair. "It is, but it needs updating. I've only just moved in here myself, so it doesn't feel like a home yet."

Gemma wraps her hands around the mug, as if savoring the warmth. "What made you decide to take me in?" she asks suddenly, her gaze direct. "I mean, you don't know me. I could be anyone."

I take a sip of my tea, considering my answer. "Honestly? I probably need you as much as you need me," I admit. "But Miranda spoke highly of you. And I guess...I guess I know what it's like to need a fresh start."

She studies me for a long moment, then nods. "Thank you," she says again. "For taking a chance on me. I imagine this must be a little strange for you."

"You're welcome." I gesture to the cookies. "Help yourself. Are you hungry? I can make you some food."

"Please, please don't worry about me," she says. "I'm here to make your life easier." She picks up one of the cookies and inhales deeply against it before she takes a bite and moans. "Mmm...this might be the best thing I've ever eaten."

My heart aches for her, but I paint on a smile. I'm not worried anymore. Far from it. She returns my smile, and I can see she's starting to loosen up too.

"So, what would you like me to do today? Miranda told me you need help with the electrics and the harvest. Maybe some home repairs? Apart from being a certified electrician, I don't have much experience with home maintenance, but I'm a fast learner."

"Not today," I say, cursing myself for making a list this morning. What was I thinking? It's her first day of freedom in many years, and I was planning on putting her to work. "Today should be special. A day to remember."

"I'd like to make myself useful, though. I don't want to be in your way."

"We can be useful together tomorrow but for now..." I pick up a cookie and take a bite. "If you could do anything, anything at all today, what would it be?"

"Hmm..." Gemma takes a beat to consider my question and the blush that rises to her cheeks is adorable. "I saw you have a bath," she says. "I'd love to have a bath and go for a walk in the orchard. Touch the trees and feel the sun on my face and real wind in my hair. The prison walls were too high to catch the wind. I've always been a city girl, but now I can't think of anything better than being in nature. When Miranda told me about your farm, it felt like a..." Suddenly, tears trickle down her cheeks. She touches them and rubs them between her fingers like she's surprised to feel them. "It felt like a godsend." She wipes her cheeks and shakes her head. "I'm sorry. I promise you I'm never like this, but it's an emotional day for me."

Without thinking, I reach for her hand over the table. "Please don't apologize. I'm so glad you're here and that I might be able to make today special for you." I squeeze her hand. "Will you allow me to do that? Please? It would make me so happy."

"You're too kind." She smiles through her tears and looks

like she wants to argue, but then she sighs, her shoulders relaxing. "Okay. Thank you."

Her tears slay me. All the lost time, the wasted years. And such simple things as a bath and a walk. I can't begin to imagine how she must feel.

"Take your time," I say, pointing upstairs to the bathroom. "I put a basket with products on the edge of the bath and there's a robe in the closet in your room. We can walk around the orchard together later, or you can go alone. Whatever you prefer." I get up and grab a pile of magazines from the counter. "Take these and your tea."

She thanks me again and heads upstairs. I hear the sound of running water, of Gemma moving around in the bathroom. The everyday sounds of a life being lived.

It hits me then, the magnitude of what I've taken on. Not just a farmhand, not just a rehabilitation project. A person, a human being with a tragic past and an uncertain future. Sipping my tea, I listen to the sounds of Gemma splashing in the tub upstairs and embrace the challenge of nurturing a connection.

9

GEMMA

*T*he sun is warm on my face as I step out into the orchard, the light filtering through the leaves creating a mesmerizing pattern on the ground. The air is filled with the heady scent of ripe fruit, a sweetness that envelops me, draws me in. I take a deep breath, savoring the freshness and the purity of it.

I feel like a new person, reborn in the most literal sense. The bath was a revelation, the simple act of soaking in hot water an almost transcendent experience. I can't remember the last time I felt truly clean. The prison showers were perfunctory at best, a hasty scrubbing under lukewarm water, always conscious of the eyes and ears around me.

But this...this was something else entirely. The luxurious lather of the bubbles against my skin, the steam rising in tendrils, the way the water seemed to leach the tension from my muscles and a little bit of darkness from my soul. I could have stayed in there for hours, pruning be damned.

And the clothes, oh, the clothes. Clean, soft, smelling of lavender and sunshine. I kept burying my nose in the fabric, inhaling deeply, marveling at the pleasure of it. My hair, too, feels like silk, the conditioner Lori left for me working magic on the tangles and snarls.

Lori walks ahead, her long, blonde hair dappled in the shifting light. She turns, a smile on her face that falters slightly as she takes in my expression.

"Gemma?" she asks, concern lacing her voice. "Are you okay?"

I nod, blinking back another sudden sting of tears. "I'm fine," I assure her. "More than fine. This is incredible."

Her expression softens, understanding dawning. "I can only imagine," she says. "It's the little things, isn't it? The things we take for granted."

"It is. Just to feel human."

Lori looks away, and I can tell I've touched a nerve, that my joy has moved her.

"Well," she says after a moment, clearing her throat. "You'll have plenty of time to rediscover all those little pleasures." She gestures around us at the lush green of the orchard, the clear blue sky above.

"It's beautiful here," I say, following her gaze.

"It is. I'm a city girl too. It was a big change for me, but a good one."

"How does it all work?" I ask. "Running an orchard, I mean. It seems like a lot for one person."

Lori laughs and deep dimples appear. "Honestly? I'm still figuring that out myself. I kind of jumped into this headfirst. Quit my job, packed up my life...I had no idea what I was getting into."

I raise an eyebrow, intrigued. "What made you do it? If you don't mind me asking."

She hesitates, chewing on her bottom lip. "I inherited the farm from my aunt, and it felt like a sign. I just needed a change. My job, my life... It wasn't me."

I nod. "And this? This is you?"

"Again, I have no idea. I guess I'll find out." Another slow smile spreads across her face. "But I'm already calmer than I've been in a long time."

We walk on in comfortable silence, the only sound the crunch of our footsteps on the fallen leaves and the distant chirping of birds. Lori leads me to the edge of the orchard, where the neat rows of trees give way to an open field, behind it, a more barren landscape with red rocks.

"I come out here sometimes," she says, settling down cross-legged in the grass. "When I need to think or just...be."

I sink down beside her, marveling at the softness of the grass, the coolness of the earth beneath my palms. In prison, the ground was hard and unyielding. Out here, everything seems to give, to welcome.

"Joseph, the old farmhand who used to work for my aunt, has been giving me some pointers," Lori continues, plucking a blade of grass and twirling it between her fingers. "But a lot of it is trial and error. Seeing what works, what doesn't."

We lapse into silence again, but it's the easy kind, the kind that feels like a conversation in itself. I tip my head back, closing my eyes, letting the sun warm my face. The act of simply sitting here is divine. No schedule, no demands, no eyes watching, judging, no threats. Just me and the sky.

"I was thinking of cooking pasta for dinner," Lori says eventually, breaking the spell. "Something hearty to ease you back into the good life. Or do you have any specific cravings? We can drive to the store and get anything you like."

I open my eyes, turning to look at her. "Actually, I love pasta, but would you mind if I cooked? I'd love to make dinner for us."

She looks surprised, then pleased. "You cook?"

I nod, a rush of memories washing over me. Standing at the stove, stirring a pan of bubbling sauce. Kneading dough for bread, the yeasty smell filling the kitchen. Chopping vegetables, the rhythmic *thunk* of the knife against the cutting board. "I used to. Before...everything. I used to find it relaxing. I always cooked when I felt anxious. It took my mind off things."

"I think that's wonderful," Lori says. "The kitchen is all yours."

We sit for a while longer and the conversation meanders like a lazy river. Lori tells me more about the orchard, about her plans and dreams for this place, and I stick to asking questions. We don't go into personal stuff. We've both been advised not to. After all, she's not supposed to ask about my background, so it's only fair that I don't get caught up in her private business either. It's difficult, though, not to go there because I'm genuinely curious about her. I remind myself that Lori is my employer. That I have a shot at life because of her, and that it's important to keep a respectable distance.

I don't realize how late it is until the sun starts to dip, painting the sky in shades of orange and pink, a giant, glowing orb in a startling tableau of color. I stare at the breathtaking display and smile as my eyes well up. It's my first sunset in seven years, six months, and twenty-two days. I sit transfixed, my eyes drinking in the sight like a parched traveler at an oasis. It's been so long, so impossibly long since I've witnessed this daily miracle. Years of sunsets, stolen from me by concrete walls and metal bars.

But now, here in this wide-open expanse of endless sky, I feel like I'm seeing it for the first time. Really seeing it, with eyes that have been starved of beauty, of nature, of the profound glory of the turning Earth.

The clouds are aflame with color, a riot of oranges and

golds, as if the sun has burst and spilled its molten core across the heavens. The light is liquid, almost tangible, bathing everything in a warm, honeyed glow. The colors are shifting and deepening, becoming richer, more saturated. The orange deepens to a burnished amber, the pink blushes into a dusky rose, and the clouds are edged in a brilliant, fiery gold.

"I can't remember the last time I cried," I say with a sniff. "But today, I can't seem to stop."

"That's understandable." Lori's hand brushes mine between us. "It's beautiful. I should stop taking sunsets for granted. Thank you for reminding me of that."

10

LORI

I lean against the kitchen counter, cradling a glass of wine, as I watch Gemma move around the space with a fluid grace. She seems utterly at home in the kitchen, in a way I haven't yet managed since I moved in. The scent of garlic, basil, and tomatoes mingling with the yeasty aroma of rising dough makes my mouth water. I don't normally eat this late but we stayed outside for hours and time flew by.

"Can I help with anything?" I ask for the third time, feeling slightly guilty for just sitting here while she does all the work.

Gemma looks up from the pan she's stirring, a smile playing at the corners of her mouth. "Absolutely not," she says firmly. "You're my host. It's my pleasure to cook for you." She nods toward my glass. "Relax, enjoy your wine. Dinner will be ready soon."

I take a sip, savoring the crisp, cool liquid on my tongue. "Are you sure you don't want a glass?" I offer. "This Gavi is lovely."

Gemma hesitates for a moment, then shakes her head.

"I'll have a glass with dinner. I love Gavi, but I want to take it slow. It's been a long time since I had a drink." She flashes me a grateful smile before turning back to the stove, giving the sauce a stir. The scent intensifies, making my stomach growl as I marvel at the surrealness of this moment.

If someone had told me a few months ago I'd be ending the day with a home-cooked meal, prepared by an ex-convict living with me on my late aunt and uncle's farm, I would have laughed in their face. But here we are, the most unlikely of scenarios unfolding in the warm, fragrant heart of my aunt's kitchen.

Gemma moves to the left side of the counter, where she's laid out a mound of flour. With deft, practiced motions, she cracks eggs into a well in the center, then begins to mix and knead, her strong hands working the dough until it's smooth and elastic. I watch, fascinated, as she rolls out the dough and slices it into thin, delicate sheets.

"You've done this before," I observe, impressed.

She looks up, a lock of hair falling into her eyes. "YouTube taught me." She chuckles. "We used to spend hours in the kitchen together."

"Maybe I should get more acquainted with YouTube myself." I laugh along as I get up. "Do you want to eat on the porch? It's such a nice evening."

"Yes." Gemma's face lights up. "That sounds perfect."

I drain my glass. "Great. I'll go set the table." I want to make this meal, this moment, special. It's Gemma's first real meal in God knows how long, and I want it to be memorable.

I rummage through the cabinets, unearthing Aunt Maggie's best china, the delicate plates edged in gold. I find crystal glasses, linen napkins, even a pair of silver candlesticks. I carry my haul out to the porch, arranging everything just so, fussing with the placement of the forks, the angle of the napkins.

As I light the candles, watching the flames flicker in the breeze, I feel a sense of gratitude to be here and bear witness to the start of someone's new life. I hear Gemma's footsteps behind me and turn. She's carrying a large, steaming bowl of pasta, the scent wafting through the evening air. Her hair is pulled back, a few loose tendrils tracing the curves of her cheeks, and her eyes are bright, almost luminous in the candlelight.

"Dinner is served," she announces, a note of pride in her voice as she sets the bowl in the center of the table.

I follow her back into the kitchen to bring out the rest, seriously impressed with the spread she's prepared. A vibrant green salad, dotted with cherry tomatoes and slivers of red onion. A basket of garlic bread, the crust golden and crisp. And the pasta...the pasta looks like something straight out of a gourmet magazine, the noodles glistening with olive oil and flecked with fresh herbs.

"Gemma..." I shake my head. "This is incredible."

Gemma ducks her head, looking pleased but slightly abashed. "I just wanted to do something nice for you." She serves me a generous portion before she helps herself and breaks the bread like a pro, turning it when the garlic oil threatens to ooze out.

I pour the wine and Gemma raises her glass, her eyes finding mine across the table. "To new beginnings," she says softly.

I clink my glass against hers, feeling a swell of something in my chest. "To new beginnings."

We sip the wine, and she closes her eyes as she savors it. "Mmm...so good." Then she twirls a forkful of pasta and brings it to her mouth. "Not bad if I say so myself." She chuckles, taking another bite. "Nothing is made from scratch in prison. Food is not a thing there and I've missed pure ingredients."

"It's delicious. You're welcome to cook anytime as long as you teach me," I say with a mischievous smile, and when she laughs, it almost feels like I'm having dinner with an old friend. "So what did you eat in prison?" I ask, then wince. "I'm sorry. You probably don't want to talk about that, and anyway, we shouldn't be discussing personal matters."

"It's okay." She shrugs. "Miranda said the same thing to me, but it might be weird if we walk on eggshells in our conversations." She pauses. "I can see why they put those rules in place, and even though I'd rather not discuss my criminal record, I don't mind talking about my time in prison. We're kind of in a unique situation, as this is your home as well as your business. It's just you and me here, no distractions, so if you prefer to keep a distance after today, I totally get—"

"No, I don't want that," I interrupt her. "But I can promise you I won't be nosey about your record or anything that led you there. You can tell me what you're comfortable with, and I'll do the same."

"That sounds good," Gemma says. "And I'm more than happy to entertain you with stories about prison food." She grins, setting her glass down. "Okay, picture this. It's your first day inside. You're terrified, you're lost and disoriented, you have no idea what's going on, and for those reasons, you're starving, as you haven't been able to get food down for days. And then they serve you dinner." She pauses for effect, her face a mask of mock horror. "It's this...slop. That's the only word for it. Spongy protein, overcooked veggies, all drowned in this grayish-brown instant gravy."

I can't help but laugh at her expression, at the vivid disgust in her voice. "That sounds...appetizing."

She snorts, shaking her head. "Oh, it gets better. Breakfast? Rubbery powdered egg scramble, burnt toast, and this stuff they called oatmeal but I swear was wallpaper paste with a few flakes of sawdust thrown in for texture."

"I don't know how you stomached it."

"I didn't at first, but you have no choice other than to get used to it. Or you learn to get creative. Like, we'd save up our fruit cups and make this sort of...prison sangria. Minus the alcohol, of course."

"Prison sangria? How does that work?"

She laughs. "You take your fruit cup, right? The syrupy peaches, the mushy pears. You drain off the juice, mix it with some powdered milk and sugar packets from the cafeteria. If you're feeling fancy, you might sprinkle in some Kool-Aid powder for color."

She mimes stirring a cup, her face a picture of exaggerated concentration. "Voila! Prison sangria. Served in a plastic cup you've rinsed out in the bathroom sink."

I'm laughing now, shaking my head. "That's...actually kind of genius. In a makeshift, prison-y sort of way."

"Hey, you make do with what you've got. Which wasn't much, let me tell you." Gemma leans in across the table. "Okay, but the worst? The absolute worst was the mystery meat casserole."

I make a face, already dreading the description. "Do I want to know?"

She grins wickedly. "Oh, you definitely do. Imagine a layer of stale Tater tots, topped with this gray, overcooked meat that could have been anything from turkey to squirrel. Then a can of cream of mushroom soup, poured over the top like some sort of unholy gravy." She shudders, the motion only slightly exaggerated. "It was like...cafeteria Jenga. You never knew what you were going to get in each bite."

"Well," I say, lifting my glass in a toast, "here's to never having to eat mystery meat casserole again."

She clinks her glass against mine, her smile wide and genuine. "Amen to that."

I study her face, marveling at the change in her demeanor. Gone is the guarded, wary woman who arrived on my doorstep this afternoon. In her place is someone lighter and more at ease. Someone who feels comfortable enough to share stories, to make jokes and let her guard down, even if only for a moment. Each time she laughs, she has this physical reaction, a flash of surprise across her face, like she hasn't laughed much and the sound of it is alien to her. Gemma's stories have given me a newfound appreciation for the simple pleasures in life, like a home-cooked meal, a clear, breezy night, and good company.

As the candles burn lower, I linger over my last sips of wine, not quite ready for the evening to end. But then I see her looking up at the stars with fascination, and sense she might want some alone time with the universe.

"I'd better call it a night," I say, faking a yawn. "Please stay out as long as you want. I'll do the dishes in the morning."

11

GEMMA

*J*olt awake, my heart pounding, my skin slick with sweat. My breath comes in short, sharp gasps and I'm disoriented, the unfamiliar room spinning around me. Then it all comes rushing back—the farm, the orchard, Lori. I'm safe. I'm free.

For a moment, I was back in my mother's cramped, dingy apartment, the air thick with the stench of cheap whiskey and stale cigarettes. I can hear the shouting, the cruel, slurred words that were my lullaby for so many years. I can see my mother's face, the fresh bruises blooming on her pale skin, the fear and resignation in her eyes. After that, the details blur together in a haze of rage and desperation. Something in my hand, heavy and solid. The sickening crunch of impact, again and again. The warm, sticky blood on my hands, my clothes, my face. The way his eyes went blank, glassy, like a doll's.

I lurch out of bed, stumbling blindly toward the bathroom. My stomach heaves and I barely make it to the toilet before I'm retching, the bile burning my throat. I clutch the cold porcelain, my knuckles white as my body tries to purge itself of the horror. But it's not that easy. It's never that easy.

I slump to the floor, my back against the wall, my legs drawn up to my chest. I'm shaking uncontrollably, my skin clammy and cold. I try to draw a deep breath, but it feels like there's a vice around my lungs, squeezing. Black spots dance at the edges of my vision and a terrible, high-pitched whine fills my ears.

I'm dying, I think wildly. *This is what dying feels like.*

But even as the thought forms, some distant, rational part of my brain whispers the truth. *Not dying. Panicking.* A panic attack, like the ones I used to get in the early days of my sentence, when the reality of what I'd done would hit me like a freight train.

I force myself to focus on that voice, to cling to it like a lifeline. *Breathe*, it commands. *In through the nose, out through the mouth. Slow and steady.* I obey, dragging in a shuddering breath, holding it for a count of three, then releasing it slowly. I do it again, and again, until the roaring in my ears starts to recede, until the black spots fade from my vision.

Gradually, the shaking subsides, leaving me spent and hollow. I use the sink to pull myself upright on rubbery legs, avoiding my reflection in the mirror. I don't want to see the haunted eyes and the pale face that I know will greet me.

Stumbling out of the bathroom, my feet carry me not back to my bed, but to the door. I need air. I need space.

The morning breeze washes over me and I gulp it in, letting it fill my lungs, my belly, chasing out the panic. The first slivers of light cast a serene glow over the orchard, but inside me, the turmoil rages on. The guilt, the shame, the sickening, gut-wrenching knowledge of what I've done.

I wrap my arms around myself, hugging tight, as if I can

physically hold myself together. As if I can stop the cracks from spreading and the darkness from seeping in.

It's been months since I've had this nightmare. During my first months in prison, it was a regular visitor, but as time passed, it faded, replaced by more immediate horrors and threats.

Now, it seems, it's back with a vengeance. Maybe it's the sudden change in environment, the whiplash shift from captivity to freedom. Or maybe it's my subconscious, reminding me that no matter how far I run, I can never truly escape my past.

I shake my head, trying to banish the memory. I've tried to push it away, along with so many other horrors. My mind is still reeling, trying to process the big shift in my life; it's bound to dredge up some ghosts.

I perch on the edge of the weathered porch steps, the rough wood gritty beneath my bare thighs. The morning carries the earthy scent of the orchard and the distant perfume of hardy desert flowers. I drink it in like a medicine fighting the last vestiges of panic and the tang of fear and guilt.

And then I hear it. The songbirds, welcoming the day. I close my eyes, letting the sound wash over me. It's a melody I'd forgotten. In the harsh, unforgiving world of prison, there was no room for such gentle pleasures. The mornings there were heralded by the clanging of metal doors, the barked orders of guards, the shuffling steps of the inmates. But here, in this oasis of green and growing things, the dawn comes on wings.

I open my eyes, scanning the trees. There, in the branches of the old oak, a flicker of russet and cream. A cactus wren, its proud tail cocked jauntily as it pours out its heart in song.

As I watch, transfixed, a hummingbird lands on the porch railing, not six feet from where I sit. It's a tiny thing, but its voice is mighty, tripping from its throat. For a breathless moment, we regard each other, the hummingbird and I.

Then, with a flick of its tail, it's gone.

I'm so lost in the moment, that I don't hear the creak of the screen door behind me. But some instinct, honed by years of vigilance, has me tensing and turning.

It's Lori, wrapped in a faded blue robe, her hair sleep-tousled and her eyes soft with concern. "Gemma?" she whispers. "Did I scare you?"

"I'm sorry. I didn't mean to wake you."

But Lori just shakes her head and settles beside me on the steps. "You didn't," she assures me. "I'm an early riser these days. Something about the farm...it makes me want to get up." She meets my gaze. "Rough night?"

"Just...bad dreams. Memories."

Lori nods. "It's special, isn't it?" she says after a long moment. "The birdsong."

"Yeah." I hesitate, unsure of how much I want to share. "In prison," I finally start, "it was always either too quiet or too loud. The silence could be oppressive, like a weight on your chest. And when it wasn't silent, it was...chaos. Screaming, crying, clanging. There was no in-between. No peace. This, though," I continue, gesturing to our surroundings, "it's like hearing the world for the first time."

Lori turns to me, shoots me a sad smile, and places her hand on mine.

We simply sit there, letting the birdsong fill the space between us. I find my gaze drawn to Lori. She's a picture of casual elegance, even in her faded blue robe with her blonde hair mussed from sleep. There's a softness to her, a vulnerability that tugs at something deep within me.

I watch as she tilts her face to the sky, her eyes drifting closed as she inhales deeply, absorbing the essence of the morning. The light catches the planes of her face, highlighting the delicate arch of her brow, the gentle slope of her nose, the fullness of her lips, and those cute dimples.

As if sensing my gaze, her eyes flutter open, and she turns to me with a smile that's both gentle and knowing. In the light, her hazel eyes are flecked with gold, warm and luminous. They crinkle slightly at the corners as her smile widens.

Objectively, Lori is an attractive woman. It's there in the classic symmetry of her features, the easy, unconscious grace with which she moves. But here, in this unguarded moment, I'm struck by a different kind of beauty. A beauty that radiates from within and speaks of kindness, strength, and compassion.

As the sun finally crests the hills, she squeezes my hand before rising to her feet. "I'm going to put on some coffee," she says softly. "Join me when you're ready?"

12

LORI

*A*s we unload the supplies from the car, Gemma is buzzing with excitement. "I can't wait to get started," she says, hefting a toolbox filled with wire strippers, voltage testers, lightbulbs, and an assortment of pliers and screwdrivers. She looks rested today and she was eager to get going. I can tell she's desperate to make herself useful, and if that makes her feel good, I'm all in.

I eye the array of tools with a mixture of curiosity and apprehension. "I'd love to learn. Can I help you? Or watch?"

"Of course." Gemma smiles. "Where would you like to start?"

We head inside, and I point to the smallest guest bedroom. "How about this one? I want to use it as a home office, but nothing works in here."

"Perfect." Gemma is already pulling out tools, scanning the walls and ceiling with a practiced eye. "Okay, first things first. We need to make sure the power is off before we do anything."

She shows me how to use the non-contact voltage tester,

carefully checking each outlet and switch. "Safety is always the top priority with electrical work," she stresses. "One wrong move and you could be in for a nasty shock, or worse."

I watch carefully as she works, trying to absorb as much as I can. Gemma is patient, explaining each step as she goes.

"See this?" She holds up a length of white wire. "This is the neutral wire. It's the return path for the electricity. And this green one here, that's the ground wire. It's like a safety net. It helps prevent shocks if something goes wrong."

I nod, fascinated by her change in demeanor. She's so in-charge, so much more confident now that she's got something to focus on.

As Gemma works on wiring the new light fixtures, I try my hand at installing an outlet. It's finicky work, trying to get the wires nestled just right, but there's a satisfaction in hearing the click as it slots into place.

"Looking good," Gemma approves, glancing over from her perch on the ladder. "You're a natural."

I laugh. "I don't know about that. But it's kind of fun, isn't it? Seeing the progress, making something better."

We work steadily through the afternoon, the conversation flowing easily between technical discussions and friendly banter. By the time we're done, the new overhead light casts a bright light, and the added outlets promise new functionality.

"One room down," Gemma says, satisfaction evident in her voice.

I step back and can imagine a desk and bookshelves in here. It's a lovely room to sit, with views over the orchard. "Thank you. This is great."

"Excellent. Ready to tackle the attic?" she asks. "You

mentioned you haven't had a proper look because it's too dark."

"Absolutely not, go and chill out." Checking my watch, I'm shocked to see the time. "I'm so sorry. You're only supposed to do five hours a day and we're already over. Keep a record of your hours and take time off whenever you want. I don't want you to think I'm taking advantage of you, and Miranda told me it can be exhausting when you're first—"

"I know what Miranda said, but I feel fine, and I would never think you're taking advantage of me." Gemma places a hand on my shoulder and smiles. "Look, I'd rather just carry on. I'm enjoying it and it's great practice for me."

I hesitate as I glance up, eyeing the pull-down stairs above the landing with trepidation. "Well, if you insist. But I wouldn't be surprised if we find mice or bats."

Gemma laughs, already gathering up her tools. "All the more reason to add some light, then. Come on, it'll be an adventure."

And so, I follow her up into the dusty, dark, cavernous space. The extended spotlight we've brought up is bright, though, highlighting the shocking amount of dust that has settled on the old furniture and boxes that are piled up high.

As Gemma works on inspecting the broken fixtures, I find myself drawn to the stacks of boxes and furniture scattered throughout the attic. It's like a time capsule, a glimpse into my aunt and uncle's past.

Inside a stack of boxes labelled "kitchen," I find a treasure trove of dishes and glassware, all in the same bold, earthy tones. Plates with geometric patterns, glasses in amber and olive green, a set of nesting mixing bowls in graduated shades of orange.

"This is amazing," I murmur, holding up a large ceramic

vase adorned with stylized daisies. "They don't make things like this anymore."

Gemma glances over, a grin tugging at her lips. "Ah, the seventies. When avocado green and harvest gold were the height of chic. I bet collectors would pay a good price for that."

I set the vase carefully aside, already envisioning it filled with wildflowers on the kitchen table. As I dig deeper into the boxes, I unearth more treasures. A set of copper canisters, tarnished but still beautiful. A collection of kitschy salt and pepper shakers in the shapes of fruits and vegetables. A fondue set, complete with color-coded forks.

"Oh my god, look at this." I hold up a large, mushroom-shaped ceramic object, turning it over in my hands with a puzzled frown. "What the hell is it?"

Gemma takes one look and bursts out laughing. "That," she says between giggles, "is a cookie jar. Collectors would go to great lengths to get their hands on that."

I blink, then snort, shaking my head. "Of course. A cookie jar. Because why would you keep cookies in some-thing boring and ordinary when you could keep them in a giant mushroom?"

I move on to a wardrobe in the corner, the wood dark and ornately carved. I tug at the handles, but they're stuck, the doors swollen with age and humidity. Gemma comes over, adding her strength to mine, and with a groaning creak, they give way.

Inside, a riot of color and texture greets us. Dresses in swirling paisley prints, a rainbow of polyester shirts, a pair of truly impressive bell-bottom jeans. And there, in the back, swathed in a protective garment bag...

"Is that...?" I reach out, my fingers hovering over the bag.

Gemma unzips it, revealing a cascade of lace and satin. "A wedding dress," she says. "And a beautiful one, at that."

I stare at the gown, trying to imagine my aunt as a young bride. The delicate lace at the collar and cuffs, the row of tiny satin-covered buttons marching down the back.

Next to the dress, I find a box labelled "Linens." Inside, a wealth of textiles unfolds. Sheets and pillowcases in sunny yellow and crisp white, embroidered with poppies. Table-cloths in rich, jewel-toned damask. A crocheted afghan in a dizzying zigzag pattern of orange, brown, and cream.

As we carefully repack the linens, a glint of metal catches my eye from the bottom of the wardrobe. I reach in, pulling out a large, flat box. Inside is a wedding album. I put it aside with the vase to take downstairs; I want to take my time going through the pictures.

As Gemma works on the electrics and I go through more boxes, the conversation turns to the rest of the house. I confess my limited budget, my concerns about being able to afford the updates I dream of.

"You know," Gemma says, "a lot of the furniture in this place is solid wood. Vintage. With a little elbow grease and some creative thinking, you could give it new life. It kind of suits the vibe of the farm, don't you think?"

"Yeah, I suppose you're right." I pause, considering. "I've always been minimalist in my style, but there's no harm in trying to make it work and seeing how it turns out." Then I remember the swanky apartment I lived in for the past four years wasn't mine. It was Cleo's, my ex. She was the one who decorated it. She was the minimalist. She was the one who made all the decisions. I always went along with whatever she wanted. Cleo didn't like to be contradicted, so it was easier that way. Truthfully, I don't even know what my style is; I haven't made any decisions of my own in a long time.

Well, apart from leaving her and quitting my job, cutting the ties in every way. For so long, I let Cleo dictate my choices, but now, standing in this dusty attic filled with possibilities, I know that I'm ready to take control of my life. Rosefield Farm is more than just a renovation project; it's a chance for me to rediscover who I am.

13

GEMMA

"That was delicious," I say, stretching my legs out in front of me. Lori's bean stew went down a treat, and I even had second helpings.

"It's nothing special, but I'm glad you liked it," she says. "It's my mom's recipe. She's into comfort food."

I nod, leaning back on my elbows and tilting my face to the darkening sky. The first stars are just starting to peek out, tiny pinpricks of light in the vast expanse. My muscles are pleasantly heavy, the satisfying feeling of a hard day's work. It's a feeling unknown to me, the sense of accomplishment that comes from tangible effort. I was always behind a desk or trotting around luxurious homes, and in prison, I didn't do much at all.

Lori nudges me gently with her elbow. "You were a machine out there today," she says, her tone a mix of admiration and concern. "I appreciate all your help, but you don't have to push yourself so hard. It's okay to take it easy, especially in the beginning."

"I enjoy it," I say and turn to her. "Is this okay for you so far? I mean, do you feel comfortable with the situation?"

"Yes, absolutely," Lori says without hesitation. "Do you?"

"Of course. As long as I can be useful and earn my keep. And I don't want to be a burden in any way," I say, voicing the fear that's been niggling at the back of my mind. "If you need space or time to yourself, I understand. I can stay out of your way, keep to my room—"

"Gemma." Lori frowns, her brow creasing. "You don't have to earn anything. I need you as much as you need me, and your company is a pleasure. Please don't ever feel like you have to stay out of my way." She squeezes my hand. "Will you promise me that?"

"Okay. I promise." I nudge her gently. "As long as it's clear that I'm enjoying this. It doesn't feel like a job."

"What did you do before..." Lori stops herself. "Do you mind me asking?"

"No, I don't mind. I was a realtor. I lost my license, though, with my criminal record, and since it's close to impossible to get any kind of job in the same paygrade with my history, I decided to retrain as an electrician. I'm still under no illusion, no company will hire me, but maybe I could work for myself one day."

"That's a smart move," Lori says. "Do you miss being a realtor?"

"You know what? I don't think I do," I say honestly. "It's a tough business with a lot of competition. There's a lot of stress involved." I regard her. "What did you do before you moved here?"

Lori's expression turns pensive, her gaze turning inward. "I was an attorney in Prescott. I worked for a big firm and specialized in family law."

I raise my eyebrows. "Wow." I try to picture her in a suit, striding down the halls of a sleek office building. "That's... that's impressive."

She shrugs, a wry smile tugging at her lips. "It was, I suppose. But dealing with divorces is also depressing. Draining. I was good at it, but I never felt like I was doing something that made me or others happy."

"Is that what made you leave?"

Lori sighs, running a hand through her hair. "It was a combination of things," she says. "The workload was crushing, for one. I was putting in eighty-hour weeks, barely sleeping, barely eating. I could feel the burnout creeping up on me." She pauses, chewing on her bottom lip. "And then there were the personal issues. I was dating my boss, you see. We were together for a few years, and it was...intense. Toxic, in many ways."

"Your boss? That must have been complicated."

Lori huffs out a laugh, but there's little humor in it. "You could say that," she agrees. "When we were good, it was fine. Looking back, I wasn't happy, but I was okay. When it was bad, though, it got really ugly. Cleo, that's her name, likes things to go her way, and that resulted in fights in the office, passive-aggressive emails, the whole nine yards. It was a mess." She shakes her head, as if trying to dislodge the memories. "When I finally left her, it was like a bomb went off. She made my life a living hell at work, undermining me at every turn, taking credit for my wins. It was untenable, so when my aunt left me the farm, it felt like a sign to get the hell out of Prescott."

"She?" I echo, trying to keep the surprise out of my voice. "Your boss was a woman?"

Lori glances over at me. "Yeah," she says. "I'm gay."

"Oh." I blink, processing this new information. It's not that I'm shocked, exactly. More that I'm reassessing, slotting this piece of Lori's identity into the growing picture I have of her in my mind.

"I dated men when I was younger," Lori continues. "But as I got older, I realized that my attraction and connection was always strongest with women. It just took me a while to come to terms with it." She crosses her legs and drapes an arm over the bench. "And you? Have you ever been married or in long-term relationships?"

"I've been in a few relationships. Gina, my last partner, ended our relationship the day I got arrested and although I didn't see it then, she did me a favor. She wasn't a nice person."

"Gina?" Lori's eyes widen.

I chuckle. "Yes, I'm gay too."

"Huh." Lori laughs along. "What are the odds?" She stares at me for a beat, and I'm dying to know what she's thinking. But then she snaps out of it and shakes her head. "It must have been so hard to lose love on top of everything.

"Honestly, I had bigger problems to deal with than thinking of her," I say with a sarcastic chuckle. "But prison gave me time to reflect on my life, and my choices. And one thing became crystal clear. My relationships, romantic and otherwise...they weren't healthy. Not by a long shot."

Lori nods, her eyes soft with understanding. "It's hard," she murmurs, "to see the patterns when you're in the middle of them. You don't recognize the dysfunction."

"Isn't that the truth? Looking back, it's so obvious. The way I kept gravitating toward the same types, over and over. The ones who treated me like I was less than them and made me feel small and worthless." I pause as I gather my thoughts and Lori waits patiently.

"I realized," I continue, "that I was repeating my mother's mistakes. She always went for the tough ones, the 'bad boys.' The ones who pushed her around and disrespected her. Some were emotionally abusive, some were physically abusive too. And I followed right in her footsteps, like it was some kind of twisted family tradition."

"It's a cycle, but the fact that you see it and that you're aware of it...that's the first step toward change," Lori says. "Do you want to date, now that you're out?"

"No. That idea is so far removed from me, I can't even begin to picture it. And even if I wanted to, how do I break it to someone that I'm an ex-convict? It's not something I can fail to mention. Anyone I let into my life deserves to know."

"Well, I think you're lovely," Lori says. "And I guess any issues people might have depends on the crime." By now, she must be burning with curiosity as to what I did to end up in prison.

"Would *you* go on a date with an ex-con, though? One you met online or in a bar?"

Lori tilts her head from side to side and remains silent.

"Exactly."

She squeezes my hand and clears her throat, a hint of hesitation creeping into her voice. "Can I ask...in prison, did you ever...were there any relationships there? I mean, I don't want to pry, but..." She trails off, looking uncertain. "I'm just curious."

I smile, touched by her concern not to overstep. "Yes, there are relationships, especially between lifers and repeat felons. They've become so used to life inside that it's like a second home to them, and everyone has their needs, I guess. I've even seen straight women convert to our team. But I mostly kept to myself and only made one friend, in my last year. It was easier and safer that way."

"Have you ever felt threatened?" Lori asks.

"Yes. I've been stabbed once, for no reason, and I've been attacked a few times." I lift my T-shirt to show Lori the scar on my belly and she gasps.

"Fuck." She runs a finger over the scar. Despite our loaded conversation, her touch makes me shiver. "Did you report it?"

"No. That would have only made it worse. I said I'd fallen onto something sharp and the guards didn't question my story, even though it was highly unlikely. The incident scared the hell out of me, but the two days in the infirmary were kind of nice."

"That's awful." Lori seems genuinely affected by my story. "You're safe now," she whispers, taking my hand.

"I know." I smile and decide to crack a joke to lighten the mood. "I love it here. It's even better than the infirmary."

14

LORI

*T*he trees in the orchard are laden with fruit, their branches bowing under its weight. It's a beautiful sight, but today, my focus is elsewhere, and my eyes are drawn to a different kind of beauty.

Gemma stands in the middle of a row of trees, a basket balanced on her hip as she reaches up to pluck a peach from a high branch. Her hair is pulled back in a messy bun, tendrils escaping to frame her face in wispy curls. Her skin is flushed and glowing, a sheen of sweat glistening on her brow.

She's wearing a pair of my old shorts, the denim frayed and faded from years of wear. On her, they look brand new, hugging the curve of her hips, the swell of her thighs. The hem of her T-shirt rides up as she stretches, exposing a tantalizing strip of skin above her belly button.

I swallow hard, my mouth suddenly dry. It's not the first time I've noticed Gemma's physical beauty, but lately, it seems to hit me with a new intensity. Like I'm seeing her through a different lens, one that amplifies every detail.

She turns then, catching sight of me, and a smile breaks

across her face. "Lori!" she yells, waving me over. "Come see the haul we've got so far. It's a bumper crop."

I make my way over to her, my legs feeling slightly unsteady. As I draw closer, I can see the freckles dusting the bridge of her nose, the amber threads running through the rich chocolate brown of her eyes. The freckles spontaneously appeared the moment she started spending more time in the sun, and they're so cute I can't stop staring at them.

"Looking good," I say, and I'm not entirely sure if I'm referring to the peaches or to her. "You've been busy."

She grins, wiping the back of her hand across her forehead. "It's a good thing you got some extra help. There's a lot more fruit than we anticipated."

As if on cue, one of the hired farmhands emerges from the next row over, a full basket balanced on each shoulder. He's a burly guy, all tanned skin and bulging muscles, and I can't help but notice the way his gaze lingers on Gemma as he passes by.

A flicker of something hot and sharp pulses through me, a sensation I don't quite have a name for. I push it aside, focusing instead on the matter at hand. "Actually," I say, "I came out here to tell you Miranda's here."

"Oh my, is it midday already?" Gemma checks her watch.

"She's a little early." I try not to gawk when her shorts ride up as she bends to place a peach in a basket, then turn to my farmhands. "Guys, feel free to take your break early if you want. I'll come and help you in an hour or so."

"I like Miranda," I say as we walk back to the house together. "I asked if she wanted to stay for lunch, but she's not allowed to do that when she's on duty."

"That makes sense. She's my parole officer." Gemma

looks me up and down and arches a brow. "By the way, you look nice today."

A nervous laugh escapes me, and I shake my head. "I just went out to meet one of the wholesalers in Sedona." A blush rises to my cheeks and I look away, hoping she hasn't noticed. I haven't dressed up since I moved here, but I pulled out one of my favorite summer dresses for the occasion and styled my hair. My old office attire won't do for the "organic farm girl" look I'm trying to pull off, but I couldn't show up in my farm rags either.

"Are you sure you didn't dress up for Miranda?"

"Miranda? What makes you think that?" I don't like the assumption she's making, and I'm not quite sure why it bothers me so much.

"I don't know. She's clearly gay and not bad looking." Gemma shrugs as if that would make total sense.

"No, Miranda is not my type, and even is she was, she's been sleeping with my best friend, Charlotte. That's how this all happened. Charlotte introduced us and came up with the idea of hiring someone through the program."

"Okay..." Gemma frowns. "So your best friend knows you have an ex-con living under your roof? And she's okay with that?"

"Yes, Charlotte knows. I know I wasn't supposed to tell anyone, but it started with her, so I had to keep her in the loop. You'll meet her. She's in court this week, but she'll drop by on the weekend." I smile. "She's lovely and she doesn't judge, I promise. We used to work together."

As we approach the house, I can sense Gemma's nervousness in the way she's fidgeting with the hem of her shirt, the way her steps slow ever so slightly. I bump my shoulder against hers, offering a reassuring smile when she glances up at me.

"It's going to be fine," I say. "Miranda's on your side, remember? She's here to help, not to interrogate you."

Gemma nods, taking a deep breath. "I know," she says, but there's a tremor in her voice that belies her words. "It's just...I'm still on parole, you know?"

I nod, understanding her unease. Of course this is daunting for her, and I'm struck by a sudden desire to protect her, but I know that's not my place. All I can do is support her, stand by her side as she navigates this new chapter.

We climb the porch steps together, and I see Miranda through the screen door, seated at the kitchen table with a file folder open in front of her. She's sipping the coffee I made when she arrived and looks up with a smile as we enter.

"Gemma." She gets up to shake her hand. "It's good to see you looking so well. Look at you—you've got a tan."

"Thanks. I've been enjoying the outdoors," Gemma says, taking a seat at the table.

I make a coffee for myself and Gemma and top up Miranda's mug before I join them.

Gemma's knee bounces nervously under the table, and I resist the urge to reach out and still it with my hand.

Miranda shuffles through some papers. "So, Gemma," she begins, her tone friendly but professional. "I just wanted to touch base, see how you're settling in. How are you finding life on the farm so far?"

Gemma clears her throat, sitting up a bit straighter in her chair. "It's good," she says, and I can hear the sincerity in her voice. "Really good. I love being out in the orchard, working with my hands. It's peaceful. I've been doing some electrical work too, and that's been fun."

Miranda nods, jotting something down in her notes.

"That's great to hear. And how about the living situation? Are you feeling comfortable, safe?"

Gemma glances at me, a soft smile playing about her lips. "Very," she says quietly. "Lori's been amazing. She's made me feel so welcome. I couldn't ask for a better setup."

I feel a flush of warmth at her words, a swell of emotion that I try to tamp down.

Miranda turns to me then. "And Lori, from your perspective? How's it been, having Gemma here, working with her?"

"It's been wonderful," I say honestly. "Gemma's a hard worker, a quick learner. And beyond that, she's just...she's a joy to have around. She brings a great energy to the farm."

I chance a glance at Gemma, catching the tail end of a pleased, slightly flustered expression before she schools her features.

Miranda nods, looking satisfied. "That's excellent. It sounds like the placement is working out well for both of you." She makes another note, then looks up again, her expression turning a touch more serious.

"Now, Gemma," she says gently, "I do have to ask. Have you been in any trouble since you got here? Socially? Any incidents you would consider confrontational?"

"No," Gemma says.

"Have you used any illicit substances since your release? Any drugs, even prescription medications that aren't yours?"

"No."

Miranda nods, making a note. "Good. As part of your parole agreement, you are subject to random drug testing. I don't have any reason to suspect anything, but I am obligated to perform a test today. Standard procedure, nothing personal."

Gemma takes a deep breath, nodding. "I understand. Whatever you need."

Miranda reaches into her bag, pulling out a sealed plastic cup. "I'll need you to provide a urine sample before I leave," she explains, handing Gemma the cup. "While you do that, I just have a few more questions for Lori."

She waits for Gemma to head for the bathroom and turns to me. "Okay, these are just for you, as Gemma's host and employer. It's all part of the process, just to make sure everything's above board and running smoothly."

I nod, folding my hands on the table. "Of course. Ask away."

Miranda consults her notes, then looks up at me. "Can you confirm that Gemma's been fulfilling her work duties as agreed upon? Showing up on time, putting in the hours, all of that?"

"Absolutely," I say without hesitation. "Gemma's been an exemplary worker. I couldn't ask for a better employee or farmhand."

"And there haven't been any issues with her living here? No conflicts, no concerns about behavior or adherence to house rules?"

I shake my head firmly. "None whatsoever. Gemma's been a model tenant. She's clean, respectful, considerate. She's a delight to have around."

Miranda makes another note, then closes her folder with a snap. "Excellent. That's really all I needed to cover today. It seems like everything's going swimmingly here." She pauses and lowers her voice. "I can see that you're a great team, but keep in mind that it's important to keep some form of boundaries. I know it's not easy when you live in the same house, but I can tell by your body language that you're..." She chews her lip. "Well, that you're quite fond of each other."

I frown, trying to grasp what that means. "Are you saying what I think you're saying? Because Gemma and I are not—"

"No, that's not what I'm saying." Miranda holds up a hand. "I just need to remind you that you are Gemma's life-line right now. You're in a position of power, not just as her employer, but as the person who provides her board and general needs. If anything happens between the two of you and it goes wrong, she'll be left with nothing."

"Of course. I wouldn't do anything to put her future in jeopardy," I say, feeling ashamed for checking her out earlier. Admittedly, I've done it a few times this week, and I've caught her staring at me too. I didn't think much of it then, but if Miranda has noticed something, I'll have to reset my boundaries.

"Good. I just had to mention it. Again, it's standard procedure."

I nod, even though I suspect that was more of a personal comment.

"And thank you, Lori," she continues, "for being such a positive force in Gemma's life. It makes all the difference."

15

GEMMA

*L*ori's been acting differently around me these past few days. It's subtle, but I can feel it—a slight hesitation in her interactions, a guardedness that wasn't there before. This morning, as I stand in the kitchen waiting for the coffee to brew, I'm acutely aware of a growing distance between us.

She's been taking her coffee inside lately, retreating to her new office instead of joining me on the porch like she used to. I miss our morning chats, the easy way we'd start the day together.

The coffee maker beeps, jolting me out of my thoughts. I make two mugs, doctoring mine with a splash of cream and take a deep breath, steeling myself. We need to talk.

I find her in the living room, curled up in an armchair with the newspaper, and she looks up as I enter.

"Hey," I say softly, holding out her mug. "I made coffee. I was hoping...could we talk? Here? Or outside?"

Lori hesitates for a beat, and I can see an internal debate playing out on her face. Then she nods, setting the newspaper aside and accepting the mug with a small smile.

"Sure," she says, standing. "Let's go outside. It's a beautiful morning."

We make our way out onto the porch, settling into our usual spots on the steps. Although the furniture is perfectly fine, it's become a morning habit, I suppose. For a moment, we just sit, sipping our coffee and watching the play of light through the trees. It's peaceful, but there's an undercurrent of tension that I can't ignore any longer.

I set my mug down, clasping my hands in my lap. "Lori," I begin, my voice trembling slightly. "Have I...have I done something wrong? Something to upset you?"

Lori's head whips around, her eyes wide with surprise. "What? No, of course not. Why would you think that?"

I shrug, looking down at my hands. "You've been... distant, lately. Like you're avoiding me. I just...I wanted to make sure I haven't overstepped or made you feel uncomfortable in any way." The truth is, I've had sleepless nights over our lack of interaction, but she doesn't need to know that.

Lori sighs, setting her own mug aside. She rubs a hand over her face, looking suddenly tired. "You haven't done anything wrong, Gem," she says quietly. "I'm sorry if I've made you feel that way. It's not you."

I frown, confusion and concern warring in my chest. "What do you mean? What's going on?"

Lori is silent for a long moment, her gaze fixed on some distant point in the orchard. When she finally speaks, her voice is low and careful. "During Miranda's visit the other day," she begins, "she pulled me aside. She said...she's noticed how close we've become, and it was clear that she was a little worried about that."

"Oh?" My heart skips a beat, a flutter of something new and strange sparking in my chest.

"She advised me to be careful," Lori continues. "To keep some distance. Professionally, you know. She's worried that our relationship might be edging into inappropriate territory. Which I assured her it wasn't," she hastily adds.

"No, it hasn't," I agree. Of course. Of course Miranda would see it that way. I'm a parolee, an ex-con. Lori's my supervisor, my host. There are lines that can't be crossed, boundaries that must be maintained. Not only that, she might be worried that if we get too close, I'll tell Lori what I've done and then she might not want to have me around anymore. "But I understand," I say. "And she's right. It's for the best."

Lori nods, but there's a tension in her shoulders that wasn't there before. "I'm sorry, I should have mentioned it," she says. "Can we talk about how we're going to move forward with this? With the boundaries?"

I nod, trying to ignore the sinking feeling in my stomach. "Sure," I say, taking a deep breath. "How do you want to handle it?"

"I think...I think we just need to be mindful," she says slowly. "Of how we interact, of how much time we spend together outside of work. We can still be friendly, of course, but maybe we need to...to pull back a bit. Keep things more professional."

"Right. Professional." The word feels wrong on my tongue, too cold and impersonal for what's already grown between us. But I nod and smile. "I can do that."

"It's not that I don't enjoy your company," Lori says quickly, as if she can read my thoughts. "I do. Very much. But Miranda's right. There are lines we can't cross. Not with our situation." She sighs. "I'm glad we're on the same page." She offers me a small smile. "And hey, now that it's out in the open, at least we can agree not to let things get too close. Right?"

I nod, but something about her phrasing catches my attention. "Too close?" I echo, trying to keep my tone casual. "What exactly do you mean?"

A blush rises on Lori's cheeks, staining them a pretty pink. She looks away, suddenly fascinated by her coffee mug. "Oh, you know," she says, waving a hand vaguely. "Just in general. I never thought of you that way, of course. But Miranda seemed to think...well, it doesn't matter what she thinks. We know the truth."

I study her profile, the sweet curve of her dimpled cheek, the way her lashes flutter against her skin. Despite her words, I can't shake the feeling that there's something she's not saying, something she's holding back.

Because the truth is, I have felt something with Lori. It's been there in the quiet moments, in the shared laughter and the easy silences. In the way my heart skips a beat when she smiles at me, the way my skin tingles when she brushes against me in the kitchen. We've never flirted, and there have been no charged comments, no lingering touches. But still, I'm sure I haven't imagined it, this subtle undercurrent of attraction.

I don't voice any of this, of course. How can I, when Lori's just made it clear that we need to maintain our distance? So instead, I paste on another smile, hoping it looks real. "You're right," I say, injecting a lightness into my tone that I don't quite feel. "We have nothing to worry about. I don't have those kinds of feelings for you either. We're just...we're just friends. Colleagues."

Lori meets my gaze again, curiosity flickering in them now. "Exactly. Friends and colleagues."

As we sip our coffee, there's a new awareness between

us, and I can't help but think it's made the already charged situation worse. Because now, all I can think of is that I can't allow my mind to go there and I wonder if that's on her mind too.

After a while, Lori clears her throat, pushing to her feet. "I should probably head into town," she says, dusting off her jeans. "I've got some errands to run, and I told Charlotte I'd meet her for coffee. Would you like me to drop you off somewhere?"

"No, thank you. I'll hold down the fort here. I was thinking I might tackle those wiring issues in the shed, if that's okay?"

"Sure. That would be great." Lori hesitates, looking for a moment like she might say something more. But then she just nods, turning to head inside. I watch her go, my eyes tracing the lines of her back, the sway of her hips.

When the screen door swings shut behind her, I let out the breath I've been holding. My heart is beating too fast and my palms are damp with sweat. *This is good*, I tell myself firmly. *This is necessary. We were getting too close, too comfortable.* But even as I try to convince myself, I can't ignore the feeling that a door has closed, a path untaken.

16

LORI

The courtyard of the Chocolate Tree is a hidden oasis amid the red-rock splendor of Sedona. Towering sycamores cast dappled shades over the stone patio, and it smells of blooming jasmine and the rich aroma of the organic, raw cacao delicacies the café is known for.

I settle into a wrought iron chair, the intricate scrollwork pressing cool patterns into my skin. The mosaic tabletop is a kaleidoscope of turquoise, lapis, and amber, the tiles forming an abstract mandala that shimmers in the sunlight.

I've barely had a moment to take in the serene surroundings when Charlotte walks in, her heels clicking on the flagstones.

"Lori!" She kisses my cheek before sinking into the seat opposite me, her oversize sunglasses glinting. "I'm so sorry I'm late. You would not believe the morning I've had."

I chuckle, shaking my head. "Let me guess. The Benson deposition?"

Charlotte groans theatrically, flagging down a waiter. "Worse. The Henderson divorce. I swear, if I have to listen to one more bitter diatribe about who gets the vacation house in Aspen, I'm going to lose it."

"Ah, yes. The perils of representing the over-privileged," I tease, perusing the menu. "Is Cleo giving you a hard time?"

"No, she's been keeping to herself. She never bugged me much to begin with. She just micromanaged you because she was a controlling witch. Have you heard from her lately?"

"Yes, she's been calling me and I've been ignoring her." I blow out my cheeks and shake my head. "I wish she would leave me alone. It's over and I just want to move on." Anyway, I don't want to talk about Cleo," I say. "Let's get coffee."

We place our orders—a dark-chocolate chia pudding for me, an acai bowl for Charlotte, and two lattes—and settle into our usual rhythm of gossip and catch-up.

"So, tell me," Charlotte says, leaning forward. "How's life on the farm? Is it everything you dreamed it would be?"

"It's good," I say, stirring my coffee. "Really good. It's a lot of work, but it's rewarding. I feel like I'm actually building something."

"I'm glad. I'm sorry I haven't stopped by lately. I've been swamped, but I'll make it up to you, I promise."

"That's okay. I've had company. You have to meet Gemma. She's lovely."

Charlotte points her spoon at me. "Oh yeah...how is your new farmhand?"

I feel a flush creep up my neck, and take a sudden intense interest in my pudding. "She's good. Great, actually. She's been a huge help. All electrics are in place, and I trust her to manage the seasonal workers."

"Uh-huh. I bet she's great." Charlotte's tone is sly, know-

ing. "Miranda let it slip that she's gay." Then she slams a hand in front of her mouth. "Oops...and I promised not to mention she'd told me that."

"Yeah, that's a breach. She's not supposed to discuss Gemma with anyone outside the system," I say in a defensive tone, feeling oddly protective of Gemma.

"I know. Trust me, she regretted it. We had too much to drink one night and I was prying. It's my fault." Charlotte shrugs. "But the fact is, I know. So...have you been mixing business with pleasure?"

"Of course not. We're keeping things professional. Boundaries, you know."

Charlotte raises a perfectly sculpted eyebrow. "Boundaries? Since when do you care about boundaries? You used to sleep with your boss."

I shift in my seat and pick at my nails. "Since Miranda reminded me that Gemma's in a vulnerable position. I'm her employer and her landlord. There's a power imbalance."

Charlotte hums, considering. "I suppose that's true."

"And anyway," I continue, "just because she's gay doesn't mean there's attraction. That's a ridiculous assumption."

"Also true." Charlotte points to my face. "But that doesn't take away the fact that you're blushing. You like her."

My head snaps up, my eyes wide. "What? No, I...I mean, yes, I like her, but not...not like that. She's just...she's easy to be around."

"Mm-hmm. And easy on the eyes, too, I bet." Charlotte leans back, crossing her arms. "Come on, dish. What's she like? What does she look like?"

I hesitate, but I can feel my resistance crumbling under Charlotte's keen gaze. "She's...lovely," I admit, my voice soft. "She's tall and lean, with this long, dark hair that she always wears in a messy bun. She's got this great, sincere smile and she's incredibly sweet."

I picture the way Gemma looks in the morning, sleep-rumpled and soft, cradling a mug of coffee. The way her face lights up when she's elbow-deep in the wiring of an old lamp, coaxing it back to life. The way her shirt creeps up when she reaches for the high-hanging fruit. *Fuck. I'm doing it again.*

Charlotte is grinning now, triumphantly. "I knew it. You're totally crushing on her."

"I'm not," I say sharply. "I'm appreciative of her help. That's all."

"Sure, sure." Charlotte shakes her head, amused. "When can I meet her?"

"Anytime. Why don't you join us for dinner when you're free? Then you can see for yourself that there's nothing going on."

"Okay." Charlotte's eyes narrow. "Can I bring a date?"

I chuckle but raise a brow when I realize she's serious. "A date? That's so unlike you. Who's the lucky lady?"

Charlotte grins, a mischievous glint in her eye. "Well, I was thinking...maybe Miranda?"

My jaw drops, and I nearly knock over my latte. "Miranda? As in, Gemma's parole officer Miranda? The casual fling?"

Charlotte has the grace to look slightly abashed, but she can't quite suppress the smile tugging at her lips. "The very same," she confirms, twirling a strand of her sleek bob around her finger. "What can I say? She's gotten under my skin. I've never met anyone who's more assertive and bossier than me. It's sexy."

I sit back, stunned. In all the years I've known Charlotte,

I've never seen her serious about a woman. She's always been the queen of casual, the master of the no-strings-attached affair. The idea of her catching feelings is mind-boggling.

"Wow," I say, shaking my head. "I thought you two were just messing around. Friends with benefits, and all that."

Charlotte shrugs, but there's a softness to her expression that I've rarely seen before. "That's how it started," she admits, tracing the rim of her acai bowl with her spoon. "But lately, it's been...different. Deeper, somehow. I find myself wanting to see her even when we're not tumbling into bed together." She looks up, meeting my gaze head-on. "She's the first woman in years that I'm genuinely excited to spend time with."

"Char," I say softly, "that's huge. I'm so happy for you." And I am. Beneath the shock, there's a warm glow of joy for my friend. Charlotte's always been the life of the party, the girl who can charm anyone with a wink and a smile. But I've also seen the loneliness that lurks beneath the surface, the yearning for a connection that goes beyond the physical.

Charlotte flips her hand over, lacing her fingers with mine and giving a gentle squeeze. "Thanks, babe," she says, then let's out an uncomfortable chuckle. She's not one for talking about her emotions, and I sense she's done. "Anyway," she says, her tone turning brisk and businesslike once more, "what do you think? About the dinner idea? I know it might be a bit...unorthodox, given the situation with Gemma. But I really want to meet her, and I thought it might be nice for Miranda to meet you in a more relaxed setting."

I hesitate as I consider the proposal. It feels like the setup for a sitcom episode; it's a recipe for disaster. "We should check with them. I suspect they'll be against the idea, but we can ask, of course. If it's not an option, you can come over alone and I can meet you and Miranda for dinner in town some other time. It might go against protocol and all that, so I'll leave Miranda for you to deal with. You know her best, after all."

Charlotte smirks. "Oh, I certainly do," she purrs, and I can't help but laugh.

"Spare me the details, please," I beg, dissolving into giggles. "I still have to look her in the eye at our next parole —" My phone pings and I stop myself. "Fuck. It's Cleo again." My stomach churns as I read the message.

Lori, we need to talk. You can't just disappear like this. You're throwing away your career and ruining your life. Come back and I'll make you partner.

Charlotte takes my phone, her eyes flashing with anger as she reads it. "She's one to talk about ruining lives. Ignore her. She's just trying to control you, like she always has."

"I've been ignoring her, but she won't stop. I've begged her to leave me alone. Should I feel guilty? Was I in the wrong?"

"No!" Charlotte shoots me a fierce look. "You've come so far, don't start doubting yourself again. That's what she does. She makes you think you're crazy for leaving her, but if you go back, she'll just make your life hell all over again."

"I know." My phone buzzes again, and I steel myself before looking at the screen.

If you don't respond, I'll come and find you. You can't just ignore me. Then, no more than ten second later, *I'll make sure you never work in the legal sector again.*

"Wow. A legit threat only two minutes after a generous offer. Looks like she's suffering from her abrupt mood swings today." It's so like Cleo, to force my hand. But not this time. I navigate to my settings, my finger hovering over the "block" button. I look up, meeting Charlotte's gaze.

Charlotte nods. "Do it. Cut her off."

I take a deep breath, feeling the weight of the moment. Then, with a decisive tap, I block Cleo's number.

"There," I say, setting my phone down. "It's done."

17

GEMMA

*T*he Sedona farmers' market is a riot of color and activity. As Lori and I stroll through the bustling aisles, I'm struck by the sheer abundance on display. Mounds of glossy, jewel-toned vegetables, pyramids of fragrant fruit, bundles of herbs tied with twine.

The air is thick with the mingled scents of ripe tomatoes, fresh-baked bread, roasted nuts, and sizzling food from the artisanal stalls. Everywhere I turn, there's something tempting that makes my mouth water and my stomach rumble.

Lori moves through the crowd with ease, her white sundress flowing around her tanned legs. It's an understated dress, but on her, it looks effortlessly chic. The light fabric dances in the breeze, and I find my eyes drawn to the sway of her hips, the graceful line of her neck.

I'm underdressed in comparison, but there's a certain confidence that comes with my outfit too. I'm wearing a pair of Maggie's old, flared jeans that I found in a box in the attic. They're soft and worn, molded to my body like a second skin, and paired with a plain white T-shirt, they make me feel both comfortable and stylish.

I catch Lori stealing glances at me as we walk, her eyes lingering on the curve of my waist, the length of my legs. It sends a little thrill through me, a spark of something warm and electric. I've noticed her looking more often lately, even though she tries to hide it.

We've both kept to ourselves more and tried not to spend long evenings on the porch together, but somehow, that's caused a heightened awareness of our chemistry, especially on days like today, when we're out doing something together. Basic things like getting groceries or just sitting in the car next to her have become a sweet torture, and I know she feels it too.

Pushing those thoughts aside, I try to focus on the task at hand. We're here to scope out the market and see if there might be a place for us here—a way to bring back Maggie's old stall, to sell fruit and maybe even some of her famous jams if we can manage to replicate them.

"What do you think?" Lori asks, pausing beside a display of handcrafted pottery. "Can you see us fitting in here?"

I take in the variety of stalls, the mix of local farmers, artisans, and food producers. There's a real sense of community here I've rarely witnessed.

"Yeah. I think we could make it work. We've got the quality produce, and with a little creativity on the presentation front..." I trail off, my mind already spinning with ideas. "Rustic crates overflowing with fruit, hand-labeled jars of jam, maybe even some samples for tasting. And how about using those vintage cloths we found to cover the table with?"

Lori smiles, her eyes lighting up. "I like your thinking,"

she says. "Because actually, I had an ulterior motive for bringing you here today."

I tilt my head, curious. "Oh? Do tell."

"I was thinking...what if you ran the stall? As your own business, I mean. You could keep the profits, use them to start building your savings."

My eyes widen in surprise and confusion. "Me? But it's your farm, your fruit. I couldn't just..."

But Lori is already shaking her head. "Gemma, you've been such an integral part of bringing the orchard back to life. You deserve to reap the rewards of that hard work. Besides, the fruit sold here is only a tiny percentage of what goes to the wholesalers, and I don't have time to do it." She reaches out, taking my hand in hers. "I want to pay you more, but I'm not in a position to do that just yet. This way, you could have a real income right away and a sense of independence. You could start saving for your future."

I swallow hard, my throat suddenly tight with emotion. It's an incredible offer, a generous gift. But it's also a daunting prospect for someone with my history. "Lori, I don't know what to say. It's an amazing idea, but..." I hesitate. "It's a customer-facing job. What if people find out about my conviction? I don't want to taint the farm's reputation."

Lori squeezes my hand, her expression determined. "Your past doesn't define you. Whatever you've done..." Her voice softens. "You're so much more than your worst mistake."

I put on a brave smile, but my stomach is churning at the mention of "my worst mistake." *If only she knew.* I take a shaky breath and paint on a smile. It's a great opportunity after all, a way for me to move forward. "Okay," I say. "I'd love to give it a go. Thank you."

Lori beams, her joy radiant and infectious. She pulls me into a hug, right there in the middle of the market, and I melt into her embrace, breathing in the soft, floral scent of her hair. *Boundaries*, I remind myself, but I don't pull away.

As we break apart, Lori's cheeks are flushed. "I'm sorry," she says, as if reading my mind. "I'm just so happy you want to do it. I'm over my head in dealing with the wholesalers, the harvest, and trying to figure out when and how many seasonal workers to employ. I couldn't handle another market gig on top of all that, but it's such a great opportunity that it seemed like a no-brainer."

"Thank you," I say again, still basking in the afterglow of the hug. There's an awkward moment of silence while my eyes meet hers, and as soon as we realize the eye contact is lingering too long, we turn and continue to walk.

"Actually, there's something else I wanted to talk to you about," Lori says. "And I want you to be honest about how you feel about it."

"Okay..." I feel the familiar flutter in my core. Is she finally going to address the elephant in the room? The fact that we have growing chemistry and no idea what to do about it?

"So my best friend, Charlotte..."

"Yes. The one who knows about me? Miranda's friend?" I ask, mildly disappointed it's not heading in the direction I hoped.

"That's right. Well, it transpires that they've been dating."

"Oh?" I chuckle. "So, it's more serious than you thought?"

"Yes. And if you're okay with it, but only if you're okay with it," Lori presses, "I thought maybe we could all have dinner together."

I suppress the urge to burst out in laughter because the idea is just absurd. "You want me to attend a social get-together with my parole officer? That is so..." I trail off, shaking my head in disbelief. "Unconventional? Bizarre? Potentially uncomfortable for everyone involved?"

Lori winces. "I know, I'm sorry, I shouldn't have asked. Please forget about it."

"It's not that I don't want to meet your friend," I say, choosing my words with care. "It's just...Miranda is my parole officer, and I doubt she'd even agree to it."

"Charlotte asked Miranda first," Lori says. "Apparently, it's a bit of a gray area. If she's off duty and happens to run into a client at a social event, it's not like she has to flee the scene. She's happy to come, but again, I totally get that you're uncomfortable with it, and I sincerely apologize for even mentioning—"

"No, please don't apologize." I linger, turning the idea over in my mind. A part of me recoils at the thought of socializing with the woman who holds my fate in her hands, but then again, chances are slim I'll get another opportunity to socialize with people I don't have to lie to. Apart from Lori, I have no friends. They all vanished from the face of the earth as soon as they heard the word "guilty." Besides, Miranda is on my side. She's not looking to catch me out on a mistake; she genuinely wants to help me. "I suppose it could be fun," I say. "And if Miranda is comfortable with it, then I am too."

"Really?" Lori studies me. "Are you sure? Because Charlotte can come alone."

"I'm sure. I mean, it will probably be a little weird at first. But like you said, Miranda's off duty. And if Charlotte's your best friend and Miranda's important to her, then I'd like to meet them both properly and..." My voice trails off as I flinch at a nearby noise. It's only a child throwing a tantrum, but my whole body goes rigid.

Lori, who has noticed it, puts an arm around me. "Hey, it's okay. We're safe here."

"I know." I take a shaky breath and square my shoulders. "I'm sorry. It's just...old habits."

"You don't have to apologize," she says. "Is the market too much?"

"No, I'm fine. I haven't been around this many people since I came out. It just takes a little getting used to. But don't worry," I hastily add, fighting a panic attack. "I can handle it." I was hoping she hadn't noticed, but Lori is observant when it comes to me and always wants to make sure I'm comfortable.

"You're not fine, you're shaking." She glances at my trembling hands and frowns. "PTSD?"

I nod. My heart rate spikes and my breathing quickens as the noise of the crowd seems to amplify around me. It's like everything is closing in, and I can't quite catch my breath. My palms grow clammy, and a cold sweat breaks out on the back of my neck. "I thought I had it under control, but sometimes it sneaks up on me, especially in new places."

Lori's brow furrows with concern. "Why don't we find a quieter spot to sit for a bit? Just until you feel more grounded."

I focus on the warmth of her touch to anchor myself as she guides me away from the market stalls, her presence a calming influence.

We find a small bench nestled beneath a juniper tree, and as we sit, Lori takes both of my hands in hers, her thumbs rubbing soothing circles on my skin.

"Just breathe," she murmurs. "You're safe here."

I close my eyes and concentrate on the sensation of her touch, the sound of her voice. Slowly, the tightness in my chest begins to ease, and the roaring in my ears subsides. I take a deep, shuddering breath, feeling the panic start to recede.

"That's it, just breathe," she repeats, and pulls me into her arms.

I close my eyes and rest my forehead against her shoulder. With each passing moment, I feel the weight of my anxiety lifting, my mind clearing. Lori's presence beside me is a reminder that I'm not alone, and I cherish her more than I can express.

18

LORI

*T*he kitchen is a war zone, a sticky, steamy, chaotic mess of bubbling pans, scattered utensils, and precariously piled dishes. I stand at the epicenter of it all, my hair frizzed from the humidity, my apron splattered with peach juice and dollops of half-set jam.

With the recipe Joseph gave me next to me, I'm so focused on stirring the three huge pans on the stove, my eyes darting frantically between them as I try to keep everything from boiling over or burning, that I don't hear Gemma come in. It's only when she clears her throat, a poorly suppressed chuckle escaping her lips, that I whirl around, nearly dropping my spoon in surprise.

"Whoa," she says, her eyes widening as she takes in the scene of culinary carnage. "Did you set off a peach bomb in here, or are you just really committed to this whole 'farm to table' thing?"

I feel my cheeks flush, half from the heat of the stove and half from embarrassment. "Ha-ha," I mutter, blowing a stray strand of hair out of my face. "Lap it up, chuckles.

We'll see who's laughing when this jam wins first prize at the county fair."

Gemma grins, sidling up to the counter and peering into the nearest pan. "I didn't know there was a category for 'most experimental texture' or 'biggest mess made in pursuit of preserves.'"

I swat at her with my free hand, but I can't help the smile tugging at the corners of my mouth. "Easy on the sarcasm. This is artisanal small-batch jam. The texture is rustic, and the mess is all part of the creative process."

She laughs, a full, rich sound that fills the kitchen. "Well, I wouldn't normally stand in the way of culinary genius, but you look like you might need some help."

I hesitate, my gaze flicking over her. She's just come in from the fields, her skin glowing with a light sheen of sweat, her hair escaping its top knot in messy strands. Her tank top clings to her curves, highlighting the lean, sculpted lines of her arms and shoulders. Her denim shorts ride up her thighs as she leans against the counter, exposing an expanse of tanned skin.

It's not the first time I've noticed Gemma's body, but here, in the close confines of the kitchen, with the heat and the steam and the sweet, cloying scent of cooking fruit, it feels way more intense.

Dragging my gaze away, I focus on the pans. "No, no, it's okay," I say, my voice a little too high, a little too bright. "You've been working all morning. You should relax. Make yourself some lunch. I have fresh bread."

But Gemma is already reaching for an apron. "I'll have some bread, but only with a dollop of your award-winning jam," she says, tying the strings behind her back. "Besides, I've made jam before." She bumps me with her hip, gently nudging me aside so she can stir one of the pans. The contact feels like an electric shock, a jolt of awareness that zips through me from head to toe.

"O-okay," I stammer, trying to regain my composure. "If you insist. I won't say no to a little help."

We settle into a rhythm, Gemma stirring the pans while I chop more fruit, the steady *thunk* of the knife against the cutting board blending with the bubble and hiss of the jam. We work in silence for a while, broken only by the occasional murmured instruction or request for an ingredient.

But as the minutes tick by, I find my eyes straying more and more often to Gemma. To the flex of her forearms as she stirs, the movements of her fingers as she adjusts the heat or tests the consistency. To the little furrow of concentration between her brows.

She's beautiful like this, I catch myself thinking. Lost in the task, unselfconscious and unguarded. There's an honest sensuality to her, an earthy, elemental allure that has nothing to do with artifice or pretense.

As if sensing my gaze, she glances at me, catching me in the act of staring. I blush, but I don't look away. I can't look away.

For a long, suspended moment, we stand there, eyes locked, the air between us thick with more than just steam. Something flickers in Gemma's gaze, a spark of heat and awareness.

But then she blinks, the spell broken, and the moment passes. She turns back to the stove, giving the nearest pan a decisive stir. "I think this batch is just about done," she says, her voice husky. She dips a spoon into the bubbling mixture, blowing on it gently before bringing it to her lips for a taste.

Her eyes flutter closed, a small, appreciative hum

escaping her throat. "Oh, wow," she murmurs. "Lori, this is amazing. The perfect balance of sweet and tart."

She opens her eyes, holding out the spoon to me. "Here, try it."

I step closer, my heart hammering against my ribs. Slowly, carefully, I lean in, wrapping my lips around the spoon. The jam bursts on my tongue, an explosion of sun-ripened sweetness cut through with a bright citric tanginess. But it's not the taste that makes my pulse race. It's the intimacy of the gesture, the knowledge that Gemma's lips have been where mine are now. I let my eyes drift shut, savoring the flavor. When I open them again, Gemma is watching me, her gaze dark and intense.

"Good, right?" she asks.

I nod, my voice deserting me. I'm suddenly very aware of how close we're standing, of the heat radiating off Gemma's body, the faint, salty-sweet scent of her skin. "It's delicious," I finally manage, my tongue darting out to catch a stray drop of jam at the corner of my mouth. "But it's missing something."

"Yeah, I was thinking the same." Gemma tilts her head, considering. "Maybe a touch of lemon zest? To add a little more zing?"

"Lemon zest," I repeat, latching on to the suggestion like a lifeline. Anything to break this tension, this electric, simmering awareness. "That's perfect. Let me just..." I step back, turning to rummage in the fridge for lemons. The cool air is a relief against my overheated skin, a momentary respite from the intensity of Gemma's presence.

By the time I find the lemon and turn back, Gemma has moved to the sink, rinsing off the spoon.

"Here you go," I say, handing her three lemons. "One for each batch. Would that do?"

"Perfect." Gemma smiles, grabbing a grater from the drying rack. "Allow me." She takes the lemon from my hand, her fingers brushing against mine in the process. It's a fleeting touch, barely there, but it sends a jolt straight through me.

If Gemma notices my reaction, she doesn't show it. She just sets to work, her hands sure and steady as she grates the peel into the pans.

"Okay," she says, setting down the grater and dusting off her hands. "Let's see what a little citrus magic can do." She gives the pans another stir and the scent of lemon rises to mingle with the aroma of peaches.

We both lean in, inhaling deeply. "Oh, that's lovely," I murmur.

Gemma dips the spoon back into the pan, scooping up a dollop of the gleaming jam. "Let's give it a taste, shall we?"

She tastes it, nods approvingly, then holds out the spoon, her eyes locked on mine. There's a challenge there, a silent dare hanging in the steam-thickened air.

Heart pounding, I lean in, closing my lips around the spoon. The brush of Gemma's fingers against my chin, catching a drop of jam, makes me shiver. Her touch lingers, her thumb stroking over my skin in a featherlight caress.

"Sweet," she murmurs, her voice low and throaty.

My eyes widen and my breath stalls. There's no mistaking the intention in her gaze, the heat simmering beneath the surface of her words.

But before I can react, the shrill beep of the timer shatters the moment, making us both jump.

Gemma steps back, a flush staining her cheeks. Grabbing a pan holder, she busies herself with removing the pan from the heat. "I think it's done. We should probably get this jarred up while it's still hot. Did you sterilize the jars?" she asks.

"Sterilize?" I frown. "The jars are new."

"For someone who makes great jam, you really don't know the first thing," Gemma jokes. She chuckles and shakes her head. "Good thing I checked. You don't want to get your customers sick. That wouldn't be a good start."

19

GEMMA

*M*elting cheese and sweet, bubbling jam welcome me as I open the oven to check on my dish. The golden, gooey brie is flecked with fragrant rosemary and studded with slivers of garlic, the peach preserves glistening on top.

I inhale deeply, savoring the mingled scents. It's been a long, busy day of harvesting, jam-making, and labeling, and Lori and I never got around to having a proper lunch. By the time we finished potting the jam, it was already getting dark.

Lori headed off to take a well-deserved soak in the tub, and I found myself pottering around the kitchen, my stomach grumbling and my mind spinning with ideas. I spotted the round of brie in the fridge, a decadent purchase from our trip to the farmers' market, and inspiration struck.

Now, as I arrange a crusty loaf of bread and a colorful salad in serving bowls, I feel a flutter of anticipation in my belly. It's not just the prospect of a delicious meal that has my pulse picking up. It's the thought of sharing it with Lori, of sitting across from her in the candlelit hush of the evening, our knees brushing beneath the table as we talk and laugh.

As if summoned by my thoughts, I hear the creak of floorboards, the soft pad of bare feet on the stairs. A moment later, Lori appears in the doorway, wrapped in her blue robe, her hair damp around her face.

"Something smells amazing," she says, her eyes widening as she peers into the oven. "What's all this?"

An uncharacteristic shyness washes over me. "I thought you might be hungry," I say, gesturing to the spread. "We never did get around to lunch, and after all that hard work…"

Lori's face softens, a smile blooming. "Thank you, but I should have done that."

"No, I enjoy it. It's nothing too fancy. Just some brie with your homemade jam and bread and salad. I figured you deserved a little something special, after making your first batch of award-winning jam."

Lori chuckles. "I already regret mentioning the award-winning part," she jokes. "Although going by the smell, your dish might be right up there."

"I'm going to have a quick shower," I say. "Just ten minutes, I'll be right back."

"Okay, I'll take this outside." Lori picks up the tray I've put on the counter. It holds plates, cutlery, and glasses, and I've put fresh candles in holders, and filled a jug with ice water and mint.

"Thank you. I won't be long."

True to my word, I make quick work of my shower, flushing away the stickiness of the day, the sweat and sugar and fruit juice that cling to my skin. Emerging refreshed and invigorated, I slip into a robe of my own.

Padding barefoot, I see Lori standing on the porch,

lighting the candles. My gaze catches on the play of light and shadow across her face, the way the candlelight gilds her skin and makes her eyes sparkle. I cross the distance between us to help her light the last candle, and we stand there for a moment, the space between us charged and crackling like a live wire. I feel the heat of Lori's body, the whisper of her breath against my skin. Her pupils flare, and her lips part ever so slightly, like an invitation. *Something is happening here.*

But then she clears her throat, the spell broken, and steps back with a soft chuckle. "We should eat," she says, gesturing to the table. "Before all your hard work gets cold."

I pull out a chair for her, and she flashes me a grin, sinking into the offered seat with a murmur of thanks. I take my place across from her, the table suddenly feeling like both too much space and not enough between us. It's been a strange day. No. It's been a strange week. Ever since we addressed the fact that we shouldn't get too close, the opposite has happened, and I can see she's struggling too.

Lori reaches for the bread, tearing off a chunk and dipping it into the molten pool of cheese and jam. She brings it to her mouth, her eyes fluttering shut as she takes a bite. A low, appreciative moan rises from her throat, sending a bolt of heat straight through me.

"Oh my god," she mumbles through a mouthful. "Gemma, this is yummy and so inspired. The sweetness of the jam, the richness of the cheese, the hint of rosemary...mmm..."

She licks her lips, and I look away because the vision is too much. She's so beautiful. I always noticed that, but now she takes my breath away. Her wet hair, her tanned skin, fresh and void of makeup. The hint of cleavage, her breathtaking eyes, and those lips...

"You're beautiful." I don't realize I've said it out loud at first, but as soon as I do, I slam a hand in front of my mouth and shake my head. "I'm so sorry...I...I didn't mean to say that."

Lori's eyes widen, her hand frozen mid-reach for another piece of bread. For a long time, she stares at me, her expression unreadable.

"I..." she starts, then stops and swallows hard. "Gemma, I..."

I feel a flush of embarrassment. "I'm sorry," I babble, the words tripping over themselves in my haste to get them out. "I don't know what I was thinking. It just slipped out. Can we forget I said anything?"

But Lori is shaking her head. "No," she says. "I don't want to forget. Because...because I think you're beautiful too, and I love looking at you."

The confession hangs between us, and I can feel the weight of it pressing against me like a physical touch.

She takes a deep breath, her fingers twisting nervously in her lap. "I'm so attracted to you," she admits, her words measured, careful. "But I know that I shouldn't be, and I'm struggling."

Our eyes lock in a silent conversation. In the depths of her gaze, I see my own longing reflected back at me, my own fear and hope and desire. It's a moment of perfect understanding, of connection so deep it feels almost spiritual.

She reaches across the table, her hand hovering over mine. For a long, aching moment, she hesitates. I can see the conflict playing out across her face, the war between desire and duty, longing and logic. But then, slowly, tentatively, she bridges the gap. Her fingers brush against mine and I feel it everywhere.

"We shouldn't," she whispers, even as her hand slides

more fully into mine. Her gaze never wavers from mine, the intensity of it stealing my breath.

The energy between us feels like a living thing. It's in the way Lori's thumb strokes over my knuckles, the way my pulse jumps at the touch. In the dark, heated looks we exchange, the way the air seems to thicken and shimmer around us.

But then, abruptly, she pulls her hand away and stands up so quickly her chair nearly topples over, the screech of wood on stone shattering the silence.

"We shouldn't," she says again, her voice tight, strained. "I can't...we can't do this."

"But..." I start to stand, to reach for her, but she steps back, holding up a hand.

"No, Gemma. Please." Her voice cracks on the last word, a pleading note threading through the firmness. "I can't. I'm sorry."

And then she's turning, striding away from the table. The slam of the screen door echoes in the sudden stillness, a punctuation mark on the end of...whatever that was.

20

LORI

*T*he digital clock on my nightstand glows 3:00 a.m., the neon numbers taunting me in the darkness. I've been tossing and turning for hours, the sheets tangled around my legs, my mind tangled around Gemma.

I can't stop replaying the scene on the porch, the moment our hands touched, the look in her eyes, equal parts heat and tenderness. The way her confession—"You're beautiful"—shimmered with promise and possibility. And the way I fled from what I want most.

Pressing the heels of my hands against my eyes, I try to block out the memory of her face when I pulled away. The hurt, the confusion, the flicker of something that might have been rejection. I hate that I put that look there, even for a moment, like she'd done something wrong.

I did the right thing, I remind myself. Because what choice do I have? The balance of power between us is already skewed. To cross that line...it would be irresponsible. Unethical, even. No matter how much I might want to. No matter how right it feels when she's near, how the world seems to quiet and sharpen and make sense in a way it never has before.

I groan, flipping over and burying my face in the pillow just as I hear a scream, muffled but unmistakable, coming from down the hall. *Gemma.*

I'm out of bed before I'm fully conscious and don't bother with a robe or slippers. I just run, my heart pounding in my throat.

Without thinking, I push open her door. The room is dark, the only light coming from the waning moon outside the window. It takes a moment for my eyes to adjust, for the shapes to resolve into furniture, into the form on the bed.

Gemma is sitting up, hugging her knees. Her shoulders are shaking, her breath coming in short, sharp gasps. She's crying and mumbling something I can't make out.

For a moment, I'm frozen by the sight of her distress. But then she lets out another sob, her whole-body trembling with it, and I'm moving, crossing the room.

"Gemma," I whisper, perching on the edge of the bed. "Gemma, it's me. It's Lori. What's wrong? What happened?" My hand hovers over her shoulder, hesitant. I want to take her into my arms and hold her until whatever demons haunt her have been banished back to the shadows. But I'm not sure I have that right, not after the way I left things between us.

At the sound of my voice, she lifts her head. Even in the dimness, I can see the tears streaking her cheeks, the wild, haunted look in her eyes. "Lori?" she croaks. "I'm sorry. I had a nightmare, but I'm okay. I didn't mean to wake you—"

"Shh," I soothe, throwing caution to the wind and pulling her into my arms. She stiffens for a moment, surprised, but then she melts into me, her face pressing into the crook of my neck, her tears hot against my skin. "I'm here. I've got you."

I stroke her hair, murmuring words of comfort as she clings to me. She's shaking like a leaf, her heart racing against my chest, and I can feel the panic rolling off her in waves.

"Breathe with me," I say. "In and out, nice and slow. You're safe. It was just a dream. You're here, with me."

I exaggerate my breaths, making them deep and even, and slowly, gradually, she begins to match them. I feel the tension start to drain from her body, the desperate grip of her hands on my tank top loosening.

"That's it," I whisper. "You're doing great. Just keep breathing."

We stay like that for minutes, Gemma's face tucked into my neck, my arms around her, rocking gently. I rub soothing circles on her back, over the knobs of her spine and her shoulder blades. She feels so vulnerable in my arms.

As her breathing evens out, she shifts, pulling back just enough to look at me. In the moonlight, her eyes are shining with unshed tears. Her hair is a wild tangle around her face, strands clinging to her damp cheeks. My hand itches to brush them away, to cup her face and run my thumb over the delicate skin beneath her eyes.

"Do you want to talk about it?" I ask softly.

Gemma shakes her head, biting her lip. "I can't," she whispers. But then, as if a dam has broken inside her, she bursts into tears again, her whole body shaking with the force of her sobs.

"I did it," she gasps out between hitching breaths. "I didn't know what got into me. I never meant for it to happen, I swear." Her words are tumbling out now, fragmented and disjointed, as if she's been holding them back for so long that they're spilling out of her in a chaotic rush. "It still doesn't feel real. I was so angry and so scared that I couldn't think straight."

I frown, trying to make sense of her scattered confessions. "Gemma, slow down. What are you talking about? What did you do?"

But she just shakes her head, pressing her face into my shoulder as a fresh wave of sobs overtakes her. "I'm sorry," she mumbles into my skin. "I'm so sorry. I'm a monster."

My heart clenches at the anguish in her voice, the self-loathing that drips from every word. I tighten my arms around her. "You're not a monster," I whisper. "Whatever happened, whatever you did...it doesn't define you. People make mistakes."

She pulls back, her eyes searching mine. "You don't know what I'm capable of..." She trails off, a faraway look in her eyes, as if she's seeing something I can't, reliving some horror I can only imagine.

"Tell me," I urge gently. "Help me understand." I shouldn't be asking questions, but something makes me think she wants to talk.

But she's shaking her head again. "I can't. You'll hate me."

"Gemma, no," I say, cupping her face in my hands. "Nothing you could say would make me hate you. I promise."

She stares at me, her eyes roaming over my face as if searching for any hint of deception. "I'm sorry. I can't talk about it," she finally says.

"That's okay. Would you like me to stay?" She doesn't reply, but sensing she shouldn't be alone right now, I shift us until we're lying down, Gemma's head in the crook of my arm, my arms still wrapped around her. I pull the quilt over us, cocooning us in warmth. She nestles closer, and her breath slowly evens out. Her weight settles more fully against me, heavy and trusting.

What did she do? What could have happened to leave such deep scars and such trauma?

When I first agreed to take Gemma in, I made a conscious decision not to dig into her past. I believe firmly that everyone deserves a second chance, that the mistakes of yesterday shouldn't define the possibilities of tomorrow. I wanted to know Gemma as she is now, not as she was then.

But now, with her broken sobs still echoing in my ears, with the feel of her tears damp on my skin, I find myself desperately curious.

I think back to the little I do know about her history. She was a realtor. She was in prison for seven years. Her relationships with her mother seems fractured, perhaps irreparably so. But the details, the specifics of her crime? Those remain a blank space in the story of her life. Part of me recoils from the idea of knowing, of peering into the darkest chapters of her past. What if she's right? What if the truth changes how I see her?

But another part, the part that aches to soothe her pain, shoulder her burdens, and help her heal...that part yearns for understanding. Because how can I truly support her if I don't know what she's been through?

In the end, though, it's not up to me. Gemma will tell me when she's ready, or perhaps she'll never tell me.

I try to quiet my racing thoughts as I focus on the rise and fall of her chest. As I hover on the edge of sleep, I feel Gemma stir slightly, burrowing deeper into my embrace. Even in slumber, she seems to be seeking comfort.

With that final thought, my eyes flutter closed.

21

GEMMA

The first thing I notice as I drift into wakefulness is warmth. It envelops me, seeps into my bones, and chases away the lingering chill of my nightmare. The second thing I notice is the scent that is distinctly Lori. It fills my nose, my lungs, and wraps around me as surely as her arms.

Those arms are draped over me, one slung across my waist, the other cradling my head. I can feel the soft press of her body against my back, the rise and fall of her chest as she breathes. Even in sleep, she's protective.

Slowly, carefully, I turn in her embrace until we're face-to-face. In the soft light of early dawn, she looks younger. Her hair is a tousled halo on the pillow, gleaming like spun gold. Her lips are parted slightly, her expression utterly peaceful. She's so beautiful.

I want to reach out, to trace the curve of her cheek. I want to commit every angle to memory. But I don't dare for fear of waking her and shattering this fragile moment.

As I watch her, the events of the night come rushing back. The nightmare, so vivid it felt more like a memory.

The way I woke screaming, tangled in the sheets. And Lori, who came running and held me as I shook.

Oh God. What did I say to her? With the rising sun, the fragments of my confessions come back to me, hazy and disjointed. I remember babbling, words spilling out of me. Apologies and self-recrimination and half-formed explanations. Did I tell her about the blood on my hands?

Then another thought hits me. What will she think of me now? Seeing me like that, broken and incoherent, a sobbing mess in the middle of the night. Will she think I'm too much trouble? Too damaged, too needy?

Lori stirs, a soft sigh escaping her. Her eyes open, hazy and unfocused at first, then widening as they meet mine. She looks startled, almost shy, and a blush blooms across her cheeks as she seems to realize the intimacy of our entanglement.

"Oh," she whispers, her voice husky with sleep. "I...I'm sorry, I didn't mean to fall asleep. I must have drifted off." She starts to sit up, but I stop her with a hand on her arm. "Don't be sorry," I murmur. "And you don't have to leave."

Lori hesitates, her eyes searching mine. I can see the conflict there, but something softens in her expression. "Okay," she says quietly.

We settle back into the pillows, our bodies relaxing into each other. The silence stretches between us, and I can feel Lori's heartbeat where her chest presses against mine. It's faster now, a rapid banging that belies her calm exterior. Is she as affected by our closeness as much as I am? Can she feel my heart racing too?

"How are you feeling?" she asks eventually, her fingers absently tracing patterns on my back. "After last night, I mean."

I take a deep breath, letting it out slowly. "Better," I say, and it's the truth. "Calm. Like I can breathe again." I pause, biting my lip. "Lori, I'm so sorry about last night. I—"

But she stops me with a finger against my lips. "Shh," she soothes. "We all have our demons. It doesn't make you weak to let them out sometimes."

I swallow hard against the lump in my throat. "Thank you," I whisper. "For being there. I haven't had someone to lean on in a long time. I hope I can do the same for you."

Lori smiles. "You already do." She pauses. "Are you still up for dinner with Charlotte and Miranda tonight?"

The social event had completely slipped my mind after last night. "Absolutely," I assure her. "It will be nice to meet Charlotte."

Lori looks relieved. "She's excited to meet you too. I've told her a lot about you."

"All good things, I hope?"

Lori chuckles. "The very best." She inches even closer, and then it suddenly hits me how bizarre this is. We're talking in bed, wrapped in each other's arms like it's perfectly normal.

"Although," I add, "we should probably keep this between us." I gesture to our current position, our limbs still tangled beneath the sheets. "I don't think Miranda would approve of such...unprofessional conduct."

Lori snorts, swatting me lightly on the arm. "No, definitely not. This is strictly off the record." She reluctantly untangles herself and stretches. "And it won't happen again. As I said, I didn't plan on falling asleep here."

"It was still nice," I say and bite my lip when I realize I've overstepped again.

Lori stares at me for a beat and smiles. "Yeah, it was nice," she says softly. Then, with a subtle shake of her head, she gets up. "I'm going to make coffee and breakfast.

Stay in bed as long as you want. I'll keep the food warm for you."

"No, you don't have to do that, it's—"

"Please," she insists, then shoots me a grin. "It's your last free Saturday before you'll be running the market stall, so enjoy it."

I stretch languidly in the bed, cherishing the warmth from where Lori lay just moments ago. The pillow still holds her scent, and I breathe it in while my mind drifts to the evening ahead. Dinner with Lori, Charlotte, and Miranda. It's daunting, the idea of facing my parole officer in such an informal setting, of meeting Lori's best friend. Will she be able to see past my record? It's one thing encouraging Lori to join the rehabilitation program, but having dinner with me and seeing how close Lori and I have become is another.

Miranda knows everything about me. She's read my file, seen the stark black and white of my crimes laid out in unforgiving detail. She knows the worst of me, the darkest corners of my history. And yet she's supporting me without judgement.

But Charlotte? Charlotte is an unknown quantity. She's important to Lori, which means her opinion matters. Her judgment carries weight. And all she knows about me is that I'm an ex-con. She doesn't know the specifics that might make her question Lori's decision to take me in.

It feels a bit like being back in the closet, back in those suffocating days of hiding who I was. The constant fear of exposure. The weight of a secret that grew heavier with each passing day. It's a different kind of closet now, but the fear is the same.

When I was younger and coming to terms with my sexuality, I remember the terror that gripped me at the thought of people knowing I was gay. I imagined the whispers that would follow me down the halls, the looks, the rejection. I pictured my friends' faces, twisted with disgust. It was a fear that gnawed at my insides like a hungry rat.

I can't control what Charlotte thinks of me, I remind myself. *I can only be authentic and hope that's enough.*

I push myself up and out of the cozy cocoon of the bed. The sun is climbing steadily into the sky, and humming softly, I gather my clothes and toiletries, my steps light as I head for the bathroom.

As I stand under the warm spray of the shower, I feel the last cobwebs of sleep and the shadows of the night wash away. I lather my hair, the scent of my shampoo mingling with the steam, and I can't help but smile through my anxious thoughts. There's something about the simple rituals of the morning—the shower, the coffee, the quiet moments—that feels indulgent now. I'm five weeks into freedom and still, every single shower, bath, meal, and breeze against my skin feels like a blessing.

I shut off the water and step out, wrapping myself in a fluffy towel. I catch a glimpse of my reflection in the foggy mirror, my skin pink from the heat, my eyes bright. Tracing the lines of my face in the mirror, I map out the changes, the softening around my eyes, the hint of a smile on my lips. For the first time in years, I recognize the woman staring back at me, a glimmer of my old self resurfacing after a long stretch of pain and isolation.

22

LORI

I hear voices on the porch, and smooth down my sundress before heading out to greet Charlotte and Miranda.

Gemma's in the kitchen, her brow furrowed in concentration as she adds the finishing touches to our meal. I've enjoyed cooking together, and under Gemma's instructions, we've put together a Mexican feast.

"They're here," I say, and Gemma looks up with a nervous smile.

"I'm almost done," she assures me. "Just need to finish plating the guacamole."

"Okay, I'll pour the drinks."

Charlotte, as always, looks effortlessly chic in a flowing maxi dress, her dark hair straightened and glossy. Miranda, beside her, is more understated in crisp linen trousers and a plain white linen shirt, but no less striking.

"Hey, guys! I'm so glad you could make it."

Charlotte sweeps me into a hug. "We wouldn't miss it. I've been dying to finally meet the famous Gemma."

I chuckle. "Famous, huh? I don't know about that. But

she's pretty great." I turn to Miranda, offering a hand. "It's good to see you again, Miranda. Thank you for coming."

Miranda shakes my hand, her grip firm and confident. "Thanks for the invite. It's great to see you again."

"Come through." I smile and lead them through to the kitchen, where Gemma is arranging a platter of appetizers. She looks up as we enter, her eyes widening slightly at the sight of our guests. I can see the nervousness in the set of her shoulders, the way she fidgets with the hem of her apron.

"Gemma," I say. "Meet Charlotte."

Charlotte steps forward first, her smile warm and genuine. "It's so nice to finally put a face to the name," she says, extending a hand.

Gemma takes her hand, a tentative smile tugging at her lips. "It's nice to meet you too."

Miranda steps up next. "Gemma, it's good to see you outside of the office," she jokes. "You're looking well."

Gemma nods. "Thank you. I appreciate you coming. I know it's a bit unorthodox."

Miranda waves a dismissive hand. "Nonsense. No reason we can't share a meal, get to know each other as people."

I see some of the tension drain from Gemma's posture. "Yeah, that would be nice," she says, and there's a note of genuine warmth in her voice. "Would you like a margarita? We just made a jug."

Miranda chuckles. "I won't say no to that."

"Why don't you take the jug outside?" I say to Charlotte. "Help yourselves and we'll bring out the food."

Gemma and I gather up the platters and bowls, and as we step out onto the porch, I hear Charlotte's appreciative whistle.

"Wow," she says, taking in the spread laid out on the

table. "This looks incredible, and it smells just like my abuela's cooking. I didn't know you could cook Mexican, Lor."

"You know I can't. Most of it was Gemma."

"Lori mentioned you loved Mexican food, so we thought we'd give it a go," Gemma says, joining them at the table.

"Thank you. I can't wait to tuck in." Charlotte spears a crisp wedge of jicama with her fork. "Mmm...you nailed it," she says after taking a bite. "But I hear cooking isn't your only talent." She leans forward, her elbows on the table. "Lori tells me you're a wiz with the electrical."

"Oh, I'm definitely not a wiz," Gemma says. "Lori was my first client, but I do enjoy the work. We rewired most of the house together."

"We?" Charlotte bursts out in laughter. "You mean you and Lori?" She looks up at the lights over the porch table. "Am I safe here or all we all going to be electrocuted tonight?"

"Hey, I'm not as big a clutch as you think." I shoot her a humorous grin. "I'm a good assistant. I can measure, cut, screw, all of that."

Charlotte shakes her head, then turns back to Gemma. "I actually have some electrical work that needs doing myself. Would you be interested in adding a second client to your list?"

"Of course." Gemma beams with genuine excitement. "That would be amazing."

"Then that's a deal." Charlotte clinks her glass against Gemma's. "As long as Lori doesn't come with the package. I don't want to die while making toast in the morning."

As they talk, I watch Miranda out of the corner of my eye. She's quieter, more reserved, but I can see her observing the interaction closely. There's a thoughtfulness to her expression, a keen intelligence in her gaze as it flicks between Gemma and Charlotte.

The conversation flows easily, jumping from topic to topic with the kind of natural rhythm that comes from a comfortable connection. Charlotte entertains us with tales of her most outrageous clients, her hands flying as she imitates their expressions and mannerisms. Miranda shares anecdotes from her work, the challenges and triumphs of helping people navigate the complex journey of reintegration. And Gemma...Gemma slowly opens up as she shares ideas for the farmers' market and possibly her own business. She seems comfortable in the social setting, excited even.

Every day, I see new glimpses of the Gemma that was, the Gemma that could be. And every day, I feel myself falling a little bit more in awe of her.

As the appetizers are cleared and the cocktail glasses drained, Charlotte leans back in her chair, one arm draped lazily over the back of Miranda's. "That," she declares, patting her stomach contentedly, "was quite possibly the best food I've had in months."

"There's a lot more coming," I warn her, and she laughs.

"Seriously? You two should open a restaurant. 'Farm to Table' is very on-trend right now."

I laugh, shaking my head. "I think we've got our hands full with the actual farm for now, but it was fun cooking together."

"It was fun," Gemma agrees, shooting me a smile. "I've always loved cooking, but I haven't had much opportunity to do it for others in...well, in a long time."

A beat of silence follows her words, a reminder of the elephant in the room. I see Miranda shift slightly in her seat, but before the moment can become awkward, Gemma clears her throat, sitting up straighter.

"So," she says, her tone deliberately light. "Charlotte, Miranda...if you don't mind me asking, how did you two meet?"

Charlotte grins, turning to Miranda. "Oh, it's quite the story," she says. "We were in Paris, the City of Love." She sighs with a dramatic, faraway look in her eyes. "I was admiring the view from the top of the Eiffel Tower when I felt a tap on my shoulder. I turned, and there was Miranda, holding a rose and smiling at me like I was the only person in the world and—"

"Charlotte, you've never been to Paris," I remind her.

Miranda chuckles and shakes her head. "She's full of shit. The truth is, we met at a coffee shop. I was in line, minding my own business, when this one," she tilts her head toward Charlotte, "stormed in, all fired up about something."

"Okay, in my defense," Charlotte interjects, holding up a finger, "I had just come from a particularly frustrating client meeting. I needed my caffeine fix."

"So she marches up to the counter," Miranda continues, "and starts ordering this ridiculously complicated drink. I'm talking half-caf, triple-shot, soy, no-foam, extra-hot latte with a dash of vanilla and a sprinkle of cinnamon."

"Hey, I know what I like!" Charlotte protests.

"Anyway, the barista gets it wrong. Apparently, they used whole milk instead of soy. And Charlotte, well..." Miranda trails off, looking at Charlotte expectantly.

Charlotte sighs. "I may have overreacted. Slightly."

"Slightly?" Miranda laughs. "You burst into floods of tears."

"I was having a bad day," Charlotte says, shrugging. "And it was that time of the month."

"So, I'm standing there, watching this unfold, and I can't help myself," Miranda continues. "I start laughing. Like, full-on belly laughing. Charlotte whirls around, ready to unleash her wrath on me, and I just put my hands up and say, 'I'm sorry, but this is the most entertaining thing I've seen all week.'"

Gemma leans forward, amused by the story. "And then what happened?"

"Well, she stared at me for a second, and then she started laughing too. We must have looked like a pair of lunatics, standing there in the middle of the coffee shop, cackling like hyenas."

"We got to talking after that," Charlotte chimes in. "Bonding over our shared love of coffee and disdain for whole milk. Numbers were exchanged, and, well," she smiles at Miranda, "the rest is history."

"That's such a sweet and funny story. You never told me that, Char." I shake my head and laugh.

"Well, it wasn't exactly my proudest moment," Charlotte says sheepishly. "But since you asked...yeah, that's how we met."

As the laughter dies down, I exchange a glance with Gemma, a private moment of shared amusement and understanding. I stand up, gathering the empty plates, and Gemma follows suit. As we reach for the same dish, our hands brush, a fleeting touch that sends a spark between my thighs. It's a reflex, an instinct to be near her, to feel her skin against mine. I glance up, hoping Miranda hasn't noticed, then rush back inside the house.

We make our way into the kitchen, arms laden with dishes, and as we set them down, Gemma turns to me with a soft smile. "This is fun," she says, her voice low and intimate. "I'm really glad we got together."

I nod, stepping closer. "Me too." Reaching out, I tuck a stray strand of hair behind her ear. "Charlotte and Miranda clearly adore you." I want to kiss her, to pour all the unspoken feelings between us into a single, perfect moment. But the sound of laughter from the porch breaks the spell, reminding us that we have guests waiting.

23

GEMMA

*A*s Miranda and Charlotte drive off, I feel a weight lift from my shoulders. It's been a lovely evening, filled with laughter, good food, and even better company, but there was a part of me that couldn't fully relax.

Throughout dinner, I tried to keep my glances toward Lori casual, to not let my gaze linger too long or too often. I was all too aware of Miranda, of the way she seemed to see everything and note every interaction. The last thing I wanted was to give her any reason to think there was something between us.

But now, in the quiet of the living room, with the soft glow of the lamps, I feel like I can breathe steadily again. Like I can just be.

Lori sinks onto the couch beside me, tucking her feet up under her. She looks relaxed, content as she hands me a steaming mug of tea, but there's also a flicker of alertness in her gaze, like she's been waiting to be alone with me.

"Well," she says, blowing on her own tea. "I think that went well, don't you?"

I nod, cradling my mug in my hands. "Yeah. Charlotte is

lovely. I can see why you are friends. And Miranda is great too. She's not at all what I expected on a personal level."

Lori chuckles. "She's a bit of a paradox, isn't she? Polite and to the point, but get a couple of drinks in her and she's all wry jokes and goofy grins." She turns, her eyes meeting mine. There's an unmistakable heated look there. She doesn't shy from the intensity of the moment, but instead, she holds my gaze, a silent challenge.

I set my mug down on the coffee table, my hands suddenly unsteady. My heart is pounding wildly. *This is dangerous*, a voice in my head warns. *This is crossing a line, stepping off a cliff into unknown waters.* But God, I want to drown in those waters. I want to sink beneath the surface and never come up for air.

"Lori," I whisper, my voice rough. "I..."

Before I can find the words, before I can give voice to this aching, desperate thing inside me, she's moving. Leaning in, closing the distance between us until I feel her breath against my lips.

"Tell me to stop," she murmurs, her hand coming up to cup my cheek.

I can't. I can't tell her to stop, because stopping is the last thing on my mind. All I can think about is her lips hovering just inches from mine. All I can focus on is the hunger that's clawing at my insides demanding to be sated.

"I want you," I breathe. "So much it scares me."

And then her lips are on mine, and the world falls away. There's no room for fear or doubt, for anything but the taste of her. She kisses me like she's been waiting for this moment, like she's been holding back and now the flood-gates have opened.

I melt into her, my hands finding their way into her hair, pulling her closer. She makes a sound low in her throat, a hum of pleasure that vibrates through me, setting every nerve ending alight.

It's hot and messy and urgent, all gasping breaths and seeking hands. Her fingers tangle in my hair, tugging, and my hands slip around her waist, splaying across the smooth expanse of her back.

She tastes like margaritas and spices, like something forbidden and intoxicating. I drink her in, greedy for more, for anything she's willing to give. The sound she lets out when my teeth graze her lower lip goes directly to my core, adding fuel to a fire that's threatening to incinerate me.

It's been almost eight years since I kissed a woman, and I'm drowning in sensation, in the scent of her hair, the touch of her skin, the soft, insistent pressure of her mouth on mine. Every touch, every taste, is like a discovery of something I didn't know I was searching for.

When we finally break apart, we're both breathing hard, our chests heaving. Lori's eyes are dark, her pupils blown wide. Her lips are swollen, glistening in the low light. She looks thoroughly kissed, and the sight sends a fresh wave of heat through me.

"Wow," she whispers, her voice low and husky. "That was..."

"Yeah..."

I'm shaking while we stare at each other, marveling at the hunger in her eyes, the desperate need for more, for closer, for everything. But there's something else there too, softer and more tender. A vulnerability that makes my heart clench.

Slowly, carefully, I reach out, brushing my fingers through her hair. She leans into the touch, her eyes fluttering closed.

"Are you sure about this?" I whisper, my thumb tracing

the delicate arch of her cheekbone. "Because if we do this... if we cross this line..."

She opens her eyes, and her gaze is raw and full of yearning. She takes my hand, linking our fingers together. The simple gesture feels weighted. "I know it's complicated." Her thumb strokes over my knuckles. "I know there are a million reasons why we shouldn't. But..." She takes a shaky breath, her eyes never leaving mine. "The way I feel when I'm with you...it's unlike anything I've ever felt. I promise I'm not messing with you."

I know exactly what she means because I feel it too. This sense of both longing and belonging, even in the midst of uncertainty. "Every time I look at you it's like something slots into place. Like a part of me that's been wandering finally finds its way back."

Lori smiles and leans in, resting her forehead against mine, and then we're kissing again, soft and slow and deep. As we lose ourselves in each other, in the slide of lips and the tangle of limbs, a little voice in the back of my mind tells me to stop because I could lose everything all over again. But I'm weak, my body aching for release and dominating my reason.

No words can describe my response to her kiss and her touch as we pour every ounce of pent-up longing into each caress of lips and slide of tongues. Her fingers thread through my hair, nails grazing my scalp, and I pull her closer still until there's no space left between us.

I break the kiss to trail my lips along her jawline, reveling in the sharp intake of breath as I find a sensitive spot below her ear. Lori tilts her head, giving me better access as I lavish attention on the column of her neck. Her pulse flutters wildly beneath my mouth.

"Gemma," she breathes, and hearing my name fall from her lips like a prayer nearly undoes me.

I recapture her mouth, needing to taste her again, to drink in her soft moans. We're both trembling now, desire coiled tightly in our veins. I know we should stop, take a moment to breathe and think. But I'm drunk on her, intoxicated by her touch and scent and the sweet sounds she makes.

My hands slip under her shirt, savoring the smooth warmth of her skin. Lori gasps and presses closer, her own hands starting to roam with more purpose. We're toeing a dangerous line, seconds from surrendering to the heat threatening to consume us both.

Lori's phone pings, the sound filtering through the haze of desire, a reminder of the world outside this room. Reluctantly, I gentle the kiss, slowing us down from the feverish pace. Lori makes a noise of protest but follows my lead.

"I don't want to stop," I whisper. "But I don't want to be the one to take it further either."

"Same here." Lori locks her eyes with mine and neither of us moves. She takes a deep breath, then shakes her head, and says, "Fuck it."

24

LORI

*W*e stumble into my bedroom, our lips still locked, and I feel like I'm floating. Gemma's mouth is like a drug, leaving me lightheaded and giddy. Her hands are clutching at me with an almost desperate intensity. Her fingers dig into my hips, pulling me closer as if she's afraid I might disappear if she loosens her grip even for a moment.

When we break apart for air, I take a moment to really look at her. Her lips are swollen, her eyes wide and dark, filled with a hunger that's almost feral. But there's something else there too, a flicker of disbelief. Like she can't quite believe this is happening.

It hits me then, with a sudden clarity. For Gemma, this isn't just a passionate encounter. It's a reawakening of a part of herself that's been dormant for so long. So many years without a loving touch, without the warmth of another body against hers. So many years of loneliness and touch deprivation.

As I lean in to capture her lips, I feel her tremble against me. Her hands are shaking as they slide under my shirt, her touch tentative and reverent, like she's handling something precious and fragile. When I deepen the kiss, my tongue slipping into her mouth, she makes a sound that's halfway between a whimper and a sob. It's a sound of pure need, of desperation and longing.

My hands soften as they map the contours of her body, and I pour all the tenderness into every caress, every brush of my fingertips. I want her to feel cherished, worshipped. I want to erase every lonely night, every touch-starved moment.

I slide Gemma's shirt over her head, letting it drop to the floor. She stands before me, bare and beautiful. Her skin is like honey, smooth and golden with tan lines begging for my lips to trace them.

My eyes roam over every inch of newly exposed skin. The elegant line of her collarbone, the swell of her breasts encased in a simple black bra. Her stomach is flat and toned, her shoulders strong. I reach out, tracing the edge of her bra, and feel the wild flutter of her heartbeat.

Gemma moans softly as my hand drifts lower, skimming over her ribs, her navel, coming to rest on the waistband of her jeans. I unbutton them, sliding them down her legs. She steps out of them, kicking them aside, and reaches behind her to unclip her bra. The fabric falls away, revealing her breasts. They're small, perfectly proportioned to her slender frame, with hard, rosy nipples.

In the soft light, her skin is smooth and unblemished. The swell of her breasts is gentle, the curves subtle but undeniably feminine. I reach out, cupping the delicate weight of them in my palms. They fit perfectly, like they were made for my hands.

Gemma gasps as my thumbs brush over her nipples, the peaks pebbling even more under my touch. They're a dusky pink, and I'm mesmerized by the contrast against the creamy pale of her tan lines. I want to taste them, take them into my mouth and feel them against my tongue.

Gemma arches into my touch, another soft moan escaping her, and the sound shoots straight between my thighs. I lower my head, pressing a trail of open-mouthed kisses along the slope of her breast, savoring the silky texture of her skin.

When I finally take her nipple into my mouth, Gemma cries out, her hands flying to my hair. She holds me there as I savor the sensitive peak, alternating between gentle sucks and flicks of my tongue. Her other breast is not neglected, my hand kneading and teasing, pinching lightly in a way that makes her gasp and writhe.

Brushing my lips down her body, I drop to my knees, my hands coming to rest on Gemma's hips in a way that borders on worship. I lean in, pressing a soft kiss on her scar, feeling the warmth of her skin against my lips. Gemma's hand comes to rest on my head, her fingers threading through my hair while I brush my lips over her scar, her belly, her hips.

She raises me back up and kisses me while she unbuttons my dress and I'm shaking with anticipation to feel all of her against all of me. Lifting my arms, she pulls off my dress and lets out a sigh as it falls away. I'm not wearing a bra, and like her, I'm only left in my panties.

I close the distance between us, and as soon as we come together, we both sigh at the contact. The intense shiver that runs through me seems to continue through Gemma like a current.

Skimming the planes of her body, I examine the dips and curves that I've only allowed myself to imagine until now. The tenderness is gone, replaced by a carnal hunger.

Gemma kisses me and gropes me hard like she's trying

to own all of me at once, and it arouses me to the point I can barely stand. It feels incredible to be wanted so badly, to be the one and only object of someone's desire. No woman has made me feel that way.

We tumble onto the bed, a tangle of limbs. The chenille bedspread is soft beneath us, the mattress giving slightly under our weight as we clumsily take off our panties.

Gemma hovers over me, her dark hair falling in a curtain around us. Her eyes are hazy with need, and she's fueled with a new assertiveness, an in-control vibe that tells me she's not the shy type in bed. She stares at me while she splays her hand wide on one of my breasts, her short nails digging into my skin while she kneads my sensitive flesh.

I trace her back and her behind, and squeeze her there, making her groan in pleasure. She feels so good, so right, and I long to make her explode.

"Let me have you," she whispers, and dips her head to kiss and suck at my neck.

I tilt my head to the side and moan as I welcome the sensation, and when she finally lowers herself on top of me and wedges a leg between my thighs, I can barely keep it together.

She feasts on me, her mouth moving to my breasts, her palms smooth and firm against my skin while she twirls her tongue around my nipples. The sensation is almost too much, too intense to bare. The tightness in my core grows and I'm so wet I know she can feel it.

Gemma moves back up, kisses me, and slides a hand down between us. She hesitates, but only for a beat, before her fingers skim the thin strip of hair between my begs. A teasing smile plays around her lips and it's sexy as hell. I want her so badly I'm squirming, and when she lowers her hand farther and skims my sex, I throw my head back and cry out.

She draws slow circles where I need it most, and I'm so fiercely reactive that I'm balancing on the edge already.

Desperate to touch her in return, I do the same, and my hand is trembling when I feel her warm wetness coating my fingers. I explore her, drag my fingers through her folds, slowly, up and down, before I find her clit.

Gemma, too, lets out a strangled cry that is muffled by my lips, and we move together in a languid rhythm. Hands exploring, mouths tasting, bodies rocking. The world narrows to this, to the slide of skin on skin, the mingling of breaths, the sighs and moans. It's a dance, a give and take, a push and pull.

She gasps, writhes and rolls, her movements building from sensual to something primal and desperate. It's a feeling of togetherness I've only ever dreamed of, an interaction of the purest kind.

The tension between my thighs coils tighter, and I feel something unfurling inside me. We're so ready it doesn't take much. In my fantasies, we've done this a million times, but reality is so much better. Mind-blowingly better. Every nerve in my body is on high alert, and when she lifts her head to look at me, we smile and push each other over the edge.

Pleasure washes over us in a blinding rush, and I cling to Gemma like an anchor. Her name falls from my lips as we shatter together and come in each other's arms. I love the sounds she makes, how she kisses me hard, pouring all her pent-up energy into me until she has nothing left to give.

I don't know if it's our deep physical and emotional connection, the fact I've been wanting this for weeks, or if it's this overwhelming afterglow, the sensation of feeling reborn, but tears start rolling down my cheeks.

Gemma's eyes well up too as she raises herself and tenderly wipes them away. "Are you okay?" she whispers.

"Yeah." I do the same for her, her tears warm against my fingertips. "Are you?"

"Yeah." She strokes my cheek as she smiles, and we can't help but chuckle at the fact that we're both crying. They're good tears, beautiful tears that prove this isn't some fleeting infatuation. They put me at ease, whisper we should have no regrets and embrace what is blossoming between us. A contentment seeps into my bones, warm and heavy. Nothing has ever felt as right as our clammy, spent bodies entangled in an embrace. I could never regret this, not for a moment.

25

GEMMA

I'm sitting on the porch, cradling a mug of coffee while I listen to the songbirds. The air is alive with their melodies, each note a tiny miracle. Getting up early to hear them has become my ritual; knowing how precious each day is, I want to make the most of each and every one.

Upstairs through the open window, I hear the shower running, the sounds of Lori moving through her morning ritual. The smile that hasn't left my lips since I woke up widens, and I take a deep breath, shivering as butterflies hit my core. I feel flutters each time my mind drifts back to our bodies pressed together, my deliciously achy muscles a reminder of our beautiful night together. We made love for hours and haven't slept very much, but somehow, I feel full of energy.

Waking up naked in Lori's arms, my body cradled against hers, was truly moving. The first rays of sunlight creeping across the sheets illuminated her sleeping face, soft and unguarded. I couldn't resist brushing a featherlight kiss across her brow, and when her eyes fluttered open, I was lost. We came together, drawn into soft, sleepy kisses that gradually deepened, igniting the embers of last night's passion.

Now, sitting here in the quiet of the morning, that warmth infuses every cell of my being. It's a feeling I haven't experienced in a long time, perhaps ever. A sense of hope and belonging.

A flicker of movement catches my eye; the hummingbird is back again. It hovers near the porch railing, its wings a blur of iridescent green. It's visited me a few times, always in the early hours when the world is still yawning awake.

I hold my breath as it alights on the railing, so close I can see the individual feathers of its throat shimmering in the sun. It's so delicate and perfect, and I marvel at its audacity. Its trust in a world that could crush it in an instant.

Lori joins me, and I glance up, my heart stuttering at the sight of her. Her hair is damp and she's wearing an oversize T-shirt, the hem skimming her bare thighs. She's never looked more beautiful.

To my surprise, the hummingbird doesn't startle at her approach. It remains perched on the railing, tilting its head as if greeting Lori.

Lori's eyes widen, a delighted smile lighting up her face. "Well, hello there," she whispers. She settles down beside me, leaning into me and brushing her shoulder with mine. "I see we have a little visitor."

I smile and nod, my gaze drawn back to the tiny bird. "It's been here before," I tell her. "I've never fed it, but it keeps coming back."

Lori leans forward to get a better look. The hummingbird regards her calmly, its dark eyes bright and curious. "In many Native American traditions," she says, "hummingbirds are seen as messengers of joy, healing, and good luck."

"Really?" I put an arm around her and pull her closer.

Lori nods. "They're also associated with resilience, adaptability, and the ability to overcome difficult times." Her hand finds mine, our fingers intertwining on her shoulder. "The hummingbird's ability to fly backward symbolizes that we can look back on our past while still moving forward in life." She turns to meet my eyes. "Maybe it's here to remind you of that."

I frown and hold her gaze. Her words resonate with me like few things ever have. "How does a former divorce attorney know about Native American bird symbolism?"

Lori smiles, a faraway look in her eyes. "My grandmother," she says. "I have Native American blood, from my mother's side. My father took off when I was young, but my grandmother was always there for my mother and me. Well, until she sadly passed away when I was fifteen."

"I'm sorry about that." I squeeze her hand. "There's so much I don't know about you."

Lori shrugs. "There's a lot we don't know about each other."

"Yeah…" I swallow hard and focus on the hummingbird, who seems determined to finish its concert. "I'm sorry I can't…"

"That's okay," Lori says softly. "We can talk about you when you're ready."

I give her a small smile and hope she knows how grateful I am for her patience. Although we might not know a lot about each other, I also suspect we have a lot in common. Neither of us had a father growing up, and we're both adjusting to a drastic change of lifestyle, albeit for the better.

"My grandmother held on to her culture," Lori continues. "Especially the folklore around animals. She used to tell me stories when I was little, teach me about the symbol-ism. She would have loved this, you know. Seeing a hummingbird up close like this. She always said they were magical little creatures that brought blessings."

When the hummingbird finally takes flight, zipping away into the trees, Lori shifts, turning to face me again. Her hand comes up to cup my cheek, her thumb brushing over my bottom lip. "Last night..." she starts. "It was..."

"I know," I whisper, leaning into her touch. "For me too."

She smiles, a slow, gentle unfurling. "I don't know what this is, Gem," she confesses. "What we are. But I know that I've never felt anything like it, and I'll never do anything to hurt you. Whatever happens...whatever you decide you need, I'll respect it. I just want you to know that your place here is safe, no matter what."

"Thank you." I feel an overwhelming swell of emotion. "I'm scared," I admit. "Scared that I'm dreaming, that I'll wake up and this will all be gone."

"I'm scared too." Lori leans in, resting her forehead against mine. "But it's not a dream." She takes my hand, placing it over her heart. I feel the steady rhythm beneath my palm. "Feel that?" she whispers. "That's because of you."

I tilt my head, brushing her lips. After last night, every-thing has changed. The barriers between us have crumbled, the lines we've been so carefully toeing have been irrevo-cably crossed. And now, in the aftermath, I'm left with a feeling of giddy disbelief, of joy so acute it borders on pain and fear of losing her.

We fall into a sweet kiss, and it's a different kind of kiss than the ones we shared last night—less urgent, less desper-ate, but no less intense. I take my time, savoring the feel of her, the taste of her. I run my tongue along the seam of her lips, teasing, exploring. She opens to me with a sigh, her hand coming up to tangle in my hair. I deepen the kiss, pouring into it all the words I'm not quite ready to say, all the emotions swirling in my chest.

It's a heady feeling, knowing that I can kiss her like this, that she wants me to. That I'm allowed to get lost in her, to let myself drown in the sensation of her mouth on mine, her body pressed against me.

"I can't believe I get to do that now," I whisper. "That I get to kiss you whenever I want."

Lori opens her eyes, her gaze meeting mine. The depth of emotions I see there brings a lump to my throat—the tenderness, the affection, the unmistakable glimmer of desire. "Believe it," she murmurs, brushing a stray lock of hair behind my ear. "Because I plan on kissing you a lot from now on."

26

LORI

The weathered leather album feels weighty in my hands as I carry it to the couch where Gemma is waiting, her long legs curled under her.

She looks up and scoots over as I approach, making space for me to nestle in beside her. I sink into the cushions, the worn fabric and Gemma's body heat enveloping me in comfort.

"I forgot about the wedding album," she says, glancing down at it.

"Me too. It completely slipped my mind with all the work and distractions going on." My lips pull into a flirtatious smile. "Only good distractions, of course."

Gemma blushes. "Of course." She leans in and kisses me. "Can I see them?"

"That's why I brought it over. I thought we could have a look at the pictures together." Realizing I'm staring at her, I let out a nervous chuckle. I've been on cloud nine for days, and every kiss still feels like the first.

My fingers trace the embossed lettering on the cover before I flip it open. *Frank and Maggie Rosefield.*

The first photo is of Aunt Maggie in the wedding gown we found in the attic. It looks beautiful on her; elegant and graceful. Her dark hair is pulled back into a chic chignon, a few artful curls framing her face. She stands firm, almost statuesque, with a bouquet of white roses in front of her and —bless her—she looks nervous.

The next picture is more cheerful. She's standing next to my mother, who is dressed in a pale-pink bridesmaid dress. They're holding hands, and unlike my mother, who looks a little out of sorts, Aunt Maggie is laughing.

"That's Mom," I say. "She must have hated that dress. I've never seen her wear one before, and she looks totally tense and uncomfortable."

Gemma chuckles. "Oh, the joys of being a bridesmaid." She turns to me. "Have you ever been a bridesmaid?"

"No. You?"

"Once, for one of my friends." Gemma winces and shakes her head. "But that was a long time ago."

I nod. "You're not in contact anymore?"

"No." Gemma refocuses on the album, so I drop the subject. It must have been hard. From once being so close to someone that you're standing next to them at their wedding, to one day losing them like they were never there...it also happened to Mom and Aunt Maggie somehow.

"She was a beautiful bride," Gemma says. "And your mother looks stunning."

"They were both beautiful," I agree, flipping the page to more pictures of Mom and Aunt Maggie. Mom looks so young. Her face is unlined, her skin dewy and glowing. And then I notice it again. There's a tightness around her smile, a distance in her eyes like she's going through the motions. "But Mom looks a bit...anxious, don't you think?"

Gemma studies the photo more closely. "I don't know her, but I suppose there's a hint of something there. Kind of like a deer-in-headlights look." She hesitates. "Your mom lives in Sedona, right? Why hasn't she been here to visit? Is it because of me?"

My eyes widen as I shake my head. "No, it's nothing like that. We do see each other about twice a month. I've been to visit her since you moved in, but she keeps making up excuses to return the favor, so I sense she doesn't like coming here."

"Because of her fight with your aunt?"

"I suppose so. She refuses to talk about it."

Gemma nods. "Aren't you a little curious about what happened?"

"Of course. I've asked her so many times, but she kept shutting me down, so I just gave up, I suppose. It was easier that way." I flip to the next page and there's Uncle Frank, tall and dashing in a crisp black tux. His hair is slicked back, and his grin is wide and confident, crinkling the corners of his eyes in a way I remember so well.

"Now that's a man who looks ready to get married." Gemma laughs. "No cold feet there." She leans in and narrows her eyes. "I see those cute dimples run in the family."

I bark out a surprised laugh. "What? No way. We're not even related. Aunt Maggie was my mom's sister, remember?"

Gemma shrugs, a sheepish grin tugging at her mouth. "Of course. I forgot he wasn't your blood uncle, given the resemblance."

I study the photo more closely and I can see what she means. There is something undeniably similar in our features, a certain cast to the cheekbones and the deep dimples. "Hmm...you're right, but I think it's mostly the dimples. Mom told me my father had dimples."

"Who can resist dimples?" Gemma shoots me a wink. She turns to the next page, where Aunt Maggie and Uncle Frank are standing in front of the altar in a church exchanging their vows.

Then we move on to the pictures of their wedding party at Rosefield Farm, starting with one of Uncle Frank carrying her over the threshold. After that, there are many family photos with both their friends and extended families—most of them whom I've never met. There's one of Aunt Maggie and Uncle Frank cutting the cake in the orchard, where long tables were set up, and another of them sharing their first dance as husband and wife.

"That must have been so romantic," Gemma says. "The lights strung up in the trees, dancing under the stars..."

"Yeah. Rosefield Farm is the perfect location for a wedding." I close the album gently, and beside me, Gemma stretches, her body unfurling like a cat in a sunbeam.

"That was lovely," she says, moving her legs onto my lap. "Especially as it worked out for them, the whole until-death-do-us-part thing. Right? It's rare, nowadays."

"Is that your way of saying you never want to get married?" I hold up a hand. "Wait. Stop. I didn't mean anything by that question. No pressure, I swear."

Gemma laughs and blows me a kiss. "I know, and I didn't say that. Just that it's a risk. One I never really saw for myself, if I'm being honest."

"Really?" I ask. "You never dreamed about a white wedding? The dress, the flowers, the whole shebang?"

Gemma shakes her head, a wry smile playing at her lips. "Nah. That was never my fantasy, and I'm definitely not a dress person."

I nod slowly, understanding dawning. Given Gemma's past, her mother's history with men, it's no wonder the idea of marriage might feel more like a trap than a fairy-tale ending.

"What about you?" she asks, her fingers playing with the ends of my hair. "Have you ever dreamed of being a bride?"

I consider the question, my mind drifting back over the years. "You know, I think I did. In an abstract way, it was always part of my imagined future."

Gemma grins. "The house, the spouse, the two-point-five kids, and a dog?"

I roll my eyes, nudging her playfully. "Something like that." I pause, chewing the inside of my cheek. "With Cleo, in the beginning, I thought we were on the same page. Building a life together, a partnership. But the longer we were together, the more she tried to control me into commitment."

Gemma looks surprised. "She wanted to get married?"

I sigh. "Yes. At least, that's what she claimed. Every time she hurt me and felt me pulling away, she'd dangle the idea of marriage in front of me and I'd come running back, even though deep down, it didn't feel right." I sigh, my gaze distant. "Thank God we never got married. Things would have been so much more complicated when I left. Splitting assets, fighting over property. Divorce lawyers like me," I add with a chuckle, "and tons of paperwork and all that ugliness."

Gemma nods and hesitates. "Do you think you'll ever want to get married now? After everything?"

"I think," I say, "that I'm open to the possibility with the right person." I meet Gemma's gaze, her chocolate-brown eyes filled with warmth and understanding. A heartbeat passes between us, the air humming with unspoken words. I reach out, giving her hand a gentle squeeze. "I'm glad we can talk about these things."

Gemma returns the squeeze, her thumb brushing across my hand. "Me too. I feel like I can tell you anything and..." She stops herself. "Okay, maybe not everything. Not yet. But that's on me, not you." She pauses. "I trust you, it's just..."

"I know. When you're ready." I lean back against the couch cushions, pulling Gemma with me. She settles into my side, her head resting on my shoulder. "How about we make some popcorn and curl up with a movie?" I suggest, changing the topic. I know she'll tell me eventually, and I'm in no rush. This thing, whatever it is that haunts her, it's bigger than this, bigger than us, and at the same time, it wouldn't change how I feel about her. Not now. "Something light and funny," I continue. "to balance out all the heavy conversation."

"That sounds perfect," Gemma says with a hint of relief. "You pick the movie, I'll handle the popcorn?"

"Deal." I press a quick kiss to her lips before standing, extending my hand to help her up. Gemma tilts her head as she places her hands on her hips.

"Sweet or salty?"

"Oh, that's a good question." I laugh. "We haven't covered this topic, but it's essential. One of my old colleagues told his new girlfriend he was happy to eat salty popcorn just to please her, and five years later, he felt it was too late to tell her so he was still eating salty popcorn. He doesn't even like it."

"Ouch." Gemma winces dramatically. "We need to be honest about these things." She shoots me a grin and wraps her arms around my waist, pulling me close. "How about this? I'll count to three and then we both say it."

I shake my head, stopping her. "No, we need to clarify something first. What if I like the combination of both?"

Carrying on the drama, Gemma cups my face. "Then you say sweet and salty. Why, is that your preference?"

"Yes," I say sheepishly.

"Sweet and salty it is," Gemma says with a triumphant glimmer in her eyes. "We happen to be on the same page."

27

GEMMA

I've finally finished setting up my stall after shifting produce around three times. Well, Lori's stall really, but she's entrusted me with it. I have no idea what I'm doing, but with the products on display, tasting platters, scale, a card machine, and a jar full of change at hand, I'm sincerely hoping I'll be able to wing it today.

Maggie's vintage tablecloths billow in the warm breeze as I take a step back, surveying my handiwork with a sense of pride. The jars of homemade jam glisten invitingly, their jewel-toned contents catching the light. Plump peaches and crisp apples, freshly harvested from the orchard and some stems and leaves still attached, spill from baskets. And above it all, the original sign we found in the attic that says "Rosefield Farm."

"Well, look at that!" A jovial voice breaks into my thoughts. I turn to see the man from the neighboring stall, his arms laden with an array of colorful vegetables as he looks up at the sign. "I was wondering who would be taking over Maggie's farm. It's good to see it's up and running again." He regards me. "Are you the new owner?"

I smile, wiping my hands on my jeans before extending one in greeting. "No, I'm Gemma," I introduce myself. "I'm helping Lori, Maggie's niece, who inherited the farm."

The man shifts his produce onto his table, freeing them to shake my hand. "Pleased to meet you, Gemma. I'm Tom. Been selling my veggies here for more years than I care to admit." He smiles. "I remember Lori. She used to come along and help her Aunt Maggie out when she was a kid, but I haven't seen her in decades. How is she?"

"She's doing well," I assure him. "Just busy getting the farm back up and running. I'm sure you'll see her soon enough."

"You make sure to tell her to stop by and say hello, you hear?" a woman's voice chimes in. I glance over to see a woman behind the stall on my other side, which sells a variety of all things lemon—jars of curd, slices of cheesecake, bottles of freshly squeezed juice. She's grinning at me, her silver hair glinting in the sun. "I remember her too. There're so many new folks here now. Tom and I are a couple of the OGs who started all of this," she jokes.

"I'll tell her to stop by," I promise, returning her smile. "And you are...?"

"Oh, where are my manners? I'm Betty, but around here, they call me The Crazy Lemon Lady." She winks conspiratorially. "Been squeezing lemons and swapping stories with Maggie since we were in our twenties. It's good to see a friendly face taking over her old spot. We all miss her."

"It's nice to meet you both," I say sincerely. "I have to admit, I was a bit nervous about today. I've never sold anything other than houses in my life. I come from the real estate business, but it feels great to be here."

"Houses, peaches...it's all the same." Tom claps me on the shoulder, his grip friendly and firm. "You've got nothing to worry about. Folks around here, they look after their own. And with a name like Rosefield Farm, you're practically family already."

As if to prove his point, a customer approaches my stall, her eyes lighting up as she spots the jars of jam. "Oh my goodness, is this Maggie's famous preserves?" she asks, picking up a jar to examine the label.

I nod, a touch of nerves fluttering in my stomach. "It is. Well, it's our attempt at her recipe, at least. Lori, her niece, and I made this batch ourselves."

"Is it the same?" she asks, looking up with a hopeful expression. "Maggie's jam was delightful. I used to add it to everything."

"I can't promise it will be exactly the same," I admit. "But we followed her recipe, and I hope we can do her name proud. Here, have a taste." I drop a generous amount of jam onto a piece of fresh bread and hand it to her.

The woman smiles. "It's delicious," she says through a mouthful. "Maggie always did have a way of bringing out the best in people." She selects a jar of peach preserves and hands over a few bills. "I can't wait to taste a little piece of the past for breakfast tomorrow."

As the day wears on, more and more customers stop by, some eager to share a story or a fond memory of Maggie. I listen and soak up every detail of the woman who meant so much to so many, so I can pass it on to Lori. She should have been here, I think, but we had no idea how much her aunt meant to the community.

With each sale, each compliment on the jam or the fruit, my confidence grows. I may be new to this, but I'm learning and realizing this has real potential. I'm almost sold out and curse myself for not bringing more. All the jam was gone within a few hours, and I've had to spread out the produce to make the stall look semi-filled.

I'm just making a mental note on how much more to bring next week, when someone pinches my behind. I jump, startled, and burst into laughter when I see Lori standing behind me.

"Hey there," she says, grinning.

"Hey." We stare at each other goofily, fighting the temptation of a kiss. "What are you doing here?"

Lori brushes my hand with hers and takes a step back, aware of the other stall holders and customers watching us. "I missed you," she whispers.

"Oh?" I arch a brow, my core fluttering. I'm so happy to see her I don't realize I'm staring until she nudges me. Her outfit doesn't help; she's wearing a short denim skirt and a white top that hugs her curves and gives me an exquisite glimpse of her cleavage.

"Not here," she whispers, shooting me a flirty look. "I'm not sure if they can handle it."

We hear whispers and turn to see Betty and Tom watching us with amused expressions.

"Well, well, look who it is," Tom says, a broad grin splitting his weathered face. "Little Lori, all grown up."

Lori's eyes widen in recognition, a delighted smile lighting up her features. "Tom? Betty? Oh my goodness, it's been years! How did you even recognize me?"

She steps around the stall, arms outstretched, and is immediately engulfed in a bear hug from Tom. He lifts her off her feet, chuckling heartily as she squeals and laughs.

"Put me down, you big oaf," she scolds playfully, swatting at his shoulder. "I'm not a kid anymore."

"You'll always be a kid to us, sweetheart," Betty says

warmly, stepping forward to clasp Lori's hands in her own. "Just look at you, prettier than a peach in July."

Lori chuckles and ducks her head. "Stop it, you'll make me blush."

"Too late for that," I tease, enjoying the pink staining her cheeks. She shoots me a mock glare, but the effect is ruined by the way her lips keep twitching into a smile.

"Gemma was just telling us about you taking over the farm," Tom says, leaning against his stall. "About damn time, if you ask me. That place needs another strong woman at the helm."

"I'll do my best." Lori's smile turns wistful, her gaze drifting over the market. "I just hope Aunt Maggie won't turn around in her grave. I know nothing about farming, and I've been clutching at straws so far."

Betty pats her hand. "She'd be proud of you, honey. Prouder than a mama hen with a clutch of blue-ribbon chicks."

That startles a laugh out of Lori. "She did love her colorful phrases, didn't she?"

"That she did," Tom agrees, chuckling. "Remember when she caught those kids sneaking into her orchard?" he says, turning to Betty. "Chased 'em off with a broom, hollering about how she was going to 'tan their hides six ways to Sunday.'"

Lori's laughter rings out again. "She was a force of nature, that's for sure."

As they reminisce, trading stories and memories, I watch Lori and smile at the way she comes alive in their presence.

"Gemma, dear, you're staring," Betty says, jolting me out of my reverie. There's a knowing twinkle in her eye, a sly curve to her smile that makes me wonder just how transparent I am.

Before I can stammer out a response, Lori's hand finds mine, her fingers intertwining with my own. "She does that," she says softly, her gaze meeting mine. "I kind of like it."

The admission, spoken so casually yet holding such weight, surprises me. I squeeze her hand, a silent acknowledgment. I didn't think she wanted anyone to know, but she clearly feels comfortable enough in their company to open up.

"Well, you girls look like you're getting on like a house on fire," Tom says.

I stifle a laugh at Tom's comment, wondering if he's being deliberately obtuse or if he truly hasn't caught on to the sparks flying between Lori and me. I catch Betty's gaze, and she gives me a wink that says she's fully aware of what's going on, even if Tom is happily living in the land of oblivion.

I head over to Betty and lean in with a grin. "Hey, Betty, do you think Tom would notice if Lori and I started making out right here?"

Betty snorts, her eyes dancing with amusement. "Sweetheart, Tom wouldn't notice if a UFO landed on his veggie patch. You two lovebirds carry on. I'll distract him with some carrot talk."

28

LORI

*S*taring at Gemma has become my favorite pastime. From my office window, I have the perfect view of her in the orchard. I should be working; I have tons of phone calls to make, emails to catch up on, but she's so deliciously distracting I've even let my coffee go cold.

The sky is turning gray, with dark patches in the distance, and it looks like we'll have some much-needed rain later, perhaps even the first thunderstorm of the summer season. They often roll in suddenly in July afternoons, announced by an eerie stillness and a prickling on the skin before the sky cracks open.

I imagine watching the storm unfold from the shelter of the porch. There's something primally invigorating about booms of thunder and flashes of lightning illuminating the night.

The rain will be good for the orchard at least, even if the lightning makes me nervous about the risk of fire, now that I'm responsible for the farm. The monsoon season is a double-edged sword that way.

A knock on the door startles me, and I open the door to find Charlotte.

"Well, well, well," she drawls, stepping inside. "Someone's got that 'just been thoroughly fucked' glow."

My cheeks flush a deep crimson as I gasp, nearly spilling the coffee I'm holding. "Charlotte!"

"What?" She rolls her eyes, plopping down on one of the kitchen chairs. "Oh, please. You and Gemma have serious chemistry. You didn't think I noticed?"

"Fuck," I mutter, biting my lip to stop the giddy smile threatening to break free. "Do you think Miranda noticed?"

"Probably not. She doesn't know you as well as I do." Charlotte chuckles. "So? Spill the tea."

"Shouldn't you be at work?" I ask in a casual attempt to change the subject.

"I had a dentist appointment so I took the afternoon off." Charlotte flashes me her teeth. "Whitening session."

I study her smile and give her an approving nod. I don't see any difference, Charlotte's teeth are always sparkling white, but she thrives on compliments. "Looks good." Do you want a coffee? Or is that a no-go after the treatment?"

"Nah, I can't, but anyway, I'm not staying long. I just came for the gossip, but you seem to be avoiding my question."

"Fine," I concede, emptying my cold coffee into the sink. "We slept together." I grin as I feel my cheeks flush. "Over and over and over and—"

Charlotte squeals, clapping her hands in delight. "I knew it! Oh, honey, I'm so happy for you. I really like Gemma. Where is she, by the way?"

"Orchard," I say, pointing at her through the kitchen window.

Charlotte follows my gaze. "She's cute, that's for sure. "So...how was it? Are you two an item now?"

"It was...incredible. I've never felt like this before." I look away, as I don't want Charlotte to see me turning bright red. "And yeah, I guess we're together." I stop her when she's about to start squealing again. "But this is between you and me, okay? You can't tell Miranda. Technically, it's unethical, given our current arrangement through the rehabilitation program."

"Of course." Charlotte pulls me into a hug. "You deserve this, Lori. After everything you've been through, you deserve someone who treats you right." She steps back and places her hands on my shoulders. "Now, about the sex. Give me details."

"No chance." I shake my head, laughing. "Why don't you tell me about you and Miranda instead? How's that going?"

Charlotte grins and ducks her head, suddenly shy. "It's... good. Really good, actually." She sighs dreamily. "Miranda is everything I could hope for. So smart and driven, but with this soft side that just melts me."

"Look at you, all smitten," I tease, poking her arm. "I never thought I'd see the day when Charlotte *Love 'Em and Leave 'Em* Carlson would be head over heels."

Charlotte rolls her eyes, but she can't hide the joy radiating from her. "Shut up. I'm not... Okay, maybe I am a little smitten."

"Did I hear smitten? Who's smitten?" Gemma, who's just walked in, shoots Charlotte a wink. She looks radiant, her smile widening when our eyes lock.

"Charlotte is," I tease and laugh when Charlotte widens her eyes at me.

"Excuse me," she says. "I don't seem to be the only one."

She turns to Gemma, waggling her eyebrows suggestively. "I heard you two have been having sleepovers too."

I groan, burying my face in my hands as Gemma laughs. "Charlotte, behave."

"Behave? Where's the fun in that?"

"I'm sorry. I told her." I wince at Gemma. "I should have discussed it with you first, but Charlotte clearly came over with the intention of interrogating me and I didn't stand a chance. I made her promise to keep it between us."

"That's okay." Gemma wraps an arm around my shoulders and pulls me in to kiss my cheek. "At least now I don't have to worry about keeping my hands to myself."

Our banter has me laughing when the first rumble of thunder vibrates the windowpanes. I hadn't realized how close the dark clouds had gotten until Charlotte quirks an eyebrow at the ominous sound.

"Sounds like monsoon season has arrived."

I'm about to make a joke in return when an enormous boom cracks overhead, rattling the glasses in the cupboard. Beside me, Gemma jolts violently, her hip slamming into the kitchen counter with a dull thud. Her eyes are wide, pupils dilated, and her face suddenly drains of color.

"Gemma?" I reach for her, alarmed, but she flinches away from my touch, her breath coming in short, sharp pants.

Another clap of thunder and Gemma practically crumples, hunching her shoulders as if expecting a blow. A strangled whimper escapes her throat and she begins to mutter under her breath, the words tumbling out in a frantic stream. "No...no, no, no, stop that. Stop it!"

The hairs on the back of my neck stand up as I realize what's happening. Gemma's not here with us anymore. She's somewhere else, someplace dark.

"Gemma, honey," I try again, keeping my voice soft and steady. "You're safe. It's just a storm."

But my words don't seem to penetrate the fog of panic that's descended over her. She's hyperventilating now, her chest heaving with shallow, rapid breaths. Sweat beads on her forehead as she rocks slightly back and forth, still pleading with phantoms only she can see.

Charlotte shoots me a concerned look. "Is she okay?" she mouths.

I shake my head but hold up my hand to stop her from approaching Gemma while I rack my brain for what to do.

Another bolt of lightning illuminates the kitchen in stark white, followed immediately by a concussive boom. Gemma sinks down onto the floor, her back against the cabinets like a cornered animal. Hugging herself, her nails dig into her upper arms hard enough to leave marks as she buries her head between her knees.

"Gemma, listen to me," I try again, pitching my voice to cut through her distress without startling her further. I sit next to her and take her in my arms. "Breathe with me, okay? In and out. Nice and slow."

I begin to exaggerate my own breathing, hoping she'll instinctively match it. Gradually, Gemma's breathing slows. Her desperate muttering trails off into shuddering inhales and exhales. I can see her struggling to surface, to find her way back from whatever hellscape she's been thrust into.

"That's it," I encourage softly. "You're doing great. Just keep breathing. Focus on my voice. Feel the floor underneath you, the wall at your back. You're safe."

I keep up a steady stream of soothing words as the storm rages outside, each crack and rumble making Gemma flinch. But slowly, painstakingly, the haze of disassociation begins to clear from her eyes. Awareness trickles in, followed by searing shame and exhaustion.

"Lori?" she rasps, her voice raw and small. "Charlotte? I'm so sorry...I'm not even sure what happened."

"I think the thunder triggered something," I murmur, tentatively reaching for her hand. She allows the touch, her fingers icy and trembling in mine.

"Fuck," she whispers. "I'm sorry. You shouldn't have had to see that again. And with Charlotte here...I'm so embarrassed."

"No," I counter firmly, giving her hand a careful squeeze. "You have nothing to be sorry for."

Charlotte joins us on the floor. "Of course not. Do you want to talk about it?"

"No." Gemma shakes her head, visibly struggling to piece herself back together. She's still far too pale, a light sheen of sweat misting her skin. "Sorry, no..."

"Come on," I say gently, extending a hand to help her up. "Let's move to the couch. I think some blankets and a cup of chamomile tea are in order."

"Or something stronger," Charlotte suggests, already moving to rummage through the liquor cabinet. "I make a mean toddy."

Gemma manages a chuckle. "If there was ever a time for a stiff drink..." She lets me help her to her feet, leaning heavily into my side as I guide her to the living room. She settles on the couch and I bundle her in blankets.

"I'm so embarrassed," she whispers again. "What's Charlotte going to think of me?"

"Shh..." I silence her with a soft kiss to her lips. "Charlotte thinks the world of you, so don't worry about anything but your breathing, okay?"

"Sorry, guys, looks like you're stuck with me for a while."

Charlotte comes in with three mugs and hands us a hot toddy. "The storm's picking up. I'm not sure it's safe to drive."

"No, you should stay. I'll cook us some food." I wince at another loud clap of thunder, but Gemma is calmer now; it doesn't affect her this time.

She takes a tentative sip, closing her eyes as she swallows. "Thanks, Charlotte," she murmurs.

Charlotte just nods, her expression uncharacteristically solemn. "Anytime. I mean that." She lingers on the spot, then glances in the direction of the kitchen. "How about I make dinner? You two stay here and cuddle up."

Somehow, that might be the sweetest thing Charlotte's ever said. She can't cook to save her life and genuinely despises being behind the stove. I'm about to object and let her off the hook, but she looks so determined that I shoot her a grateful smile. "Thank you, that would be lovely."

29

GEMMA

"I'm afraid." The words leave me in a whisper and I'm not even sure if I've said them out loud until Lori replies.

"What are you afraid of?" she asks, softly trailing her hand up and down my back. Charlotte has finally been able to leave and we're in bed, snuggled underneath the blankets. Outside, the storm has died down a little, but it's still raining.

"That I'll lose you because I have too much baggage. That you'll realize I'm too much with my panic attacks and my history."

Lori smiles sadly and shakes her head. "You're never too much. I want to help you."

"But what's in it for you?" It's a question I've asked myself many times, especially since Lori and I have gotten intimate.

Lori shifts to face me fully, her eyes searching mine in the dim light of the bedroom. "Gemma," she says, "you're not a burden. You're not some charity case. Being with you makes me happier than you can ever know."

"But my past is not just going to go away. Tonight was proof of that."

Lori nods, her hand coming up to cup my cheek. "I know that, and I'm not expecting it to. Your trauma is part of you, but it's not all of you." She takes a deep breath, her thumb brushing over my cheekbone. "Gemma, I need you to hear me. Really hear me. There is nothing, absolutely nothing, that could make me walk away from you. Not your past, not your trauma, not the challenges we might face together." She pulls back slightly, tipping my chin up so she can look me in the eye. "I'm in this, all the way. The good, the bad, the nightmares, and the panic attacks. I'm here for all of it. Because I lo—" She catches herself, swallowing hard. "Because I care about you. So much."

My heart stutters in my chest, a fragile hope unfurling. "But what about everyone else? Your friends, your family. What will they think when they find out you're dating an ex-con?"

Lori's jaw tightens, a flare of fierce protectiveness in her eyes. "Frankly, Gemma? I don't give a damn what anyone else thinks. The people who matter, the ones who truly care about me? They'll see what I see."

I stare at her, a little awed and a lot humbled. Here is this amazing woman, ready to take on the world for me, ready to stand by my side through thick and thin. It feels like a gift I'm not sure I deserve, but one I'm desperate to cling to with both hands. "Okay," I whisper, a small smile tugging at the corners of my mouth. "Okay."

Lori returns the smile. "Okay," she echoes, leaning in and brushing her lips against mine. "I'm in this for the long run."

"So am I." I hesitate. "What does that look like to you? The long run? Or even the near future?"

Lori considers my question, her fingers absently tracing patterns on my arm. A rumble of distant thunder punctuates the silence, but it doesn't startle me anymore. "Well," she starts, "I suppose in the immediate future, it looks a lot like this. Us, together, taking each day as it comes. Learning about each other, supporting each other. I want to really know you."

"You will," I promise. "The good and the bad. I'm almost there."

"I know." She shifts slightly, propping herself up on one elbow. The dim light from the bedside lamp casts soft shadows across her face, highlighting her dimples and the fullness of her upper lip. "I'm here for you, no matter what. On the hard days, the days when the past feels like it's crushing you, I want to be your safe place. I want to hold you through the flashbacks, remind you how to breathe when the panic sets in."

My throat tightens, emotion welling up. "I don't think I could've made it through these past months without you in my corner."

Lori catches my hand, pressing a kiss to my palm. "You would have made it with or without me. You're stronger than you think."

It's not the first time she's told me that, and despite my breakdown today, I'm almost starting to believe her.

A flicker of something vulnerable crosses her face. "And as far as the long-term future is concerned, I know it might be too soon to talk about forever, but Gem, when I think about my life, all I can see is you."

"Yeah?"

Lori nods, her eyes shining. "Yeah. I see us here, on this farm. Watching the sunsets from the porch, arguing over whose turn it is to do the dishes. Maybe expanding the orchard, trying out new crops. You running it with me or doing whatever it is you want to do."

The image blooms in my mind, achingly vivid. A future filled with early mornings and soil-stained hands, with laughter through the rows of trees. A future that, for the first time, feels within reach.

"I want that," I whisper, the words raw and utterly honest. "I want that with you."

Lori's smile is radiant, brighter than the sun. She leans down, capturing my lips in a kiss. I sink into it, letting her warmth and her certainty seep into my bones.

When we break apart, I rest my forehead against hers, breathing her in. "You make me so happy and I…" I want to tell her I love her. That she has my heart, my trust, my soul, and everything in between. But I want to wait until she knows everything about me. It's not fair to throw something as huge as love onto someone when they're still in the dark. I wish I could tell her right now, but fear keeps holding me back. Yes, I do trust her, but the reality is that I killed someone. I took a life, and that will haunt me forever. "I'm crazy about you," I say instead.

"I'm crazy about you too." Lori grins. "In fact, I've been making a mental list of all the things I adore about you."

I raise an eyebrow, curiosity piqued. "Oh? Do tell."

Lori clears her throat dramatically, as if preparing for a grand speech. "Well, for one thing, I love the way you always sniff your coffee a few times before taking the first sip in the morning. Like you're savoring the promise of caffeine and a new day."

"Okay, that's oddly specific," I say. "I hadn't even realized I do that."

"Uh-huh. I also love how you talk to the trees and all things growing in the orchard when you think no one's listening. Encouraging the little saplings, scolding the weeds. It's adorable."

I laugh and bury my face in my hands. "They respond better to positive reinforcement."

"I've noticed that. They've been flourishing lately." She points to my face. "And I love the way you blush. The way it starts at your neck and works its way up, like a sunrise."

I squirm a little under her intense gaze, equal parts embarrassed and pleased. "Okay, now you're just trying to make me blush more."

"Guilty," she acknowledges with a shameless grin. "But I'm not finished. I also love your secret sweet tooth, the way your eyes light up when I bake those double chocolate chip cookies you sneak from the jar when you think I'm not looking."

A surprised laugh escapes me, breaking the building emotional tension. "Hey, I have a lot of cookie-free years to make up for," I protest, poking her side playfully.

Lori yelps, squirming away from my tickling fingers. "But my absolute favorite thing?" she continues, slightly breathless from laughter. "My very favorite thing is your smile. Not the polite one you give to strangers, but the real one that starts slow, a little hesitant, like it's not quite sure it's allowed. But then it grows, spreading across your face until you're lit up from the inside out. That smile makes me melt, every single time." She hesitates. "I'm going to visit Mom tomorrow, and I want to tell her about you, if you're okay with that."

I stare at her, utterly speechless. "Of course, but...what are you going to tell her?"

"Nothing in specific. She always worries about me, so I guess I just want her to know that I've met someone and that I'm truly happy." Lori shrugs. "I'm taking the wedding album I found in the attic. Aunt Maggie is a sore topic, so it's probably best I go alone, but maybe next time, you could come along and meet her?"

"I'd love to meet your mom." I place my hand over hers. Although the prospect terrifies me, it would also be an honor to meet the person who raised such a wonderful, kind woman. "She must be something special. But why are you showing her the album if it's a sore topic?"

Lori remains silent for a beat, frowning as if she's not quite sure herself. "Something doesn't sit right," she says. "I don't know what it is, but since moving here, the past has been bugging me, and I need to know what happened."

The determination in Lori's voice, the set of her jaw, tells me this is important to her. That she needs to untangle this knot in her family tapestry.

"I understand," I say. "I hope you find the answers you're looking for."

30

LORI

$\mathcal{T}$he scent of my mother's favorite lavender candles greets me as I step into the living room. It's a smell that's always been synonymous with home, with comfort.

Mom is already settled on the couch, a steaming mug of coffee cradled in her hands. She looks up as I let myself in, a smile touching her lips. "Lori, honey."

"Hi, Mom." I lean down to press a quick kiss to her cheek before sinking into the armchair across from her and pick up the mug waiting for me. "I'm glad I could catch you at home."

"It's good to see you. You look great." She takes a sip of her coffee, her gaze flicking to the bag I've brought. "What's that you've got there?"

I take out the album and show it to her. "It's a photo album I found. Uncle Frank and Aunt Maggie's wedding album."

Mom stiffens, her fingers tightening around her mug. "Oh?"

"I found it in the attic." I hesitate, studying her face.

There's a tightness around her mouth, a wariness in her eyes that I don't understand. "Actually, that's part of the reason I wanted to come by today. To show you some of the pictures."

"I'm not sure that's necessary, dear." Mom's voice is light, but there's an undercurrent of tension that sets my teeth on edge. "The past is the past, after all. You know Maggie and I didn't get along."

"But why? You've never told me, and I never asked. Suddenly, we stopped visiting the farm and then years later, I went off to college and then I moved to Prescott. Life happened, I guess, and weirdly, I never thought about it much until now—now that I'm living Aunt Maggie's life, in a way." I lean forward to set the album on the coffee table between us. "Don't you want to see them? You and Maggie looked like you were so close."

Mom's smile is strained, brittle around the edges. "I remember just fine, Lori. I don't need pictures to remind me."

The unease in my stomach twists. "You haven't even been out to the farm since I moved in," I say, hating the note of accusation in my voice but unable to hold it back. "I thought...maybe looking at these might make you want to visit. It's my home now. Are you just going to avoid it forever?"

Mom sighs, setting her mug down with a clatter. "I've been busy, honey. You know how it is, with the shop and the book club and the church bazaar coming up..."

"Too busy for your own daughter?" The words taste bitter on my tongue, but I can't seem to stop them.

"Lori..." There's a warning in her tone, a plea for understanding. But I'm tired of trying to understand and making excuses for her absence.

"Just look at the pictures. Please." I flip open the album. "Look, here's one of you and Aunt Maggie at her wedding. You look so happy together."

The photo is beautifully faded with age. They're standing arm in arm, Aunt Maggie's wedding dress and Mom's bridesmaid dress billowing in the breeze. Aunt Maggie's smile is radiant with love and laughter, and Mom's head is thrown back in a laugh.

"You were her maid of honor," I say, tracing the edge of the photo with a fingertip. "What happened? What went wrong between you two?"

For a long moment, Mom is silent, her gaze fixed on the picture. When she finally speaks, her voice is so soft I have to strain to hear it. "We grew apart, Lori. It happens some-times, with sisters. Life gets in the way, priorities change..."

"That doesn't make any sense," I press, frustration bleeding into my tone. "You were practically inseparable, from what I remember, and from what I see here. And then one day, it was like she just...disappeared. No more visits, no more phone calls. It was like she and Uncle Frank stopped existing."

"It's complicated, honey." Mom's fingers twist in her lap, knotting and unknotting. "There were things that happened, that made it difficult for us to stay in touch."

"What things?" Frustration is rising in my voice, pent-up questions bubbling to the surface. "What could possibly have happened to make you turn your back on your own sister?"

Mom's head snaps up, her eyes flashing. "You have no idea, Lori."

"Then tell me!" I'm on my feet now, the album clutched to my chest like a shield. "Make me understand, because from where I'm standing, it looks like you abandoned her."

Mom flinches as if I've struck her, her face draining of color. For a moment, I think she's going to lash out, meet my anger with her own, but then, to my shock, she crumples. Her shoulders sag and her head drops into her hands as a shudder runs through her.

"Yes, I turned my back on her," she whispers, her voice muffled and thick with tears. "I had to. It was in everyone's best interest."

I stare at her, my anger giving way to a creeping sense of dread. I've never seen my mother so broken, and it scares me in a way I can't put into words. Slowly, I lower myself back into my chair. "What do you mean, you didn't have a choice?"

Mom takes a deep breath, lifting her head to meet my gaze. Her eyes are red-rimmed, her cheeks wet with tears. "I did something unforgivable, Lori."

"Mom...what did you do?"

She closes her eyes, her face twisting with a pain. "I had an affair," she whispers, the words hanging in the air like shards of glass. "With your uncle. Maggie was away visiting a friend in Vegas, so Frank and I met up for dinner one night."

"You...you what?"

"It was a terrible mistake." Mom's voice is pleading, desperate. "We were young and foolish and...and it just happened. Frank and I used to have a thing for each other, before he and Maggie got together, and old feelings surfaced. It wasn't worth it, of course. I swear I've never regretted anything more. And then, years later, Maggie found out, and she was so angry and hurt. Frank was the love of her life. She was crazy about him. She told me she never wanted to see me again. I have no idea if their marriage truly recovered after that, but they stayed together, and Frank passed away seven years later, way too soon. She never reached out to me. I found out through a family member."

I can't speak, can't think. The revelation is like a physical blow, knocking the wind out of me. All these years, all this time, and I never knew. Never even suspected.

"I'm sorry, Lori." Mom's voice cracks, fresh tears spilling down her cheeks. "I'm a terrible person."

"You're not, Mom," I say, my voice softening. It was wrong, but it happened decades ago, and it's sad that the guilt still eats away at her.

Mom shakes her head, a small, miserable motion. "I went to see Maggie in the hospital before she passed away. But she was in and out of consciousness, and I couldn't really have a conversation with her. I told her how much I regretted it, though." A sob catches in her throat, her shoulders shaking with the force of it.

Perching on the armrest next to her, I rub her back. The secrets, the lies, the years of estrangement...it all makes a terrible, twisted sort of sense now. But there's something else, a nagging feeling at the back of my mind. A question that I'm almost afraid to ask.

"Mom..." I start. "When...when did this happen? The affair?"

She looks up at me, her face a mask of anguish. "Lori, please..."

"When, Mom?" I press, my heart hammering against my ribs. "I need to know."

For a terrifying moment, she's silent. And then, in a voice so soft I almost miss it, she speaks the words that shatter my world.

"It was thirty-seven years ago. A few months before they got married," she whispers. "Lori...Frank is your father."

The room spins around me, the walls closing in. I feel like I can't breathe. "No..." I whisper, shaking my head in denial even as the truth settles like a lead weight in my stomach. "No, that's not...that can't be..." But even as the words leave my lips, I know. Deep down, in a place I've never dared to look too closely, I've always known. The nagging doubts, the half-formed questions, the pieces that never quite fit...it all falls into place with a sickening clarity.

"Lori, honey, please...say something." Mom's voice seems to come from far away, echoing and distorted. "I'm sorry, I'm so sorry. I never meant for you to find out like this."

"You mean you never meant for me to find out at all?" Her words are meaningless, empty platitudes that can't begin to touch the depth of my betrayal. For years, I've asked about my father. My mother told me he was a one-night stand who disappeared before she could tell him she was pregnant. How could she do this?

I push to my feet, stumbling slightly as the world sways around me. "I have to go," I mumble. "I can't be here right now."

"Lori, wait!" Mom reaches for me, her hand outstretched, but I flinch away from her touch. I can't bear it. "I can't lose you too."

"Did he know he was my father?" I ask. "Did Aunt Maggie know?"

"Frank knew." Mom pauses. "When I told them I was pregnant, it didn't take him long to figure out he was the father. But Maggie didn't know, not at first. We couldn't tell her. When she eventually found out Frank and I had had an affair, she took one look at you and put two and two together. She couldn't have children, so that made it even more hurtful for her."

I'm moving toward the door, my feet carrying me of their own volition. I need to breathe air that isn't tainted with secrets and lies. I pause at the threshold, my hand on the doorknob. I can hear Mom behind me, her sobs echoing in the stillness of the house. A part of me wants to turn back, but I can't.

31

GEMMA

$\mathcal{T}$he sun-warmed grass feels soft beneath me as I sit cross-legged under the sprawling oak tree, its branches providing a welcome respite from the heat. Lori leans back against the rough bark beside me, our shoulders brushing.

She's just finished telling me about her conversation with her mother, about the secrets that have shattered the foundation of her world. Her voice is hoarse, her cheeks damp with tears.

"I'm so sorry, Lori. I can't imagine how you must be feeling right now."

She swallows hard, blinking back fresh tears. "I don't know how to feel," she confesses. "I'm angry, I'm hurt, I'm... I'm lost."

I nod, my hand finding hers in the grass. "That's understandable. It's going to take time to process all of this."

Lori squeezes my hand. "My whole life, I consoled myself with the fact that my father didn't know I existed. That if he did, he might want to know me." She pauses, the old ache evident in her voice. "My mother made up some story about a traveling kitchen salesman she met in a bar. She said she couldn't remember his last name or the company he worked for. I spent years digging and doing research on who might have been in the area, what companies operated there." A bitter laugh escapes her, the sound harsh in the tranquil stillness. "I've wasted so much energy researching a lie."

My hand tightens around Lori's. "She should have told you."

"Yes." She sniffs, and I pull her closer, letting her head rest on my shoulder. "I suppose she wanted to save me from disappointment. My father knew who I was, yet he never reached out after Mom and Aunt Maggie broke contact."

The words seem to physically pain her. Frank, her uncle, her father...he knew.

"Maybe he wanted to," I suggest gently. "Maybe he felt like he couldn't, because of the situation."

Lori sighs, picking at a blade of grass. "Maybe. But it doesn't change the fact that he chose not to be in my life. He chose to let me grow up without a father."

"I don't think it was about you not being wanted, Lori. I think...I think sometimes people make choices that they believe are for the best, even if those choices end up hurting the people they love."

Lori turns to me and shoots me a sad smile. "Everything I thought I knew about myself, and about my family, it was all built on a lie. I would never do that to someone."

My hand leaves hers to wrap around her shoulders, pulling her into the solid warmth of my side. "You're still you, Lori. You're still the same strong, compassionate, resilient woman you've always been. This doesn't change who you are."

She burrows deeper into my embrace, and I know she wants to believe my words.

"I think," I continue, "you take it one day at a time. You let yourself feel what you need to feel—the anger, the hurt, the confusion. You talk about it, with me, with your mom, with a therapist, with anyone you trust. And you remember that you're not alone in this."

"I don't want to talk to Mom." Lori wipes her cheeks. "She betrayed me."

"I understand you're hurt right now, but she's still your mom, and she loves you more than anything." I shrug. "Trust me. I know a thing or two about family dynamics."

"What do you mean by that?"

"I did something bad, and my mother tried to take the blame for it," I say, swallowing hard. "But I couldn't let her."

Lori tilts her head. "Gemma, what happened? With your mother?" When I don't reply, she hesitates before asking the next question. "You told me your belongings are at her house. Are you planning on picking them up?"

"I don't really need anything. I'd rather start with a clean slate."

"But your mom. Don't you think she'd like to see you?"

"Our relationship is complicated." I hope I don't sound like I'm being short with her. As soon as our conversations turn to my past, I feel myself withdraw. It happens every time. Part of me wants to confide in Lori, but I also know I might lose her. Whatever happens, she'll never look at me the same way again. I shake my head, not ready to touch the surface. "Not yet." I'm repeating myself, but what else can I do?

Lori nods, and we sit in silence for a moment, both lost in our thoughts. Then, she speaks, her voice soft. "When we were going through Aunt Maggie and Uncle Frank's pictures..." She winces. "You did mention how much I look like him. I thought it was a funny coincidence, but now it makes sense."

I study her profile, taking in her beautiful face. "Yeah." I can see the wheels turning in her head. "You know," I say, "there are still a lot of boxes in the attic that we haven't gone through yet. Boxes that belonged to Frank."

"Yeah, there's quite a lot. I've been busy, so I've been putting off sorting them out for the Goodwill."

"Maybe now is the time," I say. "At the very least, it could be a way for you to get to know him a little."

Lori considers this, chewing on her bottom lip. "Yes...it might help me understand him a bit better." She leans over and presses a soft kiss to my cheek. "Thank you," she murmurs. "For being here."

I turn my head, capturing her lips in a kiss. "I wish I could take away your pain."

Lori cups my cheek and smiles. "I feel that with you all the time."

"That's sweet, but I'm fine," I say. "I'm healing. This place and you...it's good for me. You're good for me."

"I hope you know that you can trust me," she whispers, brushing her lips against mine. Although she's incredibly patient with me, Lori is clearly getting tired of being in the dark, and I can't blame her. We're together, sharing a home and a bed, and she knows nothing about me.

"I trust you. And I want to open up, but..." I blow out my cheeks. "Look, I know you need this. It's only fair that I let you in, and I'm working up to it, I promise."

"I know," Lori whispers. "When you're ready."

32

LORI

Shafts of sunlight pierce the small, circular window, illuminating the dance of dust motes in the attic. I feel nervous as I open the first box labeled "Frank." I suspect they're boxes Aunt Maggie packed up after his passing.

Gemma's hand rests on the small of my back, a comforting warmth that grounds me. "We don't have to do this today if you're not ready," she says when she notices me shaking.

I take a deep breath, steeling myself against the onslaught of emotions. "No, I want to." I wasn't all that interested in the boxes before, but now they hold so much significance.

The first box reveals a stack of old books, their covers faded and spines cracked with age. I pick one up, brushing my fingers over the embossed title. "*The Great Gatsby*," I murmur. "It was one of my favorites in high school."

Gemma leans over, peering at the book. "A classic," she agrees. "I wonder if it was one of Frank's favorites too."

The thought we may have had more in common than

just dimples makes my throat tighten, and setting the book aside, I open the next box. This one is filled with postcards, their edges worn and colors faded. Each one bears a different postmark, a different date, sent to him and Aunt Maggie by what I assume were their friends. *New York City, 1978. Paris, 1985. London, 1991.* "I don't think they traveled much themselves," I say. "I suppose it was pretty special to get a postcard from a European destination."

I spot a box that looks different from the rest. It's smaller, more compact, and tied with a faded blue ribbon. I tug at the knot, letting the ribbon fall away. Lifting the lid, I find myself staring at a stack of photographs.

"Oh," I whisper.

Gemma moves closer, her shoulder brushing against mine as she looks into the box. "Pictures."

Gently, I lift out the first photograph. In it, a young Maggie and Frank stand arm in arm, their faces alight with laughter. Maggie's hair is styled in a soft eighties perm, a polka-dot dress hugging her slim figure, and Frank looks dashing in a navy suit.

"They look happy," Gemma murmurs, echoing my thoughts.

I nod while my eyes trace the lines of Frank's cheek. They're the same dimples I see in the mirror each morning. There are pictures of them in the orchard, proudly standing underneath the trees heavy with ripe fruit. Christmases around the fireplace with Mom and me as a baby, the mantel dripping with garlands and stockings. Birthdays, anniversaries.

"He was always smiling," Gemma remarks softly. "In every picture."

"He was. That's how I remember him." I pause when I see a picture of Frank sitting in a rocking chair on the porch, cradling a bundle in his arms. A baby, swaddled in a soft, yellow blanket. And he's looking down at that bundle with an expression of such pure, unadulterated love that it brings a lump to my throat.

"Is that...?"

"Yeah," I whisper. "That's me." For a while, I can only stare at the photograph, at the man who was my father, holding me with such tenderness.

The tears come then, hot and fast, spilling down my cheeks in an unstoppable torrent. Gemma gathers me into her arms, holding me close as I cry for the father I never knew I had.

She doesn't shush me, doesn't try to stem the tide of my grief. She just holds me, her embrace strong and unwavering, anchoring me in the storm of my emotions.

When at last my sobs subside, I pull back, swiping at my tear-stained cheeks. "I'm sorry," I whisper, my voice hoarse.

Gemma shakes her head, her eyes gentle with understanding. "This is a lot to process, Lori. It's okay to feel overwhelmed."

I nod, and my gaze drifts back to the photograph. "I just wish I'd known."

Gemma's hand finds mine, her fingers lacing through my own. "I know. And I'm so sorry you didn't get that chance. But Lori..." She pauses, waiting until I meet her gaze. "He loved you. Even if he couldn't show it, even if circumstances kept you apart...he loved you. That picture doesn't lie." She squeezes my hand. "You can't change the past, but you can choose to move forward with acceptance."

"Yeah." I realize how lucky I am to have her here. "When did you get so wise?" I tease.

Gemma chuckles. "I have my moments." She holds up a particularly adorable photo of a baby me on Mom's lap, my chubby cheeks split in a gummy grin. "Look at you. You were such a cute baby."

I laugh, the sound surprising me with its lightness.

As we continue to sift through the boxes, the attic becomes a treasure trove of memories, each item holding a piece of the puzzle that was Frank's life.

One of the boxes yields a collection of men's clothes, creased from years of storage, and underneath it is a wooden chest. Inside, I find a beautiful, hand-carved chess set. The pieces are exquisite, each one a miniature work of art depicting medieval figures. I also uncover a series of notebooks filled with game notations and strategies. It seems Frank was quite the chess enthusiast, meticulously recording and analyzing his matches.

In the corner of the attic, a long, slim case catches my eye. I open it to reveal Frank's old fishing rods, and tucked into the case is a small tackle box, filled with lures and hooks.

"What do you remember about him?" Gemma asks.

I close my eyes, casting my mind back to those sun-drenched summers on the farm, and the hazy memories of a little girl. "Bits and pieces," I say. "He was tall, I remember that. He seemed like a giant to me." A smile touches my lips, the memory warming me from within. "He used to let me ride on his shoulders," I continue. "He'd run through the orchard, weaving between the trees, and I'd shriek with laughter, feeling like I was flying."

Gemma chuckles. "That sounds adorable."

"He had a laugh like a bear," I say, the sound rising in my mind. "Deep and rumbling, like it came from his belly. And he was always laughing, always smiling. He made everyone around him feel good."

I pause, another memory surfacing. "He used to call me

'sunshine,'" I murmur. "'Where's my little sunshine?' he'd say when I'd run to him." I lean my head on Gemma's shoulder, feeling the solidness of her, the steadiness. "The last summer I saw him," I say quietly, "I was eight. He took me fishing at the creek." The memory rises, vivid and bittersweet. The cool, clear water rushing over the rocks. Frank's large, gentle hands guiding my small ones as he showed me how to cast the line. I haven't thought of that day since.

"I think that's the last memory I have of him," I say. "Before everything changed."

33

GEMMA

I lurch awake, my heart pounding, my skin cold with sweat. A scream catches in my throat, strangled and raw. For a moment, I'm disoriented, but then I feel her, warm and solid beside me.

"Gemma?" Lori's voice is thick with sleep but laced with concern. She reaches for me, her hand finding mine beneath the tangled sheets. "Another nightmare?"

I nod, not trusting my voice yet. The images still linger, vivid and visceral. The sound of something shattering, the thud of flesh. The coppery scent of blood and my mother's screams somewhere in the back of my conscience.

Lori pulls me closer, and I go willingly, pressing my face into the crook of her neck. She smells like soap and sleep and safety.

"I'm here," she murmurs, her lips brushing my temple. "You're safe."

But am I? The thought rises, insidious. Because the truth is, the nightmare is not just a figment of my sleeping mind. It's a memory, a brutal reality that I've tried so hard to lock away.

Lori strokes my hair, and maybe it's the obscuring blanket of night that gives me courage. Maybe it's the raw vulnerability of the moment, the need to unburden myself of this weight. Or maybe it's simply because it's Lori, who has shown me more compassion and acceptance than anyone I've ever known. One thing I know. With her here, I'm not falling into my usual pattern of a panic attack. I can breathe because she's here.

The words come, halting at first. "My mother," I begin. "I told you she had a kind of type."

Lori's hand stills in my hair, but she doesn't speak.

"She always went for the worst guys." A humorless laugh escapes me. "The violent ones, the drunks, the manipulators. It was like she was drawn to the darkness in them." I take a shuddering breath, fighting the onslaught of memories. The sounds of shouting, the sharp slap of a hand across a cheek. The sight of my mother, huddled and weeping, grotesque bruises on her skin.

"I was on the receiving end of it too," I continue in a near-whisper. "When I was younger. They'd lash out. Sometimes I was just in the way and sometimes they simply took pleasure in beating a child."

Lori makes a sound, a soft, wounded noise, and her arms tighten around me, pulling me impossibly closer. "Oh, Gemma..."

"I got out as soon as I could, at seventeen. But Mom stayed. Every time, she stayed."

I tell Lori about the last one, the worst one. The one who put my mother in the hospital, not once, but twice. The one who twisted her mind, made her believe she deserved the pain and the fear.

"I begged her to leave him," I say, my voice cracking. "I offered for her to move in with me. But she wouldn't. She couldn't. It was like he had this hold on her..." I trail off, flashes of the past threatening to drown me. The pity in the doctor's eyes, the cold dread in my gut each time the phone rang, not knowing what fresh hell awaited on the other end.

"Then one night, I went to check on her. I had a key, from before. And I heard..." A sob wrenches from my chest and Lori rocks me gently. "I found him," I manage. "Beating her. She was on the ground, and he was just...he was..." I can't finish, can't voice the brutality of what I witnessed. "I snapped. I grabbed something. I don't remember the details. It's all a blur, but later, I found out it was a heavy vase. And I hit him. Again, and again, and again." The memory tears through me like a storm. "I killed him," I choke out, the confession ripped from the deepest, darkest part of me.

For many minutes, there's only the sound of my muffled sniffs, and the weight of my words hangs heavy in the air before Lori speaks, her voice steady and certain.

"You saved her," she says softly as she continues to stroke my hair. "You saved your mother's life."

I shake my head, but Lori cups my face, forcing me to meet her gaze. "You saved her," she repeats, each word weighted. "You were protecting her."

"But I killed someone," I whisper. "According to the pathology report, I hit him fifteen times. Apparently, I kept hitting him even after he was dead. I'm a murderer."

She shakes her head. "No. You're a survivor. You're a loving daughter who did what she had to do in an impossible situation." Her thumbs brush my tears. "You're not a monster, Gemma. You're human, and you're healing, and I love you. Every part of you, even the parts you think are unlovable."

A sob hitches in my chest, but it's different now. Not the wrenching, tearing kind, but a release. Lori's words wash over me, through me, filling the cracked and broken places with something that might mend them over time. "I love you too," I whisper. "But this isn't a petty crime I've got to my name. It's huge. And I'm scared that when the weight of it really sinks in, you'll change your mind."

"Gemma, no," Lori says. "That's not going to happen."

I give her a sad smile. "You can't know that. Maybe not today. But someday, you might wake up and realize life has become too complicated. Every time you introduce me to someone new, every time my past comes up, you'll have to either lie or tell the truth. And neither of those options is easy."

"I don't care what anyone else thinks," she says. "I know who you are."

"You say that now," I manage. "But you don't know what it's like. In prison, I used to get these letters. Hate mail, from the victim's sister, his parents, and his friends. They campaigned against my parole, said I didn't deserve to breathe free air."

"You didn't plan on killing him," Lori days. "It was self-defense."

"Technically, it wasn't. He was attacking my mother, not me. I could have just knocked him out and called the police, but I didn't. That's why I got a fifteen-year sentence for second-degree manslaughter. I was only lucky to get out early on good behavior."

"Listen to me, Gemma," Lori says. "I know this won't be easy. There will be challenges, and perhaps not everyone will understand, but I'm in this with you. You're not a bad person."

"Thank you." I smile, because I'm almost inclined to believe her. I lean in, capturing her lips in a salty kiss while I wrap my arms around her. "Although my mother has probably found someone else to abuse her."

"Maybe not. Have you spoken to her?" Lori pauses. "You told me she tried to take the blame..."

"I was in shock after it happened," I say. "Mom was the one who called the police while I was just sitting there shivering on the floor. I couldn't move or speak. It's all a blur, but I have a vague recollection of the police arriving. She told them she had done it, that it was self-defense. But it was pretty clear what had happened. I was the one covered in blood. When I managed to find my voice again, I confessed, and from there, it was a pretty straightforward case."

Lori nods and cups my cheek. "I think you should talk to your mother."

"I'm not sure if I can face her because there's something else..." I blow out my cheeks. "She was a witness in court and the prosecutor showed pictures of her boyfriend, the victim. Of what he looked like after I..." I pause, the image flashing before my eyes, vivid and gruesome. "His face was unrecognizable, and when my mother saw it, she broke."

Lori meets my eyes. "What do you mean?"

"She burst into tears and cried for him on the stand. After everything he'd done to her, she still mourned him."

"Oh, honey," Lori whispers.

"She didn't cry for me," I say, a bitter laugh escaping my lips. "I was about to lose my life, but she cried for him. For the monster who beat her and made her life a living hell. She clearly still loved him, in some sick, twisted way." I pause and almost choke on my emotions. "It felt like it had all been for nothing."

Lori crushes me against her chest. "I'm so sorry," she mutters.

"I think," I manage between shuddering breaths, "I think

a part of her blamed me. For taking him away from her and ruining the life she thought she had. She's my mother. Shouldn't she have been on my side? Shouldn't she have understood?"

"Yes," Lori agrees softly. "She should have stood by you. But Gemma...her failures are not your fault. Her inability to see the truth, to break the cycle...that's on her."

"That's the other reason why I didn't want to see her while I was in prison," I admit. "I felt like I was better off without her in my life."

Meeting Lori's eyes, I search for signs of judgement, but I find nothing but kindness and compassion. It's a relief that she knows now, but only time will tell if it will push her away.

34

LORI

I place an apple in my basket, already heavy with the morning's pickings. Beside me, Gemma is doing the same, her face flushed with exertion. She looks irresistible like this—dressed in nothing more than a pair of tiny shorts and a tank top, her hair pulled back and a frown of concentration on her face as she works.

Gemma's confession, the raw pain and vulnerability she shared, still hangs in the air between us. I glance over at her, watching as she reaches for a high branch, my eyes fixed on her scar when her shirt rides up. Knowing her scars aren't just skin-deep, it's humbling to be trusted with someone's darkest truths.

On the other side of the orchard, I can hear the cheerful chatter of the seasonal workers. Their laughter mingles with the rustle of leaves and the occasional thud of an apple hitting the ground. It's peaceful, this rhythm, and there's a satisfaction in it, a sense of connection to the earth.

My reverie is broken by the buzz of my phone in my pocket. I sigh, already knowing who it is without looking.

My mother has been calling incessantly for days, and I've been ignoring her.

Gemma glances over at me, a question in her eyes as I let the phone ring on. "Not going to get that?" she asks, her tone gentle.

I shake my head, reaching for another apple. "It's my mother again," I say, trying to keep my voice neutral.

Gemma nods, but I can see the concern etched into her features. "I know it's hard, but maybe you should give her a chance to explain."

"There's nothing to explain. She did what she did, end of story," I say, grabbing another apple.

Gemma sets down her basket and steps closer to me. "I understand," she murmurs. "Believe me, I do. But holding on to that anger will only poison you in the end. The weight of the past can crush you if you let it."

"I don't know. I really don't want to face her right now."

"The longer you leave it, the harder it will become. I've learned that the hard way."

I meet her eyes and give her a sad smile. Perhaps she's right. I'm not sure what I'm trying to accomplish by ignoring her, but I'm just so hurt. "I will talk to Mom," I finally say. "If you visit your mother in return."

I can see the instant protest in her eyes and the way her body tenses. "Lori, I don't—"

"I know," I say quickly. "I know it's different, that your situation is so much more complicated. But Gem...I think it could be good for you. The chance to say your piece, to let go of that part of your past." I pause, squeezing her hand. "I'll come with you, if you want me to."

Gemma is silent, her gaze distant. I can practically see the warring emotions playing out across her face. Finally, she sighs. "Using my own advice against me, huh?"

I grin, bumping my shoulder against hers. "I learned from the best."

Gemma laughs, lightening the mood. "Okay, I'll think about it."

My belly flutters as I stare at her. She's so beautiful when she smiles, and I can't get enough of looking at her. It's the little things she does. The way she frowns and bites her lower lip when she's concentrating, her teeth sinking into the soft flesh. The way she stretches up on her tiptoes to reach a high branch, the lean muscles of her legs flexing.

When she laughs at something one of the workers says, her head thrown back and her throat exposed, I'm over-whelmed by the urge to press my lips to that slender column, to feel her pulse jump beneath my touch. Even the way she handles the fruit, her fingers gentle as she plucks each apple from the branch, has my mind wandering to other, more intimate scenarios. I picture those same fingers skimming over my skin and imagine them tangled in my hair, tugging me closer to kiss me.

It's the little noises she makes too, the soft grunts of effort as she stretches and twists, the contented sighs when she pauses to wipe the sweat from her brow. Each sound sends a jolt straight to my core, my body responding to hers on a primal level.

"What?" Gemma raises a brow, a question in her eyes.

"Nothing," I say, shaking my head. "I just...I love you."

Her smile blooms into a full-fledged grin. "I love you too." She slides her arms around my waist as I loop mine around her neck, and we stand there, foreheads touching. She kisses me, soft and sweet and full of promise, and I melt into her, my hands tangling in her hair. The feel of her lips on mine, the press of her body, the intense chemistry that flows between us makes our kiss wilder, deeper, hungrier, and I'm vaguely aware that we should probably stop in case the workers see us.

Gemma's eyes sparkle with mischief when I pull away and glance around me. "Come with me," she whispers, taking my hand and leading me toward the old shed at the edge of the orchard.

My heart races with anticipation as I follow her and slip inside, and as soon as we're hidden from view, Gemma presses me against the weathered wood, her body flush to mine.

"I've been wanting to do this all morning," she whispers, her breath against my ear.

I shiver, my hands finding her hips, pulling her closer. "Then what are you waiting for?"

Her tongue swipes across my bottom lip, and she softly bites and tugs.

I lose myself in the sensations—the slide of her lips, the nip of her teeth, the searing heat between us. My hands slip beneath her shirt, tracing the curve of her spine, feeling the ripple of muscle beneath soft skin.

Gemma groans into my mouth, the sound sending a bolt of arousal straight to my core. Her hands are everywhere—in my hair, skimming my sides, dipping teasingly beneath the waistband of my jeans.

I arch away from the door, craving more of her touch, her taste, and the intoxicating scent of her surrounding me.

She breaks the kiss, trailing her lips down my jaw, my neck. I let my head fall back, a gasp escaping me as she finds a particularly sensitive spot just below my ear.

"Gemma," I breathe, her name a plea.

She hums against my skin, the vibration sending shivers down my spine. Her hands find the hem of my shirt, tugging insistently.

I raise my arms, letting her pull the garment over my head, and she takes a step back, her gaze raking over me with an intensity that makes me flush from head to toe. "God, you're gorgeous," she murmurs.

I reach for her, needing to feel her skin against mine, and she closes the distance between us again, discarding her shirt along the way. The press of her bare skin is electric, igniting a fire in my veins as we come together in a tangle of seeking hands and gasping breaths. Gemma's thigh slips between mine, pushing deliciously against my center, and I rock into her, chasing the friction and the building pressure.

Her hand lowers between us, popping the button of my shorts, sliding beneath the fabric. I cry out as her fingers find me, hot and slick and aching.

"Shh," she soothes, pressing a finger against my lips, even as her touch drives me higher. "You have to be quiet."

I bite my lip, stifling a moan as she circles, teases, explores. My hips move of their own accord, matching the rhythm of her hand, the tempo of my racing heart. And then she inches two fingers inside me and stifles my cry with her lips.

She fucks me, slowly at first, then faster as my body begs for release. My arms clasp around her neck and I hold on tight as the shed door bangs with each thrust.

The coil in my belly winds tighter, tighter, my breath coming in shallow pants. Gemma's eyes lock with mine, dark with desire so fierce it steals the air from my lungs.

"Let go," she whispers, her fingers curling, hitting that spot that makes stars explode behind my eyelids.

And with a final thrust, I do. I shatter in her arms, my cry muffled against her shoulder as waves of pleasure crash over me.

Gemma holds me, watches me, her moans mingling

with mine, and as the world slowly comes back into focus, I lift my head from her shoulder, finding her lips again in a slow and tender kiss.

"We should probably get back before they send out a search party," she jokes, even as she makes no move to let me go.

"Mmm, probably," I agree, trailing kisses along her jaw. "But I think I need a minute. You've thoroughly wrecked me, woman. I'm not sure if I can walk yet."

Gemma laughs, low and husky, and meets my lips again. "How about we just move to the bedroom?" she asks. "You're the boss, after all."

35

GEMMA

*M*y stall is laden with boxes of fresh produce from the farm, as well as jars upon jars of our homemade jam. The sight of it all, the tangible fruits of our labors, makes me smile every time.

The idea of it seemed a little daunting before my first market day, three weeks ago. The crowds, the questions, the social interaction...I imagined it would be overwhelming after years of isolation.

Instead, I feel a sense of belonging and community that I never thought possible. The other vendors have become familiar faces, greeting me with warm smiles and friendly waves, and the regular customers, too, have started to make small talk.

"Morning, Gemma!" Tom calls out as he starts unpacking. "I'm only a little late today, but you look like you've been here for hours."

I grin, holding up my Thermos with coffee. "I'm getting the hang of it," I say. "But the jam's been flying off the shelves faster than I can make it. It was a late night, potting it all."

Tom chuckles, shaking his head. "I'm not surprised. That jam of yours is something special. My Millie eats it by the spoonful, straight from the jar!"

Sipping my coffee, I greet Betty, who is late too, and narrow my eyes at the wicker basket she's carrying. Something's moving in there; they're definitely not lemons. The "Crazy Lemon Lady," as she's affectionately known, is a fixture at the market, her stall always a riot of yellow and green, but today, she's brought something brown too, it seems.

Instead of her usual brisk stride, she's moving more slowly, carefully, and as she gets closer, I see why.

Nestled in the basket, their tiny heads poking out, are three of the most adorable puppies I've ever seen. Chihuahuas, by the looks of them, with oversize ears and inquisitive eyes like big, black marbles.

"And who are these little cuties?" I ask, getting up as she sets the basket on her table.

"These," she says, "are the newest additions to my menagerie. My friend's dog had puppies. It was an accident, so she's looking for a home for them." She reaches into the basket, scooping up a particularly tiny pup with a coat the color of caramel. It yawns widely, its pink tongue curling, and I feel my heart melt into a puddle.

"Oh my goodness," I whisper, reaching out a tentative hand. The puppy sniffs it curiously, then licks my finger with a tiny, rough tongue. "They're so adorable!"

Betty cradles the puppy close. "They are, aren't they? I'm keeping the two girls for myself, but this little guy..." She holds up the caramel-colored pup. "He still needs a home."

As if on cue, the puppy wriggles in her grasp, straining toward me with an eager whine. I laugh, taking him into my arms, and he immediately burrows into my shirt, his warm little body vibrating with excitement.

"Well, aren't you a lover," I murmur, stroking a finger down his silky soft ears. The puppy nips playfully at my hand, his tail wagging furiously.

Betty watches the interaction with a knowing smile. "You don't have a dog, do you?"

I chuckle and raise a brow at her. "I see what you're doing here, and I'm not falling for it."

"Are you sure?" Betty scrunches her nose as she watches me with the puppy. "He likes you."

"I like him too, but I'm living in Lori's home. I can't just bring a dog back."

"But you too are together, right?" Betty asks.

"Yes, but it's all very new and—"

"And I'm sure Lori won't be able to resist this little bundle of joy either."

"I can't," I protest, even as I let the puppy lick my face and kiss his little head. "As I said it's—"

"Yeah, yeah. I know. New love and all that," Betty says. "And what would be better than completing your fresh family with a fur baby? Take him home, see how it goes. If Lori doesn't want him, bring him back to me. He's cute as pie. I'll easily find him another home." She puts on a high-pitched tone and continues with a chuckle. "Mommy, mommy, please take me."

I stare at Betty, torn. On one hand, the practical side of me knows that bringing a puppy home unannounced isn't exactly the most responsible move. Pets are a big commitment, one that requires discussion and planning. But on the other hand...I glance down at the little dog in my arms, at the way he's snuggled so trustingly against my chest.

I've never had a pet before. Growing up, it was impossible with my mother's string of boyfriends, and then later, my hectic job didn't lend itself to caring for a pet. In prison, of course, it was out of the question. But now, with the farm, with Lori...

"You know," I say, a grin tugging at the corners of my mouth, "Lori did mention wanting a guard dog for the farm..."

"Well, there you go!" Betty claps her hands together. "Chihuahuas are excellent guard dogs."

I raise my eyebrows, looking down at the tiny, wriggling puppy in my arms. "Hmm...I think you mean alarm dogs, and this little guy doesn't exactly scream 'intimidating.'"

Betty laughs. "Don't let his size fool you. Chihuahuas are fiercely loyal. They were originally bred to alert their owners to threats or intruders. Their keen senses and high-pitched bark made them perfect for the job." She reaches out, giving the puppy a gentle pat. "You see, Chihuahuas are incredibly observant. They're always on the lookout, ready to sound the alarm. It's a trait that's been bred into them for centuries."

"Yeah...still not convinced about the guard-dog pitch, but he certainly is cute." I look at the puppy and kiss him again, inhaling the scent of innocence.

Betty beams. "Wonderful! So you'll take him? I've got some supplies for you—a leash, some food, a few toys. Just to get you started."

"Wow, slow down. I didn't say that."

But Betty doesn't hear me. She's already bustled off to get the items from her car. While she's gone, I lift the puppy up before me, meeting his big, bulgy eyes. "Hear that, little man?" I murmur. "It looks like you're coming home with me."

The puppy whines, as if in agreement, and I can't help

but laugh as I place him back in the basket with his sleeping siblings. He curls up and immediately falls asleep. He's so precious I can't stop looking at him until Betty returns with a small bundle in her hands.

"Here you go," she says, passing it over. "The basics."

"Thank you, Betty. I'll take him home, but I can't promise we'll keep him. It all depends on Lori."

"Don't worry about Lori. But yes, if you change your mind, you know where to find me." She winks. "So, what are you going to call him?"

I glance at the puppy, the smallest one of the bunch, who fits into the palm of my hand. "I think his name should reflect his background," I say. "How about Lemon?"

36

LORI

I pull into a parking lot of a weathered apartment complex on the outskirts of Sedona. Glancing over at Gemma in the passenger seat, I notice how her hands are clasped tightly in her lap, her knuckles white with tension.

"You ready for this?" I ask, reaching over to cover her hands with my own.

Gemma takes a deep breath, then shakes her head and chuckles nervously. "No."

I give her a reassuring smile. "I'm here. And if you want me to stay in the car with Lemon, I can do that too."

At the sound of his name, our Chihuahua puppy pokes his head out of the travel bag nestled between us. His oversize ears perk up, his little black nose twitching. I scoop him up, cradling his warm body against me. When Gemma first brought him home from the farmers' market this weekend, I couldn't have been more surprised. A puppy was the last thing I'd expected her to return with. But the moment I saw his little face, those big dark eyes, I melted. Just like Gemma melted.

Gemma leans in to kiss me and smiles when Lemon starts licking her face. "I'd rather have you both with me," she says, stroking him. "But be warned. I have no idea what situation we'll walk into. When Mom's single, she's fairly stable, but when she's in a relationship..." She sighs and shakes her head.

"I'm here," I say again, cupping her cheek. "If you want to leave, we'll leave. If you want to stay, we'll stay. Just say it." I tuck Lemon securely into his bag. He's still so young, and he loves to nap in there when we take him on outings.

Gemma's gaze is fixed on one of the apartment doors, and it hits me then, as we head up the worn concrete steps, that this is where she grew up. These dingy walls, these chipped railings—they hold the memories of her childhood, however scarred and fractured it might have been. It's a stark contrast to Mom's welcoming apartment, and to the cozy warmth of Rosefield Farm. I try to imagine Gemma here, a little girl with skinned knees and guarded eyes, and the thought makes my heart ache.

We reach the second-floor landing, and Gemma pauses outside a door with peeling green paint.

"Hey," I say softly, touching her elbow. "You've got this."

Gemma turns to me, a fragile smile on her lips. "Thank you," she whispers. "For being here. I don't know if I could do this without you." She takes a deep, steadying breath, then knocks on the door. For a minute or so, there's silence, then the sound of footsteps, a lock turning.

The door swings open to reveal a woman who can only be Gemma's mother. She's thin, almost painfully so, with dark hair streaked with gray and eyes that are a mirror of Gemma's—the same deep brown, the same guarded intensity. For a moment, she stares, her face slack with shock.

Then her hands fly to her mouth, a choked sob escaping her.

"Gemma?" she whispers, her voice cracking around the name.

"Mom," Gemma says.

The next moment, Gemma's mother has flung herself forward and wrapped her arms around her daughter. Gemma stiffens for a split second, as if she's forgotten how to hug back, but then, slowly, her arms come up, circling her mother's waist.

I step back a bit, giving them space. Tears are streaming down the woman's face as she clings to Gemma, murmuring broken endearments into her hair. Gemma's eyes are shut tight, but I can see the shine of moisture on her lashes. It's a reunion of aching emotion, of still-open wounds.

Lemon chooses this moment to let out a small, curious whine from his bag, breaking the spell. Gemma's mother pulls back, her eyes widening as she notices me for the first time.

"Oh," she says, wiping at her cheeks. "I'm sorry, I didn't realize..." Her glance flicks between Gemma and me, a question in her eyes.

Gemma clears her throat, stepping back to my side. "Mom, this is Lori," she says, her voice steadier now. "My partner."

The word sends a thrill through me, even as I watch for her mother's reaction. To my relief, her face softens into a warm, if slightly watery, smile.

"It's wonderful to meet you, Lori," she says. "Please, come in. Both of you." She gestures into the apartment, inching back to let us pass.

As we step over the threshold, Lemon secure in my arms and Gemma's hand finding mine, I know this isn't going to be easy. There are years of hurt to unpack, wounds that might never fully heal.

We move into a small, tidy living room, and I keep a close watch on Gemma, trying to gauge her emotional state. Her shoulders are tense, her jaw tight, but there's a determined set to her chin as she glances around, taking in the details of her childhood home.

The apartment is modest, the furniture a bit worn but clean and well-cared for. There are a few framed photos on the walls, and I catch a glimpse of a younger Gemma, all gap-toothed smile and pigtails.

Gemma's mother bustles off to the kitchen, murmuring something about getting water for Lemon and making coffee. As soon as she's out of earshot, Gemma leans into me.

"No boyfriend," she whispers, her eyes darting around the room. "No beer cans, no ashtrays. She only smokes when she's really stressed, so that's a good sign."

I nod, giving her hand a reassuring squeeze. "It seems like she's doing okay."

"For now, at least. But it's always temporary. She has a way of finding the worst possible men, and then..." She trails off, shaking her head.

Before I can respond, Gemma's mother returns, carrying a small bowl of water, which she sets down for Lemon. He scrambles out of his bag, his little tail wagging furiously as he laps at the water.

"He's adorable," she coos, crouching to pet him. "What's his name?"

"Lemon," Gemma says, a hint of a smile touching her lips as she watches the puppy.

Her mother glances up at me, her expression warm. "That's lovely. He seems like a little ray of sunshine."

"He is," I say. "We've only had him for a few days, but he's already spoiled rotten."

Gemma's mother straightens up, wiping her hands on her jeans. "I made coffee," she says, a touch of nervousness in her voice. "Why don't we sit and catch up?"

She leads us to the small kitchen table, where three steaming mugs await. I take a seat next to Gemma, our knees touching under the table. Her mother sits across from us, her hands wrapped around her mug.

For a moment, there's an awkward silence, then Gemma's mother takes a shuddering breath.

"Gemma, I..." Her voice cracks, and she has to pause to compose herself. "I'm so sorry. For everything. It's all my fault, all of it."

Gemma stiffens beside me. "Mom, don't," she starts, but her mother shakes her head, the words spilling out of her now.

"No, I need to say this. I should have said it years ago." She swipes at her cheeks. "I failed you, honey. I brought those men into our lives, I let them hurt us. Hurt you." A sob catches in her throat. "They should have locked me up instead of you. It was my fault, all of it. I've had years to think about it since they took you away—and trust me—that's all I do."

"No, I did it. I deserved my punishment." Gemma is trembling now, and I press my leg against hers, trying to ground her. "You were a victim," she says. "It wasn't your fault."

But her mother is shaking her head, tears streaming down her face. "I should have left. I should have protected you from all of that. And then they took you away and you refused to see me." She chokes back a sob. "I understand why. I ruined your life."

Gemma's muscles tighten against mine, and when I turn to look at her, I see her expression has hardened. "Mom, you cried for him in court."

"What?"

"You cried for him, when you saw the picture of his bashed-up head," Gemma says, her voice suddenly stern.

"I didn't cry for him, honey. Yes, I was shocked when I saw the photograph. I don't remember the details of that night. It was all a blur. But when I saw how badly you'd injured him..." Gemma's mother closes her eyes for a beat, then covers her face with her hands and breaks out into a flood of tears. "I realized how hurt you must have been to do that, and my heart broke for you. I've been a terrible mother and..." Her voice trails away. "Did you really think I was upset because I'd lost him?"

"Yes," Gemma whispers, and I can see she's fighting back tears of her own.

"I promise you, honey, I wasn't. He was a terrible man, and I was terrified to leave him. He said he'd kill me if I ever did." Gemma's mother reaches across the table, grasping Gemma's hands. "I'm so sorry," she whispers. "I know I don't deserve your forgiveness, but I need you to know how much I regret my shitty parenting, and how much I wish I could go back and do it all differently."

Years of unspoken pain and guilt linger in the silence that follows, and I feel like an intruder, witnessing something so private. I'm about to get up and excuse myself when Gemma puts a hand on my knee and finally speaks.

"Let's not look back," she says softly. "There's no point. It won't change anything."

Her mother nods. "I'm getting help now. Therapy, support groups. I have a job at a florist, and it feels good to be independent."

Gemma nods. "That's good, Mom. Really good. I'm proud of you."

"I was hoping you'd stay with me when you got out," her mother continues. "But when your parole officer told me you would be working on a farm instead, I was happy for you. It's a much healthier environment than here, between these four walls with painful memories."

I feel Gemma relax slightly beside me as she takes my hand.

Her mother notices the gesture, her eyes flicking down to our hands, then back up to Gemma's face. "You seem happy," she says softly. "Settled."

"I am happy." Gemma turns to me. "We're happy."

The atmosphere in the small kitchen shifts, the tension giving way to a fragile, tentative hope. Gemma's admission of happiness seems to lift a weight from her mother's shoulders, and for the first time since we arrived, I see a genuine smile on the older woman's face.

"That's great. I would love to see where you live sometime," she says, looking at both of us before fixing her gaze on me. "Thank you, for being so good to my daughter."

"Gemma's been good to me too," I say with a smile. "And you're always welcome on Rosefield Farm."

37

GEMMA

*A*s we navigate the winding roads back to the farm, Lemon is cradled in my arms, his head on my shoulder so he can see out the window. I stroke his silky ears, marveling at how much has changed in such a short time. A few months ago, I was in prison, my future a bleak, uncertain thing. And now, here I am, driving home with my girlfriend and our puppy, my heart fuller than I ever thought possible.

The conversation with my mother plays over in my mind, each word a puzzle piece slotting into place. For so long, I've carried this certainty that she blamed me for what happened that night. That some twisted part of her mourned the man who made our lives a living hell. But hearing her words, seeing the raw anguish in her eyes as she begged for my forgiveness…it's shifted something in me. Not absolution; not quite. The scars are too deep, the wounds too old for that. But understanding, perhaps. A tentative bridge across the guilt that's separated us for so long.

I think about the woman I saw today—not the cowering

victim of my memories, but someone fighting to reclaim herself. The job, the therapy, the determination in her eyes. It gives me a flicker of hope that maybe we can find our way to a new relationship. One not defined by the traumas of our past, but by the strength it takes to survive them and choose to heal. There's still so much to untangle, but for the first time in years, I feel like I'm standing on solid ground.

Lori's been quiet since we left my mother's apartment, giving me space to process and feel whatever I need to feel.

"Thank you," I say softly, breaking the silence. "For coming with me today. It meant a lot, having you there."

Lori takes one hand off the wheel, reaching over to squeeze my thigh. "Of course. How do you feel about it?"

"It was good," I say, my voice a bit rough with emotion. "Seeing her, talking to her. Better than I expected, honestly. I should have gone sooner or let her visit me in prison. It's been too long."

Lori's thumb strokes over my knuckles. "She loves you. And it seems like she's getting the help she needs."

"Yeah." I blow out my cheeks, feeling a weight lift off my shoulders. "I finally feel like I can breathe around her. Like I'm not constantly waiting for the other shoe to drop, you know?"

Lori smiles. "So you'll stay in touch?"

"I will." I smile, leaning my head back against the seat. "I'll take it slow, but I want her in my life. In the end, I love her, and she only has me."

"I'm glad to hear that," Lori says. "Speaking of forgiveness, I've been thinking about my mom."

I nod, encouraging her to continue.

"Seeing you with your mother today made me realize I can't keep avoiding mine." She sighs, her fingers tightening around the steering wheel. "I need to talk to her."

"You should. I know it's not easy, but holding on to that anger isn't healthy."

"Yeah." She hesitates. "I think I need a few more days to get my head straight. But I will talk to her, soon."

"Whenever you're ready."

Lori's shoots me a sideways smile. "I love you," she says. "And I really want you to meet my mom."

"I love you too," I say, the truth of it filling every corner of my heart. "Do you think we should tell her? About my past, about why I'm really living with you?"

Lori is quiet for a moment, considering. "What do you think?"

I chew on my bottom lip, turning the question over in my mind. I've thought about it a lot lately. "I don't want to start off on a lie," I finally say. "I don't want to have to watch every word I say, worry about slipping up. And if she finds out some other way...I don't want her to think we were trying to deceive her."

"Those are all valid points," she says. "But Gem...it's your story to tell. If you're not comfortable sharing it yet, that's okay too."

"No. I want to tell her. If I'm going to be a part of your life, I want it to be with honesty. No more secrets."

Lori takes her eyes off the road for a moment, her gaze locking with mine. "Okay. Then that's what we'll do."

Lemon stirs in my lap, his little head popping up, ears perked. He lets out a high-pitched yip, his tail wagging furiously as he scrambles to look out the open window.

I follow his gaze and laugh when I see what's caught his attention. We've stopped at a red light, and in the car next to us, a large, fluffy golden retriever has its head stuck out the window, tongue lolling.

Lori and I burst out in laughter and stare at Lemon in adoration. "Did he just bark for the first time?"

Lemon looks a little confused as he stares up at me, like the noise that just escaped him startled him. Then he turns his attention back to the golden retriever and gives another excited bark, his little tail thumping against me.

"Watch out, world. I think our little guard dog has finally found his voice," Lori jokes. "Look at him. He's practically vibrating."

We burst out laughing as we watch Lemon's reaction. His eyes are wide, his whole body quivering with excitement as he strains to get a better look at this much larger canine companion.

Lemon yips repeatedly now, louder and more insistent. The golden retriever turns its head, regarding our tiny pup with what I swear is an amused expression.

"Careful there, little man," I murmur, stroking Lemon's head. "That dog is about ten times your size. Let's not start any beef we can't finish, okay?"

Lori snorts, shaking her head. Lemon has been a welcome distraction for her. The past week has been tough, and it's good to hear her laugh again. "Somehow, I don't think size is going to stop Napoleon here," she says. "He's got a big-dog attitude in a fun-size package."

Lemon wriggles in my arms, his bark rising to a fever pitch as the light turns green and the golden retriever's car starts to pull away. I have to tighten my hold to keep him from leaping right out the window in his excitement.

"Whoa there, buddy!" I laugh, pulling him back into my lap. "Where do you think you're going? You've got some growing to do before you can play with the big boys." Kissing the top of his head, I turn to Lori. "Want to swing by

Betty's house on our way home? She said we could stop by anytime so he can play with his siblings."

"Yeah, let's do that," Lori says with an amused grin. "I think he needs to let off some steam and show off his brand-new intimidation techniques."

38

LORI

*G*emma is beside me as we walk through the cemetery. She doesn't try to fill the silence with platitudes or reassurances, and I'm grateful for that. There's nothing to be said, really. Nothing that can change what was taken from me.

We weave through the rows of headstones, some weathered and crumbling with age, others gleaming and new. I scan the names and dates, feeling a pang for each life cut short.

Finally, we reach the one I'm looking for. It's a simple marker, unadorned granite with the name "Frank Rosefield" etched in neat, unpretentious lettering. The dates beneath span a life ended too soon, and the inscription beneath brings a lump to my throat. "Beloved Husband."

It could have said "Beloved Husband and Father," if things had gone differently. I stare at the headstone, and Gemma takes my hand. "Where's your aunt buried?"

"She was cremated," I say. "She preferred to have her ashes scattered over Rosefield Farm."

I take a shuddering breath. I came here for some form of

closure, but now that I'm standing in front of his grave, I don't know what to do or say. How do you have a conversation with a ghost? How do you unpack a lifetime of secrets and lies to someone who can no longer answer?

"Hi, Frank," I begin. "It's me. Lori. Your... Your daughter." Saying it out loud, here in this place of final rest, makes it real in a way it hasn't been before. "I know you knew," I continue, the words coming faster now. "I know you and Mom...that you had an affair. That you knew I was yours. And I just...I don't understand. How could you let me grow up not knowing that?"

The summer breeze whispers through the trees, and for a moment, it almost sounds like a sigh.

"I loved you, you know. I looked up to you. You were everything I thought a father should be—kind, funny, always ready with a hug or a word of encouragement. When we'd come to visit the farm, I felt like I belonged. And now..."

Gemma shifts, her hand coming up to rub soothing circles on my back, and I lean into her touch, drawing strength from her presence. She knows a thing or two about living with the consequences of other people's choices, about grappling with a past that can't be changed. If anyone understands the tempest of emotions raging inside me, it's her.

For a few moments, we just stand there, letting the silence settle around us like a shroud. The birds continue their songs in the trees, the breeze carries the distant hum of traffic from the road. Life goes on, even in this place of endings.

"I'm angry," I say. "I'm so fucking angry, Gemma. At Mom, at him..." I point to the headstone. "At the whole situation. And I don't know how to forgive that." I pause "But holding on to rage is exhausting, so I'm going to try."

"That's good," Gemma whispers. "That's a start."

I kneel down, my hand resting on the sun-warmed granite of the headstone. It's smooth beneath my palm, the edges worn soft by time and the elements.

"I wish you were here," I whisper. "I wish we had a chance to be a family, in all the ways that matter. But we don't get that chance. All I can do now is try to make peace with that."

Gemma kneels beside me, her arm slipping around my waist.

"He loved you," she says softly. "I didn't know him, but I know that much. The way you talk about him, the memories you have…that kind of love doesn't come from obligation or guilt. It's real, even if it was complicated by circumstance."

I nod, not trusting myself to speak around the lump in my throat. She's right, of course. For all the secrets and lies, I never doubted Frank's affection for me. It was there in every ruffle of my hair, every conspiratorial wink, every warm hug.

The tightness in my chest eases a fraction, the knot of anger and grief loosening its hold. It's not gone, not by a long shot, but it feels…manageable. Like something I can carry without being crushed by its weight.

"Why is this so hard?" I ask, not sure if I'm speaking to Frank or Gemma or some higher power. Maybe all three.

I lean into her, letting her strength flow into me. Slowly, I get to my feet, my hand trailing over the headstone in a final, gentle touch.

"Goodbye, Frank. I'll be back soon to clean up your grave. It looks like it's been neglected for some time." Blowing out my cheeks, I square my shoulders.

"Are you sure you're ready to go?" Gemma asks.

"Yeah. I'm done dwelling on the past. Let's just look forward together."

"Okay." Gemma takes my hand and kisses my cheek. "Do you want to go home? Help me make jam?" She shoots me a lopsided smile, lightening the mood. "I can barely keep up with the demand by myself—any more customers and we'll have to build a factory."

I chuckle, welcoming the distraction. "You know I love helping you in the kitchen. There's nothing more therapeutic than stirring pans of bubbling fruit with you," I say, nudging her. "But you're right about the demand. We should probably get someone to help us one day a week. Maybe one of the seasonal workers would be interested?"

Gemma narrows her eyes and seems to ponder over that. "Can I make a suggestion?"

"Of course. Always. It's your business."

"It's a little unconventional, so just be honest if you're not up for it."

"Go on."

"Well, there's this woman I met in Perryville. She was supposed to get out after me. I gave her my number, and I have her cousin's number, as she was going to move in with her, but she hasn't contacted me, so I'm not sure if she actually made it out. If she did, I really think she could do with some help. I may be wrong. She might already have a job, but..."

"Ask her," I say. "Do you trust her?"

"That's the thing. I don't know much about her life outside prison, and she's a repeat offender. But she really seemed genuine about wanting to turn her life around. I trusted her *in* prison. In fact, she was the only person I trusted there, and that says something. And she's from around here."

"Then call her. See if she's interested." I smile. "Everyone deserves a chance, repeat offender or not, and if it doesn't work out, so be it." I shrug. "Anyway, even if she came with bad intentions, what's she going to do? Steal preserves?"

Gemma laughs. "Okay, if you're on board, I'll try to get hold of her." She squeezes my hand. "Thank you. I've been blessed with your help, and it would feel really good to pay it forward."

39

GEMMA

*T*he farmers' market is in full swing and I'm surrounded by the chatter of customers and the enticing scents of fresh produce and baked goods. I've been at my stall for a few hours now, and the morning rush has finally started to die down. Lemon is sleeping in his basket; he's been a real attraction today, running around with his siblings and making customers laugh with his high-pitched welcome barks. While they're awake, Betty and I take turns watching the pups, and when they're sleeping, we talk in whispers and stare at their adorable little faces.

I'm just finishing up with a customer, handing her a bag of apples, when I notice a woman browsing the stall. She's elegant, with perfectly coiffed blonde hair and a crisp white blouse tucked into tailored black trousers. There's an air of authority about her, a no-nonsense vibe that sets her apart from the usual market crowd.

"Good morning," I greet her with a smile. "Let me know if you have any questions about our produce."

The woman looks up, her piercing blue eyes assessing me. "Actually, I was hoping to see Lori," she says. "Is she here? I'm an old friend of hers, and I heard she inherited Rosefield Farm. I've been wondering how she's doing."

"Lori's doing great," I say. "The farm keeps her busy, so it's usually just me at the market."

"I'm glad to hear she's well." The woman's gaze never leaves my face. "So you work for her?" she asks, a hint of something sharp beneath her polite tone.

"Yes, but she's also my partner. We live together."

A strange expression flickers across the woman's face, gone too quickly for me to decipher. "Partners," she echoes, her lips curving into an artificial smile. "How...lovely."

I feel my guard going up, an old instinct from my prison days. This woman is fishing for something, but I'm not sure what. Or perhaps she's homophobic; it's impossible to read her. "I'm sorry," I say, keeping my tone light, "I didn't catch your name."

The woman waves a dismissive hand. "Oh, how rude of me. I'm Diane." She extends a hand, her grip firm when I shake it.

"It's nice to meet you, Diane. I'm Gemma. Gemma Walker. I'm sure Lori will be thrilled to hear from an old friend. Why don't you stop by the farm some time?"

"I might do that." Diane clenches her jaw as she turns her attention back to the stall, running a finger along the edge of a jam jar. "So, Gemma, where did you live before moving to the farm? What were you doing?"

The question may be innocent, but something about her tone, the intensity of her gaze, makes me uncomfortable, and now I wish I hadn't given her my last name. "I grew up in Sedona, but I've been away for a while," I say vaguely. "I was in...a transitional period, I suppose you could say."

Diane raises a perfectly sculpted eyebrow. "Oh? Transitional how?"

I'm saved from having to answer by the arrival of another customer, an older man with a basket full of vegetables. "Excuse me," I say to Diane. "I just need to help this gentleman, if you don't mind."

As I bustle around, bagging up the man's purchases, I can feel Diane's eyes on me. She's not even pretending to browse anymore, just watching me with a calculating expression.

When the customer leaves, Diane steps closer, her head tilted to the side. "You know," she says, her voice deceptively casual, "you're awfully mysterious, Gemma Walker. A woman of few words, it seems."

I force a laugh, trying to ignore the knot of unease tightening in my stomach. "Not much mystery to me," I say, shrugging. "Just an ordinary farm girl, living a quiet life." Lemon has woken up and is now yipping excitedly, his little tail wagging a mile a minute.

"Well, hello there," Diane coos, her attention diverted. "Aren't you just the cutest thing?" She crouches down, extending a hand for Lemon to sniff. "What a sweet pup. What's his name?"

"Lemon," I say, still on guard despite Lemon's apparent ease with this woman. "He came from Betty, who has the lemon stall next to mine." I smile at Betty, who has been listening in on our conversation.

Diane chuckles, shaking her head. "Lemon. How unusual." She straightens up, brushing off her trousers. "Do you mind if I take a picture of him? He's just too adorable."

"Sure. Go ahead." Something about this woman feels off, but passers-by take pictures of Lemon all the time, so I can't exactly say no. I move out of the way a little so she can focus on Lemon, who stares at her adoringly like he was born for the limelight.

Instead of taking a close-up though, Diane steps back and makes sure to get the whole stall in the picture. I suspect I might be in it too, and that doesn't sit well. I don't like to have my picture taken anymore. Before my trial, I deleted all my social media accounts, and as far as I'm aware, there's little trace of me online. I like to keep it that way in case one of my fellow inmates recognizes me.

"Don't worry. You both look great," Diane says. "Anyway, I'd better get going. It was lovely to meet you, Gemma."

"Likewise. I'll be sure to tell Lori you stopped by."

"Please do. I look forward to catching up with her." With that, Diane turns on her heel and strides away.

"What a nice lady," Betty remarks from her stall. She's been watching the whole exchange, her keen eyes missing nothing.

"Really? I found her a little...I don't know. I felt like she was fishing for information or something." I pause and shake my head. "Maybe I'm just paranoid. She was friendly, I suppose. Have you seen her here before?"

"No. Not that I can recall. But she seemed keen to catch up with Lori." Betty shoots me a teasing grin. "Are you jealous? Do you think she might be an old flame of Lori's? Because you have nothing to worry about. Lori is clearly smitten with you and—"

"No, I'm not jealous," I interrupt with a chuckle. "Lori and I are great. I don't worry about such things."

"Good. Because you shouldn't," Betty says, picking up one of her pups. "Speaking of that pretty girlfriend of yours, it was so nice to get a surprise visit from you all last week. We should make it a regular thing."

"Sure, that would be lovely, I'm always up for a coffee-puppy-playdate. Why don't you come to the farm next time?"

"What about me?" Tom chimes in with a comical grin. "I want to come to the coffee-puppy-playdate too."

"You don't have a puppy," Betty says matter-of-factly.

"But I have a dog. He's just at the farm, guarding the premises."

Betty waves her hands. "Exactly. So who's going to guard the farm when you're drinking coffee with us?" I know she's only teasing. Betty and Tom have been friends for years, but they love winding each other up.

"My wife," Tom jokes. "She's a hell of a lot feistier than Brutus, that's for sure." He turns to me. "Anyway, this supposed get-together will be on Gemma's turf, so it's up to her, not you, Betty."

"Sure, Tom." I laugh. "You and Brutus can come too. And of course, your wife is always welcome."

40

LORI

*T*he warm glow of the morning sun filters through the curtains as I stir, my body deliciously heavy with the remnants of sleep. Beside me, Gemma shifts, her arm tightening around my waist as she nuzzles into my neck.

"Mmm, morning," she murmurs, her voice husky with sleep. At the foot of the bed, Lemon stretches and yawns, his little pink tongue curling. He blinks at us sleepily before settling back down with his head on his paws.

I smile, turning in Gemma's embrace to face her. Her hair is tousled, her eyes still heavy-lidded, but she's never looked more beautiful to me. "Morning, love," I whisper, pressing a soft kiss to her lips.

"Good morning, babe. What's on the agenda for today?" she asks, pulling me into a tight hug. "Orchard work?"

I shake my head. "Actually, I was thinking...what if we just stayed here today? Spent the whole day in bed?"

Gemma's eyes sparkle with mischief. "Why, boss, are you trying to seduce me?"

I laugh, trailing my fingers down her arm. "Maybe I am. Is it working?"

In answer, Gemma leans in, capturing my lips. "What do you think?" she murmurs against my mouth, and deepens the kiss. Her hand traces lazy patterns on my hip, igniting a familiar warmth in my belly. I lose myself in the taste of her, the feel of her skin against mine.

We take our time, unhurried kisses slowly building into something more heated, more urgent. Gemma rolls on top of me, her weight a delicious pressure. My hands roam the expanse of her back, feeling the play of muscles beneath her smooth skin.

As our kisses grow more heated, more insistent, I feel the last remnants of sleep fall away, replaced by a hunger that's bone deep. Gemma's mouth trails from my lips to my jaw to my neck, leaving a path of fire in its wake. I arch into her touch, my fingers tangling in her hair, holding her close.

"Gemma," I breathe. "I want you."

She lifts her head, her eyes dark and needy as her hand slides down between my thighs. "I know," she teases, her hand lowering, her fingers skimming my wetness. "I can feel it."

She kisses me again, deep and thorough, like she's trying to pour every ounce of desire into this one moment. I moan at the slick slide of her tongue against mine, the nip of her teeth on my bottom lip, her fingers sliding inside me, filling me up deliciously slowly. Her other hand traces the dip of my collarbone, the curve of my breast, the jut of my hip. My back bows off the bed, my hands fisting the sheets as she works me higher and higher. She knows my body so well, knows just how to drive me wild.

Spreading my legs with her knees, she pushes into me, and I lose all control while she fucks me slowly and deeply, watching me like she's never seen anything so fascinating. Meeting her eyes, I suspect she can make me come with that dark look alone; it's incredibly sexy.

"Does that feel good?" she whispers, a mischievous smile playing around her lips. She knows it does; I'm moaning and writhing underneath her and barely know what to do with myself. I can't even answer, and it doesn't matter. Her thumb circles and strokes my clit while she moves in and out of me, finding that perfect rhythm that has me gasping against her mouth. The tension in my belly coils tighter, my hips rocking in time with her hand.

"Come for me, babe," she whispers against my lips. "I love it when you let go."

I try to hold off because it feels so good, but I can't. Shattering in her arms, my cry is muffled against her lips as my legs wrap around her hips and my walls clench around her fingers. Instinctively, my whole body squeezes her as if trying to hold her in place forever, and Gemma holds me through it, her fingers slowing but not stopping, drawing out my pleasure until I'm boneless and spent.

Gemma brushes a damp strand of hair from my forehead, her touch infinitely gentle. "You're so beautiful," she whispers.

A blush rises to my cheeks, heat blooming under my skin as I capture her hand, bringing her palm to my lips. I press a lingering kiss there, my lashes fluttering as I breathe her in. Gemma's pulse thrums beneath my lips, and her skin is warm and slightly salty. Her eyes are luminous, shining with desire. It's a look I've come to know, to crave—a look of pure, unfiltered adoration.

Under the intensity of her stare, I feel seen, wholly and completely. Laid bare in a way that should be terrifying but instead feels like coming home.

I lean up, capturing her lips in a kiss, and Gemma sighs into my mouth, her body melting into mine as if we were made to fit together. When we break apart, I trace the line of her jaw, marveling at the softness of her skin, and roll us over. I take my time kissing down her body, worshipping every inch of her. When I finally settle between her thighs, she's already glistening, ready for me.

The first touch of my tongue has her arching off the bed, a broken moan falling from her lips. I lose myself in her taste, in the little gasps and sighs I draw from her with each stroke, each flick. Her fingers tangle in my hair, guiding me, urging me on.

It doesn't take long before she's teetering on the edge, her thighs trembling, her breath coming in short, sharp pants. I double my efforts, delirious with the need to see her fall apart, and when she finally does, she lets out a long, throaty moan that makes me smile. I work her through it, my tongue gentling as the aftershocks ripple through her body. Only when she tugs at my hair do I relent, pressing a final, soft kiss to her center before crawling back up her body.

Gemma pulls me into a kiss, no doubt tasting herself on my lips. It's erotic and intimate, and when we break apart, we're both breathing hard, giddy smiles on our faces.

I rest my head on her chest, my fingers stroking her stomach. "I don't want to move."

"Me either. Let's stay in bed." Gemma kisses my temple, then lifts her head. "By the way," she says, "I forgot to tell you about the woman at the market yesterday. Diane."

I frown. "Diane? Who's that?"

Gemma props herself up on her elbow. "There was this woman," she begins. "She came up to the stall and started asking all these questions. She said she was an old friend of yours."

"I don't think I know a Diane. What kind of questions?"

"She said she'd heard you'd inherited the farm and wanted to know how you were doing." Gemma hesitates. "She asked how we knew each other, so I told her we were partners, and she got this...look on her face. Like she'd smelled something bad."

I frown. "What did she look like?"

"Blonde. Really put together, you know? Expensive clothes, perfect hair. And she had this air about her, like she was used to getting what she wanted."

Dread solidifies into a hard knot in my gut. I know that description. I know it all too well. "Cleo," I whisper, the name tasting bitter on my tongue.

Gemma's eyes widen. "Your ex?"

I nod. "I bet it was her. She kept calling and messaging me after I left, but I never responded."

Gemma takes my hand. "What does she want?"

I let out a shaky laugh. "Honestly? I don't know. To tell me what a mistake I'm making, probably. How I'll never make it on my own. She hates not being in control."

"I'm so sorry. I had no idea she was bugging you," Gemma says.

"Not anymore. I blocked her. Maybe that's why she decided to investigate." I take a deep breath, meeting Gemma's gaze. "I didn't tell you everything," I confess. "About how bad it got at the end." And then it's all spilling out of me. The constant criticism disguised as "constructive feedback." The way Cleo would build me up one moment, only to tear me down the next. The realization that I'd never be enough, never measure up to her impossible standards.

The digs, the mean comments, the pleasure she got from putting me down in meetings if I didn't do what she wanted.

Gemma listens, her eyes shining with empathy. When I finish, she pulls me into her arms. "I'm so sorry," she whispers. "You know it was all on her, not you, right?"

I give her a small smile. "I do now, but for so long, I believed her."

Gemma presses a kiss to my temple, her arms tightening around me. "I got a bad vibe from her. I knew I wasn't crazy."

"The longer I'm away from her, the clearer I can see how toxic she was." I pull back, meeting Gemma's eyes. "Leaving her and my career was the best move I ever made, and as scary as it was, it opened the door to something so much better." I tuck a strand of hair behind Gemma's ear. "Because it brought me here, and it brought me to you."

41

GEMMA

$\mathcal{T}$he farm is filled with the hum of voices, the rumble of engines, and seasonal workers are walking back and forth, bringing crates filled with fruit to the driveway. It's a busy day, the kind that leaves me exhausted but satisfied, knowing we're making progress.

I'm in the kitchen, stirring a pan of jam, when I hear another vehicle approaching. Peeking out the window, I see a familiar wholesaler's truck pulling up to collect the weekly harvest.

Wiping my hands on my apron, I turn the stove down to a simmer and head outside to check if they need help with loading. Lori is already standing on the drive with iPad in hand, ready to handle the business side of things. We've fallen into a natural rhythm, a division of duties that plays to our strengths. She's the negotiator, the organizer, and I'm more hands-on.

Stepping out into the bright sunlight, I wave at the driver. "Hey. Do you need help?" He's been here before, a regular on our route, and he's always friendly, but today there's something different in his eyes. A curiosity, tinged with what might be unease.

"Thank you, but I've got this," he says, avoiding my gaze.

"Are you okay?" I ask. "You look like you've seen a ghost."

The driver hesitates, glancing between Lori and me before pulling out his phone. "I wasn't sure if I should say anything," he says. "But I figured you'd want to know." He taps his screen, then holds the phone out to me.

I take it, and my heart starts to thud in my chest as I read the post on the screen. It's posted in a local community group, the kind where people share news and gossip. But the image that stares back at me isn't a lost pet or a reminder for a community event. It's me. A candid shot, taken at the farmers' market, and underneath is my mugshot.

"Would you buy from a murderer?" it reads, and below, in damning black and white, are the details of my conviction. My sentence. My shame laid bare for all to see.

I feel the blood drain from my face, a sick, sinking feeling opening up in my gut. Lori sucks in a sharp breath, her hand coming up to cover her mouth.

"I figured it had to be some kind of sick joke," the driver says, his voice sounding far away through the ringing in my ears. "Maybe a rival farmer, trying to stir up trouble. I reported the post. Hopefully, it'll be taken down soon."

I can't speak or tear my eyes away from the screen. It's my worst nightmare, come to life. My dark past dragged into the unforgiving light of day.

Lori takes the phone from my numb fingers, her jaw tight with anger as she scans the post. "Cleo," she mutters, her voice low and furious. "It has to be. She's the only one who would stoop this low."

The driver's eyes dart between us, his expression uneasy.

"It's not true, right?" he asks hesitantly. "I assumed that mugshot was Photoshopped."

I close my eyes, fighting back a sudden sting of tears. This is it. The moment of truth. I could lie, deny it all and hope the rumors die down. But what's the point? My past will always come back to haunt me.

"It's true," I finally say, my voice shaking. "I was in prison. I..." I swallow hard, forcing the words out. "I killed someone."

The driver's eyes widen, shock and something like fear flashing across his face. Beside me, Lori's hand finds mine and she gives me a squeeze.

"Gemma, you don't have to..." she starts, but I shake my head, cutting her off.

"No, I do. Cleo's clearly out to get me and she's not going to stop." I turn back to the driver, taking a deep breath. "It's a long story," I say. "And not a pretty one. But the short version is, I was protecting my mother. The man I killed was beating her up."

The driver's face softens, and his mouth pulls into a grim line. "Right," he says. "Well, it's not my business, but I appreciate your honesty." His gaze flicks to Lori, then back to me. "For what it's worth...you're good people."

"Thank you," I manage. "That means a lot."

The driver nods. "Look. Again, it's none of my business, but I've been around the block a few times. I've seen good people make bad choices, and I've seen bad people get away with worse. What matters is what you do after, you know?"

"I'm trying," I say, meeting his gaze head-on.

"Anyone with eyes can see that. You're not hiding out here, you're contributing. Making something of yourself." He shrugs. "Anyway, I'd better get these crates to the warehouse before the fruit starts to ferment. Take care, Gemma. I hope this doesn't cause you too much trouble."

I help him load, and as the truck rumbles down the driveway, I let out a shaky breath. The adrenaline is starting to fade, leaving me jittery and weak in the knees.

Lori, who has been practically speechless all along, turns to me, her hands coming up to cup my face. "Babe, are you okay?"

I start to nod, an automatic response, but then I pause. Am I okay? The post is still out there, a ticking time bomb of shame and exposure. Cleo is on the warpath, intent on destroying the fragile peace I've found.

"I'm sorry. Of course you're not," she whispers and lets out a deep sigh. "I'm going to make her pay for this."

"Maybe it's best if we just ignore it," I say. "I'll try to get that post removed. Although rumor spreads fast around here. I wouldn't be surprised if everyone has shared it already." I feel sick and hold on to my stomach. "Oh, God. Everyone is going to know. It can take hours, sometimes days to have something public removed."

"I won't let her get away with this." Lori is already heading for her car. "I'll make her take it down right now." I rush after her, trying to stop her.

"Lori, wait," I plead, reaching for her hand. "Please don't do anything rash."

But Lori is shaking her head, her eyes hard with determination. "I can't just sit back, Gem. She's crossed a line."

"I know," I say, trying to keep my voice steady. "Believe me, I'm as angry as you are. But confronting her, giving her a reaction…it's exactly what she wants. She's trying to provoke us, to get under our skin."

Lori pauses, her brow furrowing. I can see the conflict playing out across her face, the warring impulses of protective fury and rational restraint. But then she shakes her head again. "I'm sorry. I can't just do nothing," she says, her voice strained. "It's one thing coming after me, but it's another coming after someone I love."

Despite the gravity of the situation, I feel a flush of warmth at her fierce protectiveness. "I appreciate you wanting to defend me," I say. "More than you know. But the truth is, my past was always going to come out eventually. I couldn't hide it forever, no matter how much I might want to."

"I know that. But sharing your story should be on your terms, not hers." With that, Lori yanks open her car door, her shoulders set in a determined line. I watch, equal parts touched and terrified, as she slides behind the wheel. She pauses, looking back at me through the open window. "I love you." She smiles, her eyes softening. "I'll be back soon, I promise."

And then she's gone, the car kicking up a cloud of dust as it speeds down the driveway and disappears around the bend. I'm left standing there, my heart in my throat, as the sound of the engine fades into the distance.

This is it. My secret is out, and I've never felt more vulnerable.

42

LORI

The familiar glass doors of my old law firm loom before me, but I barely register them as I storm through, my anger propelling me forward like a hurricane. The receptionist, a young woman named Nancy, looks up startled as I breeze past her desk.

"Excuse me!" she calls after me, half-rising from her seat. "You can't just...Ms. Hawthorne is in a meeting!"

I ignore her, my strides never faltering. I know this office like the back of my hand, know exactly where I'm headed. Cleo's corner office, the one with the best view of the city, the one she always lorded over me.

I can hear Nancy's hurried footsteps behind me, her heels clicking on the polished marble floors. But she doesn't dare stop me, the former star attorney who's clearly on the warpath.

Cleo's door is closed, her muffled voice emanating from behind the frosted glass. She's on a call, but I don't care. I don't care about her precious clients or her precious reputation. All I care about is making her answer for what she's done.

I burst through the door, the glass rattling in its frame with the force of my entrance. Cleo looks up from her desk, her phone pressed to her ear, her perfectly painted mouth falling open in shock.

"I'll have to call you back," she says into the receiver, her eyes never leaving mine. She sets the phone down with a click, leaning back in her high-backed leather chair. "Lori. What a surprise." Her voice is smooth, unruffled, but I can see the calculation in her cool blue gaze, the wheels turning behind her carefully constructed facade. "You look...different." She takes in what I'm wearing—jeans, sneakers, and a plain T-shirt. She's never seen me like this, without my heels and makeup. I always felt like I had to be perfect around her and even did my hair before bed.

"Cut the crap, Cleo," I snap, slamming my palms down on her gleaming mahogany desk. "I'm not here to discuss my outfit. I know it was you. The post about Gemma, the smear campaign. It has your fingerprints all over it."

Cleo blinks at me, a perfect picture of innocence. "Gemma? You mean your new...partner?" She says the word like it leaves a bad taste in her mouth, her nose wrinkling in distaste.

"Don't play dumb," I seethe, my hands curling into fists. "You couldn't stand that I blocked you, that I wasn't at your beck and call anymore. So you started digging, looking for dirt. And you found it, didn't you?"

Cleo's lips curve into a smile that's all sharp edges and cold satisfaction. "I was just trying to help. You needed to know what kind of person you were associating with and, more importantly, the kind of person you were letting into your bed. Surely, you would want to know if your girlfriend was a..." She drops a pause. "A murderer."

The word hangs in the air between us, ugly and damning, and my nails bite into my palms, my anger boiling over. "How dare you," I whisper, my voice shaking with barely contained rage. "How dare you try to paint yourself as some kind of concerned friend. You didn't do this to help me. You did it because you're a spiteful, jealous woman who can't stand to see anyone else happy."

Cleo's mask slips, her carefully crafted composure cracking. "You have no idea what you're talking about," she hisses, her eyes flashing. "I made you, Lori. I built you into the brilliant attorney you were. And this is how you repay me? By running off to play house with a convicted felon? God, you couldn't possibly sink any lower."

A bitter laugh escapes me. "You didn't make me. You tore me down, piece by piece, until I didn't recognize myself anymore. You made me think I needed you, that I was nothing without you." I lean in, holding her gaze unflinchingly. "But you were wrong."

"Come on. You're making me out to be some kind of monster. I only ever had your best interests in mind."

"Sure. You keep telling yourself that." I straighten up, looking down at the woman who once held such power over me. She seems smaller now, diminished somehow. "I am so much more than you ever allowed me to be. And Gemma sees that. She loves me for who I am, not what I can do for her career or her ego."

Cleo scoffs, rolling her eyes. "Love? Please. What does a woman like that know about love? She's using you, Lori. Your status, your influence. She needs you to rebuild her life, and when she's done, she'll leave."

I shake my head, a wry smile tugging at my lips despite the anger still simmering in my veins. "You just can't stand it, can you? That I've found something real. Because that's what this is, a love that isn't based on mind games and manipulation." I lean across her desk until we're almost nose to nose. "Gemma is the best thing that's ever happened to me. She's kind and brave, and honest in a way you can't even begin to understand. What she did...it was a mistake, yes. But it was also an act of protection and love, which you wouldn't recognize if it bit you in the ass."

Cleo's face is flushed now, splotches of red standing out starkly against her pale skin. "You're delusional. That woman is a criminal. And when this little fantasy of yours inevitably implodes, don't come crying to me."

"I won't," I say, my voice steady and sure. "Because I'm done with you, Cleo. Leave us alone. I'm sure you have better things to do with your precious time than running some petty hate campaign."

"And I thought you'd have better things to do than letting yourself go." Cleo's eyes drop to my hips. "It seems farm life is making you pack on the pounds."

And there it is. I'd forgotten what it felt like to be insulted. Her defense didn't work, and now she's going in for an attack, hoping to hurt me. I don't care that I've put on a bit of weight. My weight was always more her concern than mine, and I actually like how I look now, but she just has to have the last word.

I don't even bother to reply. I let her have her precious last stab and with that, I walk out, letting the door slam shut behind me with a satisfying finality. Nancy is hovering anxiously outside, her eyes wide and wary. She's heard everything and I don't care.

"I'm sorry," she stammers. "But you really have to leave now. Without an appointment—"

"I know," I interrupt her. "I'm already gone. You won't see me again."

She nods, looking a little shell-shocked. I can't blame her. I'm feeling pretty shell-shocked myself.

As I step outside, the adrenaline starts to fade, leaving me shaky and drained. I lean against the building, closing my eyes and tilting my face up to the sun. It's over. The confrontation I should have had months ago, even before I met Gemma. The final severing of ties. I expected to feel relieved, but mostly, I just feel tired. Beneath my emotional exhaustion, though, is a tiny spark of victory. It was about time I stood up to her.

43

GEMMA

*L*emon scampers around my feet while I unload fresh produce from the car, his little tail wagging furiously as he darts between the crates, sniffing at the bright colors and enticing scents. Despite my nerves, I can't help but smile as I watch him, his unbridled joy a balm to my frayed emotions. We haven't really trained him; he just tends to stay by our side at all times.

"Lemon! Come here, buddy!" Betty's voice rings out from the neighboring stall. I glance over to see her kneeling, arms outstretched, as Lemon's littermates tumble over each other in their eagerness to greet him. "Oh, look at you, you're growing bigger every week."

Lemon lets out an excited yip and bounds over, immediately engaging his siblings in a game of chase.

For a moment, I'm lost in their play, in the innocent, pure delight of it. But then I feel it again—that prickling sensation on the back of my neck, the weight of eyes on me. I look up, scanning the market. Are people staring? Or is it just my paranoia getting the better of me? I barely slept last night, my mind spinning with worries about facing members of the community who have seen the post. Lori checked this morning; it's been taken down, but nowadays, things never really disappear entirely.

Trying to shake off the unease, I focus on setting up my stall, arranging the jars of jam, the baskets of fruit, but my hands are clumsy, my movements jerky, a far cry from my usual smooth efficiency.

"Morning, Gemma." Tom's voice startles me, and I nearly drop the crate of peaches I'm holding. He's standing at the edge of my stall, his weathered face creased with concern. "How are you?"

I swallow hard, forcing a smile. "I'm fine," I say, but the words sound hollow even to my own ears. "A little tired, is all."

Tom nods, but I can see he's not buying it. He glances around, then leans in closer, lowering his voice. "You look tired. Have you been working too hard?"

I blow out my cheeks, letting out the breath I've been holding. He hasn't seen the post, and from the looks of Betty, she hasn't either. But then again, this is market day, the day that gossip is exchanged.

"No, I just had trouble sleeping," I assure him and continue to busy myself with the produce. I'm in fight-or-flight mode today, terrified about confrontation, accusation, public humiliation, all of it, and I'm grateful when Lori arrives to distract me. She looks tired herself, shaken after confronting her ex yesterday.

"Hey, babe." I pull her into a hug and kiss her temple. "How did you get here?"

"I got a lift with Joseph," she says. "I wanted to check in on you and..." She hesitates. "Well, I was thinking, maybe it's best if I run the market today."

"Why? You should stay at home and get some rest."

"I'm fine." Lori lowers her voice. "It's just that..." Another pause, and I know nothing good will follow. "I got a few emails. About you."

"Fuck. So it's happening."

"Yeah. No one I know personally. Just some random locals who saw the post." Lori lowers her voice to a whisper. "They were warning me about you. They thought I didn't know." She squeezes my hand. "Please let me do this today. Take the car, go home, and pick me up later."

"This is the last thing I wanted," I say. "Now you're getting dragged into all of this. Maybe it's best if I stay away for a while and—"

"No!" Betty looks up when Lori raises her voice. "Absolutely not. I'm not worried about my reputation," she says, dialing her voice down to a whisper again. "I'm worried about you. I love you and I don't want you to go anywhere."

"I love you too, but I can handle it."

"Gemma, you're trembling," she says, rubbing my shoulders. "Please, let me help you."

I let out a deep sigh. A part of me wants to stay and face whatever comes. But a larger part, the part that's still raw and aching from the wounds of my past, is desperate to flee and hide away until the storm passes.

"Okay," I finally say, my voice small. "I'll go. But Lori, please be careful. I don't want you to get in trouble because of me."

"I'll be fine," she says sweetly. "It's you I'm worried about. Go home, take a bath, and try to get some sleep. I'll see you later."

I nod, not trusting my voice, and with a final squeeze of her hand, I turn and head for the car.

The drive home is a blur, my mind whirling with dark thoughts. What if this is just the beginning? Almost on autopilot, I reach for my phone, scrolling through my contacts until I find Miranda's number. She picks up on the second ring.

"Gemma? Is everything okay?"

At the sound of her voice, something in me cracks. A sob wrenches from my throat, tears blurring my vision. "No," I choke out. "No, it's not okay."

"What happened?" Miranda's tone sharpens, alert now. "Are you safe? Is Lori all right?"

"We're fine. Physically, at least." I swipe at my cheeks, trying to steady my breathing. "It's just...someone found out about what I did. They posted about it online, and now..." My voice breaks. "Now everyone knows."

There's a beat of silence, then a soft exhale. "Oh, Gemma. I'm so sorry. That must have been a terrible shock."

"That's an understatement. I feel like my worst nightmare is coming true."

"I can only imagine." Miranda's voice is gentle. "But Gemma, listen to me. You've worked so hard to rebuild your life. Don't let this setback erase all that progress. Lean on the people who love you. Where's Lori?"

"At the market. She insisted on taking over the stall today, to spare me from...from whatever fallout there might be."

"She's a good woman. You're lucky to have her in your corner."

"Yeah." Despite everything, a wobbly smile touches my lips. "But I don't want to get her in trouble. Her business could suffer just by association."

"Don't get ahead of yourself," Miranda says calmly. "Now, here's what we're going to do. I'm going to drive up tomorrow, and we'll sit down and figure out a plan. How to handle any questions that might come up and how to navigate this going forward. Okay?"

I nod, then remember she can't see me. "Okay," I say, my voice a little steadier now. "Thank you."

"You don't have to thank me. This is what I'm here for. In the meantime, be gentle with yourself."

44

LORI

*T*he bathroom is a sanctuary of warm light and soothing scents, the candles on the edge of the bath casting dancing shadows on the tiled walls. The aroma of lavender and vanilla mingles with the rich, earthy notes of the red wine in our glasses as Gemma and I wind down from a very stressful day. The rest of the world feels far away, held at bay by a cocoon of steam and shadow.

I lean back against Gemma's chest and her arms encircle me. Her skin is slick and warm, a much-needed respite from the turmoil.

"I'm sorry about today," Gemma murmurs, her breath tickling my ear. "I hate that you had to deal with it."

I tilt my head back to look at her, tracing the line of her jaw with my gaze. Even now, with weariness etched into her features, she's the most gorgeous thing I've ever seen. "Don't apologize. It's my fault, and I should have seen this coming. If I hadn't dated such a control freak..." I sigh and shake my head as Gemma's arms tighten around me.

"How was it today?" she asks after a moment. "Were people...did they say anything?"

I take a sip of my wine as I consider my answer. "Honestly? There were a few looks and whispers, but no one said anything outright. A few people asked where you were, and I told them you weren't feeling well."

"Do you think they knew about the post?"

"Some of them, maybe. There was a certain...curiosity in their eyes." I could spare Gemma by sugar-coating it, but I want to be nothing but honest with her.

Gemma is quiet for a moment, and I can practically hear the gears turning in her head. "I feel like I'm tainting you, just by association."

The pain in her voice breaks my heart. I shift slightly so I can face her, the water sloshing and taking out one of the candles. "Listen to me," I say, holding her gaze. "You are not tainting me. You could never taint me. Your past has made you who you are, and who you are is the woman I love."

"I love you too." Gemma takes my hand and presses a kiss to my palm. "Was Cleo there?"

I stiffen at the mention of my ex's name. "No, she wasn't. And I'd be shocked if she ever showed her face around here again after what she did. I made it very clear I wanted nothing more to do with her."

Gemma nods. "What attracted you to her?" she asks. "I mean, I know she was awful to you, but you must have loved her too, otherwise you wouldn't have stayed."

I take a deep breath, letting it out slowly. The memories still feel tender. "She was...intense. Driven. Ambitious. That's what drew me to her initially. Her passion, her fiery intelligence. I was an ambitious junior lawyer. She was a partner, also twelve years my senior. I looked up to her, I suppose. But over time, that intensity turned toxic. I didn't realize it was happening. It was such a slow process until one day, I realized I'd lost myself. That I was only thinking about her needs, what she wanted. How she wanted me to dress, how she wanted me to act, who she wanted me to be."

Gemma kisses the top of my head and inhales against my hair.

"It started small," I continue, closing my eyes as I let myself drift back. "Little comments, about my clothes, my hair. How I could stand to lose a few pounds, how I wasn't quite polished enough for the image she wanted to project. I brushed it off at first, told myself she was trying to help me be my best self." I pause. "But it got worse. She started questioning my decisions at work, undermining me in front of clients and colleagues. If I argued back, she'd twist it around, make it seem like I was being irrational or overly sensitive."

"Lori, I'm so sorry," Gemma says.

I shrug, the water rippling with the movement. "I didn't see it for what it was at the time. Emotional manipulation, gaslighting. I just thought I wasn't trying hard enough. She had a way of making me doubt myself and making me feel like I needed her approval at all times."

"I know how that feels," Gemma says quietly. "Gina, my ex...she was like that too. Always making little digs and finding ways to chip away at my self-esteem. I thought that's what love was supposed to be like. Tumultuous, all-consuming, painful. It was the only example I had growing up, so I assumed it was normal."

I nod. "We have more in common than we thought."

"Yeah. It's crazy how things that seem unthinkable now were normal then. My mother's boyfriends were all cut from the same cloth. Violent, manipulative, cruel. I swore I would never end up like Mom, but I guess I just traded one kind of abuser for another." Gemma nuzzles my neck. "And then I met you..."

"I'm so grateful we met," I whisper. "I'll be honest. I had my doubts at first, and although Miranda assured me there was nothing to worry about, I still had sleepless nights after I'd agreed to enter the program."

"You thought I'd be a violent criminal?" Gemma chuckles, and the sound of it lightens the mood. "I don't blame you. There are plenty of violent woman in Perryville, although the program would have never matched you up with any of them."

"I know. I didn't think you'd be violent, but I had some pretty wild expectations after watching a ton of prison TV shows before you arrived."

"Oh, really? Do tell," she says in a teasing tone.

I grin, taking another sip of wine before setting the glass on the small side table next to the tub. "Well...I pictured you as this tough, hardened ex-con. You know, covered in prison tattoos, biceps bigger than my head..."

Gemma throws her head back and laughs. "Oh, absolutely. And I'd have a shaved head, a permanent scowl, and a pack of cigarettes rolled up in my sleeve, right?"

"Exactly!" I chuckle, tracing Gemma's arm, unmarred by any ink. "I was fully prepared for you to start a riot in the orchard or threaten me if I looked at you wrong."

Gemma snorts, shaking her head in amusement. "Damn, I missed my chance. And here I was, happily pruning trees and rewiring the house like a chump."

"I know, right? Such a disappointment." I heave an exaggerated sigh. "Where's the drama, the danger? I was promised a criminal, and instead I got..." I pause, turning my head to kiss her. "I got you."

"And that's a good thing?" she asks, meeting my eyes with a smile.

I reach up, cupping her cheek, my thumb tracing the delicate arc of her cheekbone. "It's the best thing. You're kind, and thoughtful, and wickedly funny. You're brilliant, and resilient, and so incredibly strong. Getting to know the real you beyond the labels and the assumptions…it's been the greatest gift."

Gemma brushes her lips against my neck and breathes into my ear, making me shiver. "Funny," she murmurs, "I was going to say the same thing about you. When I first got here, I was so scared of messing up and not being good enough. Scared that you'd take one look at me and send me packing."

"Oh, Gem…"

"But you didn't. From day one, you treated me like a person. Not an ex-con, not a charity case, but an equal. A friend. You saw past the surface, past all the labels society slapped on me, and you gave me a chance," she whispers. "You have no idea how much that meant to me. It made all the difference."

Gemma kisses my neck and shoulder, soft and sweet. I sink into her caress and moan as her hands roam over my breasts, massaging them in slow circles. Her tongue teases my earlobe, and she bites it softly while she pinches my nipples and rolls them between her fingers.

Another low moan rises in my throat, and I push myself back, firmer against her.

"God, Lori. I want you all the time," she pants, trailing her lips along my jaw and the column of my throat. "Even after a day like today, you make me forget about everything." I tilt my head to the side, giving her better access, my eyes fluttering shut as she finds that sensitive spot just below my ear that makes me squirm. I'm about to turn around, but she stops me. "Stay there. Just enjoy it." And then her hands are everywhere, urgent and demanding, leaving no inch of skin untouched.

I tilt my head to meet her mouth in a searing kiss and gasp against her lips as she slides a hand between my thighs. She swallows the sound with her kiss, her fingers teasing me while I jerk into her touch.

The water sloshes around us, some of it spilling over onto the floor as our movements grow more frantic. But neither of us care, too lost in the slide of skin against skin, in the mounting ache of need.

And then her fingers are inside me, filling me, and I cry out, my head falling back against her shoulder, my hands clasping onto her thighs. She sets a deep, steady rhythm, her thumb finding my clit, rubbing in tight, perfect circles. I'm climbing rapidly, my body quivering when Gemma's lips find my ear.

"I'm going to fuck you all night," she whispers, her voice like pure sin. "All night long."

It's so sexy when she takes charge. I know she will, and her words send me over the edge. I shatter with a hoarse cry, my body shaking, clenching around her fingers. Gemma moans and shivers as I come undone. The sound of our labored breathing breaks through the sloshing of the water, and Gemma presses soft kisses to my face, my hair, my neck, anywhere she can reach.

I giggle when I open my eyes and see the floor is covered in water. "Oops!" I shoot her a playful smile.

"Yeah, you've made a mess," she jokes. "Maybe it's best if we continue this in the bedroom."

45

GEMMA

"Thanks for coming," I say to Miranda, placing three mugs of coffee on the porch table. "I know you're busy."

Miranda shakes her head and smiles. "As I said, don't worry about it, it's my job." She sips her coffee, her keen eyes studying me over the rim of her mug. "How are you today?"

I take a deep breath, my fingers tightening around my own mug. "Anxious," I say honestly. "Nervous about leaving the farm. Afraid of the inevitable judgment." I found my escape in red wine and Lori last night, but as soon as the sun came up, the harsh reality hit me again. "I feel like I'm right back where I started," I continue. "Like all the trust I've built in the community has just been wiped away."

"Unfortunately," Miranda says, leaning forward, "what you're experiencing is very common for individuals reentering society after incarceration. The stigma, the judgment, the feeling of being 'othered'—it's a heavy burden to bear."

"I don't know what to do," I confess. "I feel so exposed. I expect everyone to be watching me now, waiting for me to slip up and prove their worst assumptions right."

Lori sits next to me and puts a hand on my thigh. We were supposed to hide our relationship from Miranda, but the small touches have become instinctive, and I suspect she doesn't even realize she's doing it.

"Whatever you do, don't hide," Miranda says calmly, her eyes briefly darting to Lori's display of affection. "It's easy to become isolated if all you think about is people's perception of you. That's why it's important to take control of your own narrative." She pauses. "Look, you can't control what people think, but you can influence how they see you."

"What do you mean?" I take Lori's hand in mine. It's too late anyway; Miranda has already seen it, and I need Lori's support.

"I mean, don't let gossip and speculation fill in the blanks." Miranda sits back, folding her hands on the table. "Be proactive. Share your truth, in your own words, on your own terms."

A flicker of unease passes through me, my stomach clenching. "You want me to...what, make a public statement? Go door to door, explaining myself?"

"Not necessarily." A small smile tugs at Miranda's lips. "Though I admire your commitment to transparency. What I'm suggesting is that you start a dialogue with the people who matter most to you in this community. The ones whose opinions and support you value."

I think of Tom and Betty, of the other vendors at the market who have become something like friends over these past months. The thought of baring my soul and my scars makes my palms sweat. "Okay," I say slowly. "I'll try my best."

"Good. That's really good." Miranda clears her throat, suddenly more businesslike. "Now, let's talk strategy. How do you want to approach these conversations? What do you want to say?"

For the next hour, we brainstorm and plan, Miranda offering guidance and perspective from her years of experience. She helps me craft my message in a way that feels authentic but also protective of my privacy and my healing process.

By the time she drains the last of her second coffee, I'm feeling marginally more prepared and a little more grounded. The anxiety still hums beneath my skin, but it's tempered now by a sense of direction.

"Remember," Miranda says, "you are in control here, Gemma. You get to decide how much you share, and with whom. Don't let anyone pressure you into disclosing more than you're comfortable with."

"Thank you, I'll keep that in mind." I give her a small smile. "Can I get you another coffee? Water? Actually, I have some homemade cloudy apple juice in the fridge."

"No thank you. I'd love to catch up on a personal note, but I have another appointment in an hour." Miranda levels her gaze at me. "But there's something I need to address before I go. I've been ignoring it, but I can't any longer." Her tone is serious but not unkind. "I can see that you and Lori are more than just friends, and as your case worker, I have to advise against it. It's my job."

Lori and I exchange a glance and simply sit there sheepishly like two kids caught stealing candy.

"You know?" Lori asks. "Charlotte promised to be discreet." Then she finally notices we're holding hands and quickly retracts hers.

"Charlotte has nothing to do with this. I see everything. I can't believe you two thought you were being subtle." Miranda rolls her eyes and laughs. "Seriously, the longing looks, the little touches over dinner the other night—which I really enjoyed, by the way, and I'd like to return the favor at my place soon—it was like watching a romance novel unfold right in front of me."

I feel my cheeks heat up and turn to Lori, who looks equally abashed. "We did try to be discreet," I mumble.

"Discreet?" Miranda snorts. "Please. You two have about as much subtlety as a bull in a china shop."

Despite my embarrassment, I can't help but laugh. "We may not be subtle, but we are happy."

"I can see that." Miranda sighs and pushes her glasses up on her nose. "There's no point in making a fuss about it. You two are clearly crazy about each other and I'm happy for you."

"Thank you." Lori clears her throat. "I know it was wrong, from my side, but it doesn't feel wrong."

"Well, Gemma's only got two weeks left on your three-month contract," Miranda says. "So I'm going to turn a blind eye and pretend I haven't noticed. After that, you're technically not her employer through the program anymore, so if anything goes wrong, it won't be my problem." She turns to me. "I will have to come back for an exit interview and support you in finding a job and a home, though I suspect you're not going anywhere."

"No, I don't think I am."

Miranda gives me a knowing look, and we both laugh.

Movement outside the window catches my eye. "That's Joseph Delaney," I tell Miranda, watching his progress up the walk to the house. "He drops by once or twice a week to check on the orchard and we have a usually coffee together. He's a lovely man, so helpful."

Miranda nods and places a hand on my shoulder. "Then

maybe now would be a good time to start sharing your story."

I chew my bottom lip, considering her suggestion. Perhaps she's right. Maybe it's time to unburden myself, and I'm comfortable with Joseph. He generally keeps to himself and doesn't gossip. I don't know him that well, but he doesn't strike me as the judgmental type.

He lifts his walking stick as a matter of greeting and Miranda takes that as a cue to leave.

"I'll see you soon," she says before heading off. "Call me. Let me know how you're doing."

46

LORI

$\mathcal{M}$om hands us each a glass of iced tea before taking a seat across from us. "I'm so glad you came, Lori," she says, her eyes shining. "I was worried I'd lost you."

Still feeling emotionally bruised, I manage a small smile. "I figured we should talk, and I'm ready to listen."

Mom, Gemma, and I are sitting on the small balcony of Mom's apartment. The space is cozy, with potted plants lining the railing and a little bistro set nestled in the corner.

Mom nods. Her gaze shifts to Gemma, who is sitting quietly beside me. "And Gemma," she says, a warm smile touching her lips. "It's wonderful to meet you, dear."

Gemma returns the smile, but I can feel the tension in her body, the slight tremor in her hand. "It's great to meet you too, Ms. Hawthorne," she says, her voice steady despite her nerves.

"Please, call me Moya," Mom insists. "Any friend of Lori's is a friend of mine."

"Actually..." I clear my throat, glancing at Gemma. "Gemma is more than a friend. She's my girlfriend."

Mom's eyebrows rise, but her smile doesn't falter. "I already suspected that," she says. "Well, then, I'm even more delighted to meet you, Gemma."

Gemma's hand squeezes my thigh gently. "Thank you, Moya. That means a lot."

I take a deep breath, steeling myself for the next part. "There's something else you should know. About Gemma, and about how we met. We wanted you to know before you find out through others."

"Go on," Mom says, her brows knitting curiously.

I glance at Gemma, and she gives me a small nod. "Gemma is living with me on the farm," I begin. "But not just as my girlfriend. She's...she's part of a rehabilitation program. For former inmates."

"Oh." Mom's gaze darts between Gemma and me. "I...I see."

Gemma leans forward, her expression earnest. "Moya, I want you to know that I'm not proud of my past. I made a terrible mistake, and I paid the price for it. But Lori has given me a fresh start, and I'm doing everything I can to make the most of it."

Mom is quiet for a moment, her gaze assessing. Then, slowly, she nods. "We all have parts of our past we're not proud of. How long were you in prison?"

"Seven and a half years."

"Right." Mom hesitates. "That's quite some time." I know what she's thinking. Long sentences are generally the result of serious crimes, which means Gemma is no angel.

"Yes." Gemma swallows hard. "About my sentence—"

"Wait." Mom shakes her head. "Let me ask you something first. Are you two serious about each other?"

"Yes," Gemma and I say in unison, and I let out a nervous chuckle.

Despite her unease, Mom shoots us an amused smile. I suspect she's relieved the attention is on Gemma. That she's off the hook for the first part of our visit because my new girlfriend has done something bad too. "Then maybe we should leave it with this, for now. I'd like to know what you did, of course. I want to know exactly who my daughter is dating, but perhaps it's best if we meet up a few times first. I don't want to fall into the trap of forming an opinion of you before I get to know you."

Gemma's shoulders sag with relief, a shaky smile touching her lips. "Thank you," she says. "I really appreciate that."

Mom reaches across the table, patting Gemma's hand. "Of course, dear. Let's save this conversation for some other day."

Her reaction surprises me. I didn't think it would be so simple, but I suppose she's not in a position to judge right now. I feel a sudden swell of love for my mother in that moment. For her compassion, and her open-mindedness. She accepted my sexuality when I came out to her, and she's always accepted my choices. It's time that I let her explain her choices.

Mom takes a sip of her iced tea, her gaze turning inward. "Well, as you're here to talk," she says, setting her glass down with a soft clink. "I'll start, if that's okay with you?"

I nod. "I'm listening."

Mom sits back, her fingers twisting in her lap. "When you were younger," she begins, "you used to ask about your father all the time. Do you remember?"

I nod. "I do. You always said he was a traveling salesman, that he didn't know about me."

Mom closes her eyes briefly, pain etching lines into her face. "As you now know, I lied," she says, her voice barely more than a whisper. "At first, I lied because I didn't want Maggie to find out I'd had an affair with her husband, and once she did find out, I lied because I was scared of losing you."

"Losing me? Why?"

Mom sighs, her shoulders slumping. "You loved being on the farm with Maggie and Frank. Every time we visited, it was like you came alive there and belonged in a way you never quite did with me."

I open my mouth to protest, but Mom holds up a hand, stopping me. "It's okay, honey. It's the truth. You were always meant for wide open spaces and fresh air. Not an apartment in the city with a single mom working long hours."

"That's not true. I was happy with you." I feel tears prick at the corners of my eyes for all the sacrifices she made.

"Perhaps I was just being paranoid," Mom says, "but the truth is, that's how it felt to me at the time. As you got older, it became harder and harder for me to take you to the farm. Maggie didn't know about what happened years prior between Frank and me. And Frank..." She pauses, swallowing hard. "Frank was getting closer to you. Letting little things slip. Calling you 'my baby girl.'"

I feel like I can't breathe, the weight of her words pressing down on my chest.

"I was scared," Mom whispers, tears slipping down her cheeks now. "Terrified that you would choose them over me."

"Mom," I choke out, my own tears welling up. "I would never..."

But Mom is shaking her head, a sad smile on her face. "You would have," she says gently. "And I wouldn't have blamed you. They could give you things I never could—a father, a stable home, and a future on that beautiful farm."

I take a few deep breaths to steady my emotions, and Gemma's arm slips around me, holding me close.

"When Maggie found out," Mom continues, "it was like my worst nightmare come true. She was furious and felt betrayed. She told me I wasn't welcome at the farm anymore, that she never wanted to see me again. But you..." She meets my gaze. "She said you could visit anytime and stay for as long as you wanted. That it wasn't your fault, what your parents had done. Maggie and Frank tried for a baby for years until Maggie found out she was unable to conceive, and her mothering instincts always came out when you were around."

I nod, remembering that last visit, the confusion when Aunt Maggie had hugged me extra tight and whispered in my ear that I was always welcome, no matter what. I was young and I had no idea what was going on.

"I was selfish," Mom says, her voice cracking. "I made excuses, let you believe that your aunt and uncle simply didn't want us around anymore. Frank called and even showed up at my door a few times, but I felt it was easier if we cut off all contact."

"He tried to see me?"

"Yes. He loved you."

Mom's words hit me like a physical blow. Frank loved me. He tried to see me, even after everything that happened between him and Mom. All these years, I thought he had simply forgotten about me, moved on with his life.

I feel a rush of emotions—shock, confusion, a tentative flicker of warmth at the thought that my father wanted me, followed quickly by a crushing sense of loss for what could have been. All the missed birthdays, the father-daughter moments that never were.

I try to remember if there were ever any hints, any clues

that Frank was trying to reach out. I rack my brain, sifting through hazy childhood memories, but come up empty. Mom kept it quiet. She made sure I never knew.

A part of me still wants to be angry at her for that, but as I look at her now, her face lined with regret and sorrow, I can't find it in my heart to hold on to that anger. She did what she thought was best, even if it was misguided.

"You should have told me," I say. "But I'm glad you told me now."

"It's too late. You deserved so much better."

"No, Mom. I was lucky to have you." I'm out of my seat before I realize I'm moving, rounding the table to engulf my mother in a hug. She clings to me, her tears soaking into my shirt, and I hold her tighter, pouring all my love into the embrace.

When we pull back, I cup her face in my hands, my thumbs brushing away her tears. "No more secrets," I say softly.

Mom stares up at me and nods. "No more secrets." She pauses. "You look so much like him."

"That's what I said," Gemma whispers. "It's the dimples."

I return to my seat beside Gemma, slipping my hand into hers.

"Yes. But you have his character too," Mom says. "Kind and hard-working."

"Will you tell me about him?" I shoot my mother a pleading look. "I know this is hard for you, but I need to know more. It doesn't have to be now. You can come to the farm, when you're ready."

Mom dabs at her eyes with a napkin, composing herself. "I will. I'll have to get used to the idea that Rosefield Farm is your home now. Even after everything that happened, you ended up exactly where you belong."

Mom's words bring a sense of comfort. Despite the pain and secrets of the past, it seems that fate has led me back to where I was always meant to be.

"It feels like home," I whisper.

"Both Frank and Maggie would be so proud of you, Lori. Seeing you take on the farm, making it your own…"

"I hope I can make it thrive." I smile at Gemma. "That *we* can make it thrive."

"I have no doubt you will." Mom looks at us, and I can see she's genuinely happy for me. "Now, I hope you don't mind if we move on to a more light-hearted subject, because I want to hear all about my daughter's dashing new girl-friend. And not your past, Gemma. Your present."

47

GEMMA

*L*ori takes Lemon for a wander around the market while I display my preserves and the apple muffins we made yesterday. She insisted on coming today, and although I feel like this is my mess to deal with, I'm grateful that she's here. I'm worried about giving her farm a bad name, perhaps causing friction between Lori and the wholesalers, but she doesn't seem worried about anything but me.

As I arrange the jars and baskets, I glance around, trying to gauge the reactions of the other vendors and the early morning shoppers. Are they whispering about me? Casting looks in my direction? It's hard to tell, but the weight of their potential judgment is potent.

Lori must sense my unease, because she pauses on her way past my stall, Lemon wriggling excitedly in her arms. "Hey," she says softly, her free hand coming to rest on my arm. "Remember what we talked about. Head up, eyes forward. You've got this."

I take a deep breath, letting her calm certainty wash over me. "I know. It's just...I'm feeling a little anxious."

She nods, understanding in her eyes. "I know, love. But you're not facing it alone, okay?" With a final reassuring squeeze of my arm, she moves on, Lemon's happy yips fading into the general bustle of the market. I square my shoulders, turning back to my display.

"Good morning, Gemma," Betty says as she finishes setting up her stall.

"Good morning." Is it me, or is she more standoffish than usual? *Of course, she knows*, I remind myself. What was I thinking? That I could be part of a small community and get away with it? Have people believe I was just like any of them? I suppose I found a spark of hope after telling Joseph. He simply listened and hasn't treated me any differently since. Needing to address the elephant before it gets too busy, I turn to Betty. "I suppose you've heard?"

"Yes." She shakes her head, her silver curls bouncing. "It's that woman from last week, isn't it? You said you had a bad feeling about her."

"I did, but..." I hesitate, fiddling with a jar of jam. "That doesn't make it any less true."

Betty keeps rearranging her lemons, her hands restless, as if she doesn't quite know what to do with herself. "Well," she finally says, "everyone has a story. Some more tragic than others, but everyone has one. It doesn't change anything. You're still the same Gemma I know, and I happen to like spending my Saturdays with you. Besides, I need someone in between myself and Tom, or we'll be bickering all the time." She winks.

I'm so grateful I want to hug her, and seeing my eyes well up, Betty walks over to me, her arms outstretched.

"Oh, come here, honey." She wraps them around me so tight she almost squeezes the air out of me. When she lets go, Tom is beside us.

"She's right." He places a large, comforting hand on my shoulder. "It doesn't change anything." He too pulls me into a hug. "At my age, I consider myself a pretty good judge of character, and you have a good heart. That's all I need to know."

"Thank you," I say, wiping my cheeks. I told myself I wasn't going to get emotional today, but these are good emotions, and Betty's and Tom's acceptance pushes back against the chill of my anxiety. "That means the world to me."

"It's all good, honey." Tom's eyes shimmer as he pats my shoulder again and turns back to his stall, where a customer is waiting.

The early birds are often out-of-towners, and I fall into the flow of greeting customers, offering samples, making change and small talk. With paranoia eating away at me, I approach everyone with a bit more caution.

"Can I help you?" I ask a woman who stares at me, her expression pinched, her eyes hard.

She takes me in, her gaze roaming over my face, then glances down at her phone. I catch a glimpse of the screen. It's my mugshot. "It really is you. You were in for murder," she says, her tone accusatory.

I'm so thrown by her directness that I can't get a word out. I expected looks, maybe some whispered comments, but nothing like this—a bold confrontation in the middle of the market.

"Well?" she arches a brow, impatience and something like disgust etched into her features.

Anxiety starts bubbling inside me, hot and thick. Yes, I did something terrible, something unforgivable. But if she has a problem with me, she can take her business else-where. There's no need for this.

My hands are shaking, and I take a deep breath, forcing myself to stay composed. Any signs of anger, or even raising my voice will only confirm what she already thinks of me. That I have a temper. That I can't control myself. "Second-degree manslaughter," I correct her politely, my voice miraculously even. It feels absurd to have this conversation, but it's happening.

"What's the difference? You took a life."

"You're right," I admit. "There's no excuse for what I did."

"Excuse me." A familiar voice cuts through the tension. "If you're not buying, would you mind moving over for a second?" It's Joseph. "Good morning, Gemma. I'll have one of these, please," he says, handing me a jar of preserves to bag. "And I'll have a few of those delightful apples."

Relieved to see him, I manage a smile. "You don't need to buy our apples, Joseph. Just help yourself, either here or in the orchard." Handing him a generous bag filled with fruit, I add, "It's all on us, for helping Lori."

"Thank you, that's very kind." Joseph glances at the woman who was interrogating me, then turns back to me, his expression warm. "A little birdie told me you're a damn good electrician. Why didn't I know about this?"

"Oh, it's just something I do on the side," I say, my eyes flicking back to the woman for a split second.

Joseph nods. "Do you have time to do a job in my kitchen?"

I stare at him, surprised. "Um, of course," I stammer, finding my voice. "Anytime for you, Joseph."

"But she's..." The woman next to Joseph frowns as she holds her phone up to him. Her face is pinched with confusion and disapproval, as if she can't quite believe he's just invited a murderer into his home.

"She's what? Kind? Helpful? As sweet as the delicious

preserves she makes?" Joseph shoots me a wink, mischief dancing in his eyes. "She sure is."

The woman sputters, her cheeks flushing an angry red, but Joseph simply takes his preserves and apples and ambles away, whistling a cheerful tune. I watch him go with a lump in my throat.

"If you're not buying..." Betty chimes in, staring the woman down, "it would be great if you could move over a little so we can serve our customers."

"Do we have a problem?" Lori has returned with two takeout coffees, and the look on her face is fierce to say the least. She tucks Lemon in his basket on the table, puts down the coffees and turns to the woman with her hands on her hips.

"No, we're fine," I say, kissing her cheek.

"Yes, we're fine. She was just leaving," Betty agrees. When the woman storms off, no doubt looking for allies, she gives Lori a knowing look. "The less attention we give people like her, the better."

Her fists balled, Lori doesn't look convinced. "Are you sure you're okay?"

"Yes, babe. Betty is right. Please let it go. I don't want to draw more attention to myself than necessary."

"Okay," Lori says softly, then settles back into one of the chairs behind the stall. "Do you need help?" she asks, sipping her coffee.

"No, everything is under control." I lean over her and plant a soft kiss on her forehead. "But it's nice to have you here." The incident has rattled me, but I continue to focus on my customers. There will be more like her; it's only a matter of time, and I'll deal with them calmly, one by one.

Lori chats to Betty and Tom and greets one of our seasonal workers who passes by with his girlfriend, and then Charlotte pays us a surprise visit. I greet her while I'm helping a customer and don't even notice she's set up the folding chair she's brought next to Lori's until I thank my customer and turn around. She's got a large Thermos and a paper bag clutched in her hands.

"Fresh croissants!" she exclaims, grinning at Lori and me as she brandishes her offerings.

I blink at her, uncomprehending for a moment. Then it hits me. She's here, right in the middle of the market, making a very public show of support, despite the risk to her own reputation. Apart from Joseph, Charlotte's the only other person I approached before today. It turned out she already knew; she saw the post a week ago and hasn't treated me any differently.

"Charlotte, that's so sweet," I say. "You didn't have to..."

She waves it off, pressing a croissant into my hands. "Of course I did. What else are friends for?" Her smile is warm, her gaze steady on mine. "Besides, I couldn't let you and Lori hog all these delicious muffins to yourselves, now, could I? So let's trade."

A laugh bubbles up through the tightness in my throat, escaping in a chuckle. "Well, when you put it that way..."

She smiles and greets a customer, seamlessly integrating herself into the flow of the market as if she's always been here, a fixture right alongside Lori and me.

I sip my coffee with Charlotte and Lori while we catch up on Charlotte's latest court dramas. Betty cajoles a customer into trying her new lemon curd recipe, and Tom haggles good-naturedly with a regular over the price of his heirloom tomatoes. And through it all, Lemon yaps and wags his tail at everyone who passes by.

With my little army of supporters, the day already feels so much more manageable, and I count my blessings. Something has started to shift inside me, and I'm almost inclined to believe that I deserve them. That I deserve all the good that has come into my life lately. Their presence and solidarity are a reminder that I'm not alone. They see the real me, and in their eyes, I'm beginning to catch a glimpse of the person I am beyond my past. Maybe I *do* deserve this.

48

LORI

$\mathcal{I}$ finish applying the last layer of crisp white paint to the kitchen cabinets and step back, admiring my handiwork. Flecks of sage green speckle my clothes and skin from the walls we finished earlier.

The once dingy and dated kitchen has been transformed. The fresh white cabinets make the space look bright and airy, while the soft green walls bring a warm, earthy vibe to our home. Pops of color from the potted herbs on the windowsill and Aunt Maggie's vase on the kitchen table add just the right amount of homey charm and a wink to the farm's heritage.

"What do you think?" Gemma's husky voice breaks the silence as she moves to stand beside me.

I turn to face her, unable to stop the grin that spreads across my face at the sight of her. Even with locks of hair escaping her haphazard ponytail and smudges of paint on her cheeks, she's utterly gorgeous. The oversize T-shirt she's sporting does nothing to hide her toned arms, and the cocky smirk playing at her lips makes my heart flutter.

"I think it's perfect," I say, my gaze roaming over her face before dropping to her lips. Those full, pink lips quirk up even farther at the corners as Gemma's eyes sparkle with mischief.

"You know, we should really celebrate a job well done."

She wraps an arm around my waist and pulls me in. The scent of her shampoo mixed with the faint aroma of paint thinner makes my head spin delightfully. Gemma's hands find my hips, her fingertips brushing up against the sliver of exposed skin between my T-shirt and shorts. It's a warm day and we're both scarcely clad, bare legs and bare feet.

"Oh, yeah?" I murmur, my voice dropping lower. "What did you have in mind?"

Gemma leans in, her lips a hairbreadth from mine. "Well—" The shrill ringing of the doorbell cuts her off and we both groan in frustration at the disruption.

Gemma lets her forehead drop against mine with a sigh. "I swear, if that's those kids from down the road doing a ding-dong-ditch again..." she mutters darkly.

Chuckling, I disentangle myself from her embrace and head for the front door.

"It's just Miranda," I call over my shoulder as I open it.

"Sorry I'm early," Miranda says. "I had a last-minute cancellation and happened to be nearby. Is it okay if we meet earlier?"

"No problem, come on in! Sorry about the mess. We've been painting all week."

"Oh, this looks great," she says, glancing around before turning to us. "Although I'm not sure who caught more paint. The two of you or the kitchen."

"It got messy under time pressure. I was just getting one last lick of paint on before Lori kicks me out on the street," Gemma jokes.

"As if I'd ever kick you out," I scoff, nudging her shoulder with mine. "I don't know what I'd do without you." Feeling my cheeks flush, I shake my head. "Anyway, where are my manners? Let me make some coffee."

"There's that amazing discretion again." Miranda observes our interaction with an amused grin and takes a seat at the kitchen table, gratefully accepting the coffee and homemade peach muffins we made.

We cover the basics first—Gemma's financial situation, employment prospects, goals for the future. I can't help but beam with pride as she talks about picking up more electrical work lately and running the popular market stall. It wasn't so long ago that she arrived with nothing but a bag of borrowed clothes, her confidence and self-worth shattered by a string of shitty circumstances.

"I feel like I finally have a life again," Gemma says softly. "After everything, I didn't think that was possible. But here I am with a job I'm good at, paying my own way..." Her gaze finds mine, and the love I see reflected steals my breath away. "Thank you, Lori."

"I'm so proud of you," I say, taking her hand.

Miranda smiles and I swear I detect a glimmer of emotion in her stern facade. I suppose with all the struggles in her job, it's nice to see something working out better than expected. "I'm very glad to hear it's going so well," she says. "What about the gossip? Has it died down a little?"

"Yeah," Gemma says. "It's gotten a lot better, and having supportive friends has made a world of difference. I get stared at, of course, and I get the odd remark here and there, but I'm learning to deal with it emotionally."

"That's good." Miranda pauses, tapping her pen against her chin thoughtfully. "You know, Gemma, I've been in this line of work for a long time. I've seen a lot of people come out of the system, and it's not an easy road. Not everyone makes it, so seeing you embracing life and succeeding makes everything worth it." She sets her notepad aside and regards us warmly. "I have to say, you two have been my favorite clients to work with over the years. Seeing your relationship blossom from friendly housemates to..." She gestures vaguely between us. "Well, you know...it's been a real joy."

My face flames, but Gemma just laughs and throws her arm around my shoulder, hugging me against her side. "What can I say? She just can't resist my sparkling charm."

I snort indelicately. "You wish."

Miranda laughs. "Well, I guess on that note, this is where the program ends and I can put a big, fat check mark behind your name. I'll still be your official probation officer, but I'll put forward a proposal that we bring our meetings down to once a month, and it will only be a courtesy phone call, either from me or one of my team members." She shrugs. "To be honest, I'd prefer to hand your case over to someone else because I really like hanging out with you guys and it would make it so much easier."

"So do we," I say. "Charlotte was threatening to drop by later. Are you busy?"

"No, not at all. You're my last clients for the day. That's why I thought I'd try my luck and drop by early. It's not often I get to sign off before five." Miranda chuckles. "But I can tell Charlotte you're in renovation mode, and we can meet later?"

"No need." Lori claps her hands together. "We were just finishing up, so let me pour you a real drink. How about some punch? We have more fruit than we know what to do with, and if I tell Char you're here, she'll drop everything and head straight over."

"Really?" Miranda arches a brow.

"Yeah. She's crazy about you. Don't you know that?" Gemma chimes in. When I'm about to get up, she nudges me back into my chair and kisses me. "Let me get the drinks, babe."

It's the first time I've seen Miranda lost for words, and it's making me laugh. "I guess I wasn't sure. I'm crazy about her too, but Charlotte's a hard nut to crack," she finally says. "She doesn't give much away."

"She just needs a little more time than most people," I assure her. "And I can tell you one thing. In all the years we've been friends, she's never even mentioned a girlfriend, so consider yourself special."

"Huh." Miranda seems to ponder over that while Gemma chops fruit for the punch. "You really think she's serious about me?"

It's so endearing to see put-together Miranda flushed that part of me wants to hug her. "Yes," I say confidently and shoot her a wink. "You have nothing to worry about."

49

GEMMA

*T*he community center is a hive of activity as I weave my way through the crowd with my toolbox in hand. Volunteers are getting the space ready for the annual Sedona Summer Fair, and they've asked me to set up the equipment for the outdoor stage. It has to be ready for a kids' talent show this afternoon, and later, there will be a raffle and live music. Inside tables are being set up for a flea market, and there will be lots of stalls and fun things to do at the back of the community center too.

It felt like such an honor when the committee asked me to help; I think someone put in a good word for me, and I'm grateful for the opportunity. It's a chance for me to mingle with the community and get to know new people. I expected some pushback from certain people who would rather see me go, but so far, it's been nothing but friendly.

As I set up my tools and start checking the wiring for the stage lights, I can't help but reflect on how far I've come. Five months ago, the idea of being here, of being trusted by people who know what I've done, had seemed impossible.

But slowly, day by day, I've been rebuilding—not just my life, but my sense of self and my place in the world.

I spot Lori walking up to the stage, in conversation with one of the committee members. She catches my eye and waves me over.

"There you are!" She greets me with a quick kiss on the cheek. "Ready to work your magic?"

I nod, surveying the tangle of wires and equipment littering the stage. "I'm ready. Want to help me untangle?"

Lori laughs. "You know I never say no to a challenge."

Someone tugs on my sleeve, and I look down to see a young girl, no more than eight or nine, staring up at me.

"Are you the lady who can fix things?" she asks, her voice high and sweet.

I crouch at her level, smiling. "I try to. What do you need fixing?"

She holds out a small, plastic tiara, a frown puckering her brow. "It broke. The lights won't turn on anymore."

I take the tiara and examine it. It's a cheap thing, probably won at one of the fair's game booths, but to this girl, it's clearly a treasure. The wiring is basic, just a small battery pack and a few LED bulbs. I fish in my toolbox for a minute, finding a small screwdriver.

"Let's take a look," I say, carefully opening the battery compartment. A quick adjustment to the connections, and the tiara springs to life, the tiny lights blinking in a cheery pattern.

The girl's face lights up brighter than the tiara. "You fixed it!" she squeals, bouncing on her toes.

I place the tiara gently on her head, adjusting it to sit just right. "There you go, Princess. Good as new."

She throws her arms around my neck in an exuberant hug. "Thank you, thank you, thank you!"

"You're very welcome," I say with a chuckle. "Now, go find your mom, Your Highness. It's that lady over there, right? The one setting up the face-paint booth?" I wave at the woman while the girl scampers off, and she waves back at me.

As I refocus on the tangled cables, I catch Lori watching me, a soft smile playing about her lips.

"What?" I ask, raising an eyebrow.

She shakes her head, her smile widening. "Nothing. Just...you. Seeing you like this. It makes me happy."

I smile. "Fixing tiaras, you mean?"

"Fixing anything. And you're good with kids. It's adorable."

I arch a brow. "Oh, you're thinking about kids now?"

Lori grins. "It was just an observation." She looks away, thinking she can hide her blush, but fails miserably.

"Do we need to talk about kids?" I ask as I pull one of the cables toward a speaker. "Is that something you want?" Tilting my head, I regard her and note she seems lost for words. "It's okay, we can talk about anything."

"I know," she says shyly. "Maybe we should discuss it sometime when we're alone. I...uh..." Lori stammers, her cheeks flushing an even deeper shade of pink. "I mean, it's not something I've given a lot of thought to. At least, not until recently." She looks down at her hands, fidgeting with the hem of her shirt. "But lately, I've been thinking..."

I drop the cable and turn to face her fully, my heart skipping a beat at the vulnerability in her expression.

"About what?" I ask softly, encouraging her to continue.

"About the future. Our future." Lori takes a deep breath, then meets my gaze. "I know we haven't really talked about it, but...I like the idea of having kids someday. With you."

Her words hang in the air between us, heavy with

promise and possibility. I feel a swell of emotion rising in my chest, a mixture of intense love and fear and hope.

Lori is watching me closely, her hazel eyes wide and uncertain. "I'm not saying right now," she clarifies hurriedly. "I know we've got a lot of other things to figure out first. But someday...yeah. I think I'd like that if it's something you might consider too." She shakes her head. "Anyway, here and now is not the time or place for this conversation. I hope I didn't scare you. I swear, I'd be fine if it's not for you, and—"

"Hey, hey, it's okay," I say, chuckling at Lori's endearing nervousness. I reach out and pull her into a tight hug, feeling her relax against me. "You didn't scare me. I'm just a little surprised, that's all."

Lori buries her face in my neck, her words muffled. "I didn't mean to spring it on you like that. It just kind of... came out."

I stroke her hair, pressing a kiss to her temple. "I'm glad it did. It's a big conversation, but it's one we should have."

"Yeah." Lori steps back and glances around, suddenly aware of the bustling crowd surrounding us. "People are watching," she whispers with a goofy grin, then turns back to the tangled mess of cables at our feet.

As I continue working on the stage setup, my mind keeps drifting to Lori's comment about kids. It's not something we've really discussed before, at least not in any serious capacity. Sure, we've joked about Lemon being our "fur baby," but the idea of actual human children? That's a whole different ballgame.

I suppose it's only natural that the topic would come up eventually. We're in a committed relationship, building a life together.

Growing up, the idea of having kids someday always

seemed like a far-off, abstract concept, something that would happen in a nebulous "future" when I had my life together. But then everything went sideways. Prison, the years lost... The future I'd imagined for myself crumbled to dust.

Even now, with the pieces of my life slowly falling back into place, the notion of parenthood feels fraught. How could I even consider bringing a child into the world when my history is so checkered? One of their mothers would be a murderer, and there's nothing I can do to change that.

But then I think of Lori. Of the unwavering love and acceptance she's shown me. She's such a kind and protective person. She'd be a great mother, and with her by my side, anything feels possible.

I picture a little boy or girl with Lori's dimpled smile. A family, built on a foundation of love and second chances. This vision of our future, once an amorphous wisp, now takes on a more tangible form in my mind's eye. It's a future I never thought I'd have the audacity to imagine, but Lori's unwavering belief in me, in us, has sparked a newfound boldness. It makes me dare to dream.

50

LORI

"I can't remember the last time I ate that much funnel cake," I say, kicking off my shoes and wiggling my toes with a contented sigh. "Or talked to so many people in one day."

"Yeah." Gemma laughs as she settles beside me on the porch. "That volunteer serving coffee was talking my head off. I know everything about her—what her kids do for a living, how many times she's been married, what time she gets up in the morning, what she's cooking for dinner tomorrow... I'm glad you came to the rescue with that vague emergency excuse."

"According to Betty, she's always on the lookout for new people talk 'at' instead of 'to.'" I chuckle. "I could tell you were looking for an escape."

Gemma's arm is draped along the back of the bench, her fingers idly playing with the ends of my hair. It's a casual intimacy, born of familiarity and trust. I'm just starting to contemplate the merits of a post-funnel-cake early night when Gemma clears her throat.

"So," she starts, her tone carefully casual. "About that conversation we had earlier…"

I feel a flutter of nerves in my stomach, but I keep my voice light. "You mean the one about the perils of deep-fried Oreos? Because I stand by my assertion that they're a culinary marvel."

Gemma snorts, shaking her head. "No. The one about…" She hesitates, chewing on her bottom lip. "About kids."

"Oh. That one." I sit up a bit straighter, turning to face her fully. The fading sunlight gilds her features, highlighting the uncertainty in her eyes. "I guess I kind of dropped a bombshell on you this morning, huh?"

Gemma shrugs. "It was a bit out of the blue," she admits. "But not in a bad way. Just…unexpected."

I nod, fiddling with the hem of my shorts. "Honestly, it kind of caught me off guard too. It's not something I've given a lot of serious thought to before. But seeing you today, with that little girl…" I shake my head, trying to find the right words. "It just hit me, you know? This glimpse of a future I hadn't really let myself imagine."

Gemma is quiet for a moment, her brow furrowed in thought. "I get that," she says slowly. "It's not something I've allowed myself to consider either. With my past…the idea of being responsible for a tiny human? It's terrifying."

"But also kind of amazing?" I venture, searching her face. "I mean, can you imagine a little mini-you, all dark hair and mischievous grins?"

Gemma huffs out a laugh. "Or a mini-you, with those killer dimples and a heart big enough to love the whole world." She sighs, her fingers resuming their gentle combing through my hair. "I don't know, Lori. I want to believe I could be a good parent. That I could give a kid the kind of stable, loving home I never had."

I reach out, lacing my fingers through hers. "Hey, you'd be an amazing mother."

"You really think so?"

"I know so," I say with conviction. "Gemma, I feel your love. Fiercely, wholly, with every part of yourself. Any kid would be lucky to have that. But I also know that parenthood is a huge, life-altering thing, and if it's not for you, I can live with that."

"I wouldn't dream of taking that away from you," she says. "If having kids is something you want, then I want it too. Because you deserve the world, and I would move mountains to give it to you."

I feel my heart swell in my chest and swallow down the lump in my throat. "Gemma," I whisper, cupping her face in my hands. "You are my world. And if parenthood is part of our future, then I want to walk that path with you. But only if it's something we both want, fully and completely. Having you is enough, always."

"I do want it," she murmurs. "Someday. The idea of creating a family with you..." She smiles. "I never thought I'd have that."

I brush my thumb over her cheekbones, marveling at the strength and vulnerability etched into every line of her face. "You deserve everything good, and I'm going to spend every day of our life reminding you of that."

A sudden bark breaks the tension. Lemon is sitting at our feet and looking up at us, his tail wagging expectantly.

"Hey there, buddy," Gemma coos, reaching down to scratch behind his ears. "You want in on this heart-to-heart too?"

Lemon yips in response, his tongue lolling out in a doggy grin. I can't help but laugh at his impeccable timing.

"I think he's saying we're getting a little too serious for

his taste," I joke, patting my lap in invitation. Lemon hops up without hesitation and curls up. I grin, a sudden thought popping into my head. "If we do have kids someday, should I be worried about your naming skills?"

Gemma's brows shoot up, a mix of amusement and indignation on her face. "What's that supposed to mean?"

I glance pointedly at the furry bundle in my lap. "Well, you did call him Lemon. Need I say more?"

Gemma gasps in mock offense, her hand flying to her chest. "Hey, Lemon is a beautiful name. It's unique, and it suits him perfectly."

I can't argue with that. Our little Lemon is certainly one of a kind. But still, I can't resist teasing her a bit more. "Sure, whatever you say."

"I think Lemon would be cute for a girl too," she says, keeping a straight face. "And how about Kale for a boy?"

"Kale?"

"Yeah." Gemma shrugs. "It's a strong name. Memorable."

"And a superfood," I add in all seriousness, barely suppressing a grin. "We could always let Lemon name them?"

Lemon looks up at me and blinks a few times.

"He's thinking about it," Gemma jokes and leans over to bring her ear to his face. "What's that? Oh, you like the name Squeaky Toy? Yeah, that's a good one."

I throw my head back in laughter. "Thanks, Lemon." I scratch his neck and turn back to Gemma. "If it were up to him, I bet 'Chicken' and 'Park' would make it to the top of his list too." Leaning in, I place a soft kiss on Gemma's cheek. "You know what I think?" I murmur, my head resting on her shoulder.

"What's that?" she asks.

"I think, no matter what we name them, our kids are

going to be pretty darn lucky, because they're going to have us as parents, and that's a gift no name could ever top."

"Even if they're called Kale?"

I smile as contentment washes over me. "Yeah. Even if they're called Kale or Squeaky Toy."

51

GEMMA

*I*t's been years since I spent more than a few hours with my mother, and having her here, in this place that has become my sanctuary, was a little unsettling at first. Nevertheless, it was really nice to have dinner with her and Lori, and now that we've had some time to get used to each other again, it almost feels normal.

Lori squeezes my hand under the table and rises, citing an early morning, and I shoot her a smile. I know what she's doing; she's giving us space.

"The dishes can wait until morning," she says, pressing a kiss to my cheek. "Take all the time you need." With a final goodnight to Mom, she slips upstairs, leaving us alone in the warm cocoon of the kitchen. For a moment, we just look at each other, the silence stretching between us, heavy with the weight of all the years apart.

We move to the wicker chairs on the porch, the ones Lori and I have spent countless evenings in, sipping wine and watching the sun set over the hills. But tonight, the beauty of the scenery is lost on me, my focus entirely on my mother.

"You're lucky to have her," Mom says, her voice soft as she gazes out over the moonlit orchard. "Lori is sweet, considerate...everything you deserve."

I nod, a smile tugging at my lips. "I know. I thank my lucky stars every day."

Mom leans back in her chair, the wicker creaking under her weight. "She's nothing like those exes of yours. Remember Gina? Or that awful—"

"Mom," I interject gently. "I'd rather not dwell on the past. I'm trying to move forward."

She sighs, her hands twisting in her lap. "I know, honey. It's just...I have so many questions still. So much I don't understand."

I feel a pang of guilt. After a few visits early in my sentence, I'd asked Mom to stop coming to the prison. The hurt and confusion in her eyes each time, the strained conversations across the metal table, the impression she blamed me for her boyfriend's death...it was too much. I thought I was sparing us both.

"I'm sorry," I murmur. "I shouldn't have pushed you away like that."

Mom reaches over, her hand finding mine in the darkness. "I understand why you did." She hesitates. "Those years...what was it like for you? In there?"

I take a deep breath. Where do I even begin? How do I put into words the isolation, the fear, the crushing monotony interspersed with sudden bursts of violence?

"It was...hard," I start, my voice sounding small in the vast quietness. "Harder than I could have ever imagined. The first few weeks, I was in a constant state of terror. I didn't know the rules, the hierarchies. I felt claustrophobic. I didn't know who to trust. I didn't know how to behave."

Mom's fingers tighten around mine.

"But I learned quickly," I continue. "I kept my head down, did the chores I signed up for, tried to stay invisible. The days blurred together...wake up, count, meals, count, chores, count, sleep, repeat. I read a lot. Sometimes I even managed to finish the books before they got stolen by fellow inmates. I did courses, attended therapy sessions whenever they were offered. Anything to break the monotony. There were fights, threats, I got attacked a few times, and the transfer to Perryville was tough too. Even though I had more privileges and freedom there, I had to reestablish myself within a dangerous crowd, and it felt like my first few weeks behind bars all over again." I pause. "But the worst was the hatred from Randall's family when I was up for probation. They sent me letters, and maybe I shouldn't have read them, but I did." It's the first time I've said his name since I got convicted, and it feels dirty on my tongue. "And the way his sister looked at me during my probation hearing...I don't think I'll ever be able to delete that look from my memory."

"They didn't know him like you and I did."

"I know. But even if they did, they're still his family, and being hated is a horrible feeling. It poisons the mind and it will always stay with me."

Mom is quiet for a long moment and then, in a voice thick with tears, she says, "I'm so sorry, Gemma. I did this to you."

"No," I say firmly, shifting to face her fully. "Mom, no. We're not having this conversation again. The choices I made...those are on me."

"But if I hadn't stayed with him," she insists, a tear rolling down her cheek, "if I hadn't let it get to that point—"

"You were a victim," I cut in, my voice brooking no argument. "For years, I watched him whittle away at you, eroding your sense of self. He isolated you, made you dependent. I saw your bruises, and even though you denied it was him, I knew better." I clench my jaw. "I hated him so much. I fantasized about killing him, so I guess in a way, it was premeditated."

Mom sniffles, wiping at her face with her free hand. "I should have been stronger. For you, if not for myself."

"You broke your patterns and turned your life around," I say. "That takes incredible courage."

She looks at me then, really looks at me, her gaze searching mine. "I don't know how you can forgive me."

"There's nothing to forgive," I say simply. "You're my mother. I love you, and I know you love me. We've both been through hell, but we survived, and we're here, together. That's what matters."

A watery smile breaks across her face and she pulls me into a fierce hug, her thin arms stronger than they look. I hold her tightly, breathing in the familiar scent of her. It's the smell of my childhood, of the good moments snatched between the bad.

When we finally pull back, both our faces are damp. Mom reaches up, brushing a strand of hair from my forehead in a gesture so tender it makes my chest ache.

"Look at you," she murmurs, pride shining in her eyes. "My beautiful, brave girl. I always knew you were destined for more than the life I gave you."

I smile, leaning into her touch. "I didn't do it alone," I remind her. "But I'm happy now."

Mom sniffles again, but it's a happy sound this time. "I'm so proud of you, Gemma. So proud of the woman you've become. And I'm grateful, more than you know, that I get to be a part of your life again."

"Me too," I whisper. "I've missed you, Mom." In the

distance, an owl hoots, a low, mournful sound that echoes through the night.

"It's so peaceful here," Mom remarks, her gaze drifting over the shadow-dappled farm. "I can see why you fell in love with it."

"Not just the farm." I smile. "With Lori."

She squeezes my hand again, a silent affirmation. We sit like that for a while longer, hand in hand, watching as the moon makes its slow arc across the star-strewn sky. It's a moment of peace, of connection, that I know I'll treasure for years to come.

Finally, Mom yawns, breaking the spell. "I suppose we should head to bed. We've got a busy day tomorrow. I'm looking forward to help you out at the market and meet Lori's mother. It's exciting. It feels so official."

I chuckle. "Yeah. The moms meeting each other..." I get up and Mom follows me inside. "We figured as you were staying the weekend, we might as well invite her over too. I think you'll like her."

I bid Mom goodnight and make my way upstairs, a smile playing on my lips. The past may be complicated, but the present is beautiful, and I'm determined to cherish every moment of it.

52

LORI

*G*emma and her mother, Cynthia, climb out, their arms laden with empty crates from the morning's market.

"Hey there," I call, waving as I descend the porch steps. "How was the market?"

Gemma grins, her face flushed from the heat. "Great! We nearly sold out of everything."

"That's fantastic!" I take a crate from her, pressing a quick kiss to her cheek. "You two look like you could do with a cold drink."

"Yes, it got pretty warm out there." Cynthia smiles. "Gemma was in her element," she continues, her voice warm with pride. "She has a real knack for connecting with people."

"She does. She—" I look up when another car pulls up behind mine. "There's Mom." I head over to greet her, and she looks the same as always—neatly coiffed hair, understated jewelry, a hesitant smile on her face as she takes in her surroundings.

"Hi, honey," she says, pulling me into a hug. Over her

shoulder, I see Gemma and Cynthia watching, identical expressions of tentative welcome on their faces.

We've all been nervous about this meeting, this collision of past and present. For Mom, Rosefield Farm holds a tangle of difficult memories. She hasn't set foot here in decades, and on top of all that, she's meeting Gemma's mother for the first time.

"How was the drive?" I ask as we pull apart, studying her face for any signs of distress.

"Oh, fine," she says, waving a hand. "I remembered it well and I always did like a good country road." But I can see the tightness around her eyes, the way her gaze keeps flicking to the farmhouse.

"Mom," I say softly, taking her hand. "Are you okay?"

She takes a deep breath, squaring her shoulders. "I'm fine, Lori. Truly. It's just...it's been a long time."

I nod, giving her hand a squeeze. "I know. But I'm so glad you're here." I turn, gesturing to Gemma and Cynthia. "Come and meet Gemma's mom."

The introductions are made, hands shaken, small talk exchanged. I can feel the undercurrent of tension, but there's warmth too, a genuine desire to connect.

We head inside, and Mom pauses in the entryway, her gaze roaming over the space. I watch her closely, trying to gauge her reaction.

"You've done wonders with the place," she says. "It looks so different but still somehow the same."

"Gemma and I have been working hard." I slip an arm around my girlfriend's waist. "We've been updating things while trying to keep the essence of it."

Mom nods. "Well, you've certainly managed that." She moves farther into the room, her fingers trailing along the back of the couch, the mantelpiece. "Is this the same fire-place? The one we used to roast marshmallows in?"

"The very same," I confirm, grinning at the memory. "Do you remember the time Frank singed his eyebrows trying to get the perfect golden brown?"

Mom laughs, the sound bright and unexpected in the quiet room. "Oh, he was so vain about those eyebrows! Sulked for weeks until they grew back in."

Beside me, I feel Gemma relax slightly, a small chuckle escaping her as we settle into the living room with wine, cheese, and crackers. Mom asks about the farm, and Gemma and Cynthia's day at the market. She listens intently, laughing at their stories, but I can't miss the occasional hitch in her voice or the way her fingers worry at her necklace as she glances around, no doubt reliving the past.

Cynthia entertains us with tales from her days as a young switchboard operator. It's a far cry from the tense, tight-lipped expression she wore when she first arrived. As her story winds down, Mom sits back in her chair, twirling the wine around in her glass.

"Are you okay, Moya?"

"Yeah." Mom lets out a long sigh. "Have they told you about the history with the farm?"

"Yes," Cynthia admits.

"Then you know that Frank, my sister's husband, was Lori's father." Cynthia nods, and Mom clears her throat with a nervous flicker in her eyes. "There are so many memories here."

"Were you close to your sister?" Cynthia asks.

"Yes. We were all close," she says. "Maggie, Frank, and me. We were inseparable as kids, always getting into scrapes, driving our parents mad with worry. But in our teenage years, Frank and I developed feelings for each other. It was intense and confusing, and for a while, I thought we might end up together. But then I moved away to study, and we lost contact. I dated through college, and he moved on too. When I returned years later, he was with Maggie, and I was happy for them, truly. They were my best friends, and seeing them find joy in each other...how could I begrudge them that?"

"But the feelings never really went away," Cynthia concludes softly.

"No, they didn't, and that resulted in that one night of weakness and selfishness that destroyed everything." Mom shakes her head. "But all things considered...I can't say I wish I could make it undone, then I wouldn't have had Lori." She manages a smile as she turns to me. "And you're the best thing that ever happened to me."

"And I'm forever grateful to have you as a mother." I return her smile and gently rub her arm. "It's okay, Mom. I think it's time to let the past be the past."

"Yes," Cynthia agrees, her gaze flicking to Gemma. "Look where we are now. Look at the love in this room."

I take in the faces of these special women. Mom, who's always been my rock, even when her own world was crumbling. Cynthia, who's fought so hard to rebuild herself and her relationship with her daughter. And Gemma...my Gemma, who's walked through fire and come out the other side, scarred but unbroken.

"In fact," Cynthia continues, "I think we should toast to the present." She raises her glass. "To love, to family, and to new friendships. Thank you all so much for welcoming me into your world, and thank you for being so good to my daughter. It really does feel like a fresh start."

"To a fresh start," I repeat, raising my glass along with the others.

As we clink our glasses together, a sudden commotion from outside draws our attention. Lemon, who's been snoozing peacefully in his bed, jolts awake, runs out through the open door, and starts barking. Gemma and I exchange puzzled glances before I head over to investigate.

There, illuminated by the porch light, stands Joseph, looking slightly bewildered as Lemon yaps and growls at his feet, his tiny body quivering with the effort of his mighty barks.

"Hey, Joseph."

"Hey, Lori. I hope I'm not interrupting," he says, raising his voice over Lemon's yaps. He glances into the living room and waves at Gemma, Cynthia, and Mom. "I was just wondering if I could grab a few of those heirloom tomatoes you have growing out back? My sister is visiting tomorrow and I'm making her a tomato pie."

"Of course. But why don't you join us for a drink first? Or you're welcome to stay for dinner. We have family over, so Gemma's made more than enough." When Joseph hesitates, I press on, as I know he's just being polite. "We have a few lovely bottles of red. Come in."

Joseph grins as he glances down at Lemon again with a mix of amusement and confusion. "Uh, that depends. Is he going to let me past?" he jokes, stepping inside.

Lemon inches back but still stands at attention, his small body quivering while he lets out a string of high-pitched barks that sound more like squeaky toys than fierce warnings.

"Lemon, calm down," I say with a chuckle, gesturing for Joseph to follow me.

Joseph greets Gemma, Cynthia, and Mom with a sheepish grin on his weathered face. "Evenin', ladies." He taps his hat. "I might join you for a tipple, if that's okay?"

"Of course." Mom scoots over on the couch and Joseph takes a seat next to her. "What's gotten into Lemon?" she asks, amused as we watch the little dog's attempts to threaten him.

"It might be because I've never shown up at night before," Joseph muses, scratching his chin. "Poor little fella probably thinks I'm some kind of intruder."

Lemon, seemingly affronted by Joseph's nonchalance, redoubles his efforts, running in circles around his feet.

"Lemon, come here." I try to grab him, but he's too quick, darting out of reach and making Cynthia laugh.

Gemma crouches down, trying to coax our furry defender, but Lemon remains adamant, his bark only growing louder and higher in pitch.

As Lemon continues to bark and run circles around Joseph's feet, the old man suddenly leans down and scoops him up, placing him gently on his lap. Lemon's eyes go wide with surprise, his little legs still running in the air for a moment before he realizes he's been captured.

The room falls silent, everyone watching to see what Lemon will do next. He looks around, his head swiveling comically from side to side as he takes in his new vantage point. His gaze lands on Gemma, his tiny head immersed in mental calculations.

"Mum?" he seems to say, his eyes pleading. *"A little help here?"*

Gemma just grins, shaking her head. "Sorry, buddy. You got yourself into this mess. You can get yourself out."

Lemon's head swivels to me, his ears drooping pathetically. *"Other Mum? Please?"*

I hold up my hands, fighting back a laugh. "Don't look at me, little man. You're the one who wanted to play big bad guard dog."

Lemon's face falls, and for a moment, I think he might start barking again. But then, as if realizing the jig is up, he heaves a mighty sigh and flops down on Joseph's lap, his chin resting on his paws in a perfect picture of doggy defeat.

The room erupts into laughter, and even Lemon's tail gives a half-hearted wag, as if he's in on the joke.

"Well, I guess that's settled," Joseph says, scratching Lemon behind the ears. "I suppose it's on me. I was the one who told you to get a guard dog."

53

GEMMA

*I*t's been five months since I last saw Tonya, yet in some ways, it feels like no time has passed at all as I engulf her in another hug. She feels the same, sounds the same, and her smile is equally radiant, but her outfit is a far cry from the drab prison scrubs I'm used to seeing her in. She's dressed to the nines, her hair styled and topped off with a sparkly headband, her makeup flawless.

"Girl, look at you!" she says, holding me at arm's length. "Out here living the farm life. It's crazy."

I laugh and hand her a coffee. "Trust me, sometimes I still can't believe it myself."

Tonya grins. "Well, you look damn good. Freedom suits you."

"It suits you too," I say, taking in her outfit again. "You're putting my flour-dusted jeans to shame."

Tonya strikes a pose, one hand on her hip. "Hey, I've got to make up for lost time. You know how it is—when you're in there, you dream about all the things you're going to wear when you get out. I've got a closet full of outfits I've been dying to wear again."

"Well, you might want to lose the heels," I joke, sipping my coffee. "We're going to be on our feet all day, stirring pans and slicing fruit."

Tonya kicks off her stilettos without hesitation, padding over to the counter in her bare feet. "No problem. I'm ready to work. I was so glad when you called me. Honestly, I didn't think you would."

"I figured you might need some help. I know I did."

"Yeah." She shoots me a grateful smile. "The coffee shop could only offer me three days a week, and life is expensive. I want to get my own place, so I'm saving up for a deposit. My cousin doesn't mind me living with her, but it's a lot with three kids in a small apartment."

"I can imagine. But it's been good so far?" I ask.

"It's been great." Tonya beams. "It's not my first rodeo, but this time, I'm not falling back into old habits. I'm going to do it right."

"I'm proud of you. It's great that you found a job so fast." I narrow my eyes, looking her over. Now that we're out, it feels okay to ask the question. "What were you in for? Do you mind me asking?"

"Possession," she says. "I'm surprised you didn't ask me before you offered me the job. Didn't Miss Hawthorne want to know?"

"No. I trust you and Lori—you can call her Lori. Well, Lori trusts me, so it really wasn't an issue. I was just curious, is all."

"Thank you. That means a lot," Tonya says. "So to be entirely transparent, the first couple of times I got caught selling stolen goods. The last time I was holding onto a stash of weed for a friend and got busted. I'm not a user myself. I just wanted to make a little money on the side." She shrugs.

"Anyway, I'm steering clear of my old buddies now. No more shady business."

"Just coffee and jam," I joke. The possession charge doesn't surprise me. Tonya isn't a violent person, and she wasn't the thieving kind in prison, so I figured it would have to be something like that. "I'm scared to ask what you think of my coffee."

"Not bad for an amateur." Tonya takes a sip and winks. "Just kidding. After Perryville, even cheap instant tastes like heaven first thing in the morning."

"Are you enjoying the barista job?" I ask.

"Yeah. The gig is great. I mean, the early mornings are a bitch, but I kind of love the chaos of the morning rush. All those grumpy people in need of their caffeine fix, and I get to be their savior, you know?"

I chuckle, nodding. "I can just picture you, charming the pants off everyone with your witty repartee and killer latte art."

"You know it," Tonya says. "I'm the latte queen, the espresso empress, the cappuccino...captain? I don't know, I'm working on the title."

"Captain Cappuccino has a nice ring to it," I say, tapping my chin thoughtfully. "Or maybe the Macchiato Maestro?"

Tonya laughs, pointing a finger at me. "Ooh, I like that one. Makes me sound all fancy and shit." She leans against the kitchen counter and looks me up and down. "What about you? What were you in for?"

I anticipated the question, and I'm ready to be honest with her. The fact that so many people know now has been incredibly tough, but on the other hand, it's made it easier to talk about it.

"Wait, let me guess," she says, holding up a hand. "Fraudulent schemes?"

"No." I take a deep breath and meet her eyes. "Second-degree manslaughter."

I expect Tonya to be shocked, but instead, she laughs. "You're funny. Seriously, though. What did you do?"

"I'm not joking. Eight years ago, I killed my mother's abusive boyfriend in a blind rage."

Tonya's expression turns serious, and she stares at me for what seems like an eternity before she breaks the silence. "Oh."

"I just wanted you to know," I say. "You'll be working with me, after all. I'll tell you about it sometime."

"Okay. Wow. I didn't see that one coming."

I shrug. "If you're uncomfortable being around me now, I understand. Perhaps I should have told you before you came all the way out here."

"No, no. Not at all," she says, staring me over once more like she's still can't believe it. "I bet he deserved it."

"No one deserves that," I say. "I'll never make excuses for what I did."

Tonya tilts her head from side to side. "I beg to differ. In my opinion, some people do deserve what's coming to them." She gives me a sweet smile. "Look, I know you, and it doesn't change how I see you. It's just the last thing I expected."

I nod. "I've heard that a lot lately."

"Does Lori know?"

"Yes. Actually, Lori and I are together."

"What? As in together-together?" This seems to surprise Tonya even more than my conviction.

"Uh-huh." My mood lifts just at the thought of Lori, and I feel my lips pulling into a grin. "She's visiting her mom, but you'll meet her later. She's pretty amazing. And beautiful," I add. "And smart, kind, funny, and super cute."

Tonya's jaw drops. "Oh my God. Says the woman who had no interest in dating."

"I know. It was the last thing I expected to happen. I've been so incredibly lucky."

"I'm so happy for you. Come here." Tonya hugs me for the fifth time since she arrived. "So, is she the one?"

"Yes," I say without hesitation. "This is it. When you know, you know." Remembering we've got work to do, I grab two crates of peaches and two large chopping boards from the pantry. "And you? Are you dating?"

"No. I only have one goal in mind, and that's to get my own place."

"Says the woman who couldn't wait to find a man," I shoot back at her.

Tonya laughs. "You know me. All talk and no action."

"Did you at least get your fried chicken?"

"Oh yeah, I got plenty of that."

"Well, you'll have more because I have some marinating in the fridge. If you're up for it, we could all have dinner together later?" I hand her a knife.

"You didn't..." Tonya looks touched. "You're making me fried chicken?" When I nod, she lets out a little shriek and waves her knife around. "My prison bestie is making me fried chicken! I didn't think this day could get any better."

54

LORI

*G*emma and Tonya are already seated at the weathered wooden table as I step onto the porch with a pitcher of iced tea in hand.

I pause for a moment, taking in the scene. Tonya, with her sparkly headband, long, fake lashes and infectious grin, looks right at home here, and she's a far cry from the image I'd conjured in my mind—a wary and guarded ex-con. Instead, she radiates a joy and ease that's almost palpable.

"There she is!" Gemma calls out, spotting me. "The lady of the hour."

I roll my eyes good-naturedly, setting the pitcher down on the table. "Please, I just made the tea. You're the real star here with that fried chicken."

Tonya grins, her fork already poised over a golden-brown drumstick. "This is such a treat. I can't begin to tell you how nice it is to have dinner with you both. I expected to be in some kind of industrial kitchen all day, chopping fruit until my hands blistered, but this has been a great day." She turns to me and bats her lashes. "So, did you taste the jam? Am I officially hired?"

"Of course you're hired," I say with a chuckle. "I'm so glad you were able to help us out." I slide into the chair next to Gemma. Lemon, ever the opportunist, immediately hops up onto my lap, his nose twitching at the enticing scents. "So, you two were pretty close in there, huh?" I ask, scratching Lemon behind the ears. "Gemma's told me a bit, but I'd love to hear more about your time together."

Tonya and Gemma exchange a look, a silent conversation passing between them. There's a depth of understanding there, a shared history that I'll never fully understand.

"Well, your girl here was a real lifesaver," Tonya says, pointing her fork at Gemma. "You never know who you're going to share a bunk with, and I couldn't have had a better cellie."

"Same here," Gemma says. "At first, I was just grateful Tonya wasn't stealing from me or threatening to kill me in my sleep." She chuckles, but I have a feeling she's not joking. "But then, she also turned out to be a decent human being. I couldn't believe my luck."

"I remember this one time, only a few weeks after I first met Gemma," Tonya says. "I was in a bad way, struggling with some personal stuff, and I guess I wasn't hiding it well." She takes a sip of her iced tea, her gaze distant. "Gemma noticed one of the COs started giving me a hard time, singling me out. It was over something stupid. I was in possession of a shampoo that wasn't on the approved list, and I was this close," she holds up her thumb and forefinger a hairbreadth apart, "to losing it on her, doing something that would've got me thrown in solitary or worse." Tonya turns to Gemma, a soft smile on her face. "But then this one, she steps in, gets between me and the CO and takes the heat, even though she didn't have to. She could've just kept her head down, minded her own business. But that's not who she is."

"I just did what anyone would've done," Gemma says.

"No." Tonya slams her hand on the table. "You didn't. In there, most people look out for number one. They don't stick their neck out for someone else, especially someone they barely know. But you did. And that's when I knew I could trust you."

The emotion in Tonya's voice, the raw honesty of it, almost makes me choke up. "She's got a habit of doing that," I say softly, "being there for the people she cares about, no questions asked." I reach over, lacing my fingers with Gemma's, feeling the warmth and strength of her hand in mine.

Gemma squeezes my hand, a silent acknowledgment. "I remember this one night," she says, "I was having a rough time. It was one of those days when the weight of everything just hits you, you know? The time, the isolation, the regrets. I was lying in my bunk, trying so hard not to let anyone hear me crying."

Tonya nods. "We've all been there."

Gemma takes a deep breath, her fingers tightening around mine. "Tonya didn't say anything. She didn't try to get me to talk about it or tell me it was going to be okay. She just started humming."

I tilt my head, curious. "Humming?"

Tonya grins, a little sheepish. "It was a lullaby my grandma used to sing to me when I was little. Whenever I was upset or scared, she'd pull me into her lap and hum that tune until I fell asleep."

Gemma smiles. "She just kept humming, this gentle, comforting sound in the darkness. I knew she was doing it to calm me, and it made me feel less lonely, like I had someone by my side."

My heart clenches, a bittersweet mix of sorrow and gratitude. The image of Gemma, curled up in her bunk, trying to muffle her sobs, is almost too much to bear, and I feel a rush of affection for Tonya.

"It's the little things, you know?" Tonya says, her gaze distant. "Those small moments of connection. They make all the difference inside."

I nod, blinking back a sudden sting of tears. "I can't even imagine."

Gemma leans into me and smiles at Tonya. "We got each other through," she says. "Day by day."

As we dig into the meal and the stories continue to flow, I feel a deep sense of contentment settle over me. Through Tonya, I'm getting a little bit more insight into Gemma's life behind bars and what it was like for her. Through it all, I'm struck by the bond they've forged, a mutual understanding of what it's like to have your identity stripped away.

When the last of the chicken is polished off and the table cleared, Tonya leans back, patting her stomach with a contented sigh. "This was amazing. Thank you both so much. Not just for the fried chicken," she jokes. "For the job. I promise I won't let you down."

"If you ever want to pick up some extra hours, we could always use an extra set of hands in the orchard too," I say. "We have seasonal workers during harvest season. It's hard physical labor, especially in the summer months when it's hot, but the option is there." I shrug. "I work in the orchard two days a week myself, and I like it, but it's not for everyone."

Tonya's face lights up. "For real? That would be amazing!"

"Consider it a standing offer," I say with a smile. "God knows we need all the help we can get when those trees start dropping fruit faster than we can pick it."

"I'm in." Tonya checks her watch and sighs. "I should get going. I borrowed a friend's car and promised I'd bring it back tonight."

"Is it difficult for you to get here?" I ask.

"I can get a bus, but the nearest stop is a half-hour walk from here, and it was hot today." Tonya fans her face. "I miss the things I took for granted...a home, a car..." She smiles. "But I'll get there. I have a plan and I'm sticking with it." She gets up and squares her shoulders.

"Good for you," Gemma says. "In the meantime, I can pick you up from the bus stop in the mornings and drop you back home at night."

Tonya shakes her head. "You don't have to do that."

"No, I insist." Gemma gets up too.

"Yes," I agree. "And if Gemma can't make it for some reason, I'll pick you up. "We all help each other out around here, it's no bother." Rising to my feet, I'm taken aback when Tonya suddenly flings her arms around me.

"Thank you, Lori."

"You're welcome, but there's really no need to thank me." I groan as she tightens her grip. "Easy," I joke. "I think I ate my weight in fried chicken. I'm so full I can't breathe."

Gemma smirks. "Lightweight. Tonya and I used to dream about meals like this."

"Oh yeah?" I laugh as I step away from Tonya. "And what else made the cut, besides fried chicken?"

"Honestly? Anything that wasn't sloppy and served on a plastic tray," Tonya says, hugging Gemma goodbye. "Imagine a life without plates and metal cutlery. I don't think anyone can appreciate the simple things until they've actually lived without them."

"Fair enough," I concede. "Remind me never to complain about doing dishes again."

As we watch Tonya go, Gemma takes my hand.

"She's lovely," I say. "Do you really think she'll stay on?"

Gemma chuckles. "Yeah. I think we'll be seeing a lot of Tonya. She's got a way of making herself indispensable."

"Just like someone else I know," I tease, bumping my hip against hers. "So, Fried Chicken Fridays?"

Gemma turns to me and licks her lips as she looks me up and down. "I think I prefer 'Loving Lori' Fridays."

"Oh? I like the sound of that," I say playfully, arching a brow. "So what happens on Loving Lori Fridays?" I let out a shriek as she scoops me up and carries me inside.

Gemma finally sets me down in the bedroom, and her eyes sparkle with mischief as she tugs me close. "How about we start off with a massage?"

EPILOGUE
7 MONTHS LATER

*T*he dawn breaks soft and golden over Rosefield Farm as I sit on the porch, sipping my coffee while I breathe in the fresh air. In these moments before the day begins, I'm still filled with wonderment over the beauty of the sunrise.

Leaning back in the old wicker chair, my feet are resting on the new stool Lori and I picked out together. The porch is looking great. The once-peeling paint has been refreshed with a soft shade of blue, complementing the vibrant green of the potted plants that now line the railing. My gaze wonders over the trailing vines of the jasmine, their delicate white blossoms just beginning to unfurl in the morning light. We've poured care and love into every corner of this farmhouse, slowly bringing it back to its old glory, and it feels like home in every sense of the word.

There's a new sign above the door, proudly proclaiming "Rosefield Farm" in elegant, hand-painted script. For her, it's a homage to her roots. For me, it's the foundation of my future.

It's been a year since I first set foot on Rosefield Farm,

my meager possessions in a single duffel. I remember that day with startling clarity. The first glimpse of Lori, silhouetted against the weathered wood of the farmhouse porch, her dimpled smile, warm and wide.

So much has changed since then. The farm has flourished under our combined care, and the orchards are bursting with life. But more than that, I have changed and healed in ways I never thought possible. I am not the same woman who arrived here a year ago, a shadow of my former self. The scars remain, but I wear them as badges of survival rather than marks of shame. In the shelter of these trees, in the steadiness of Lori's love, I have found a space to unfurl and discover a strength I never knew I possessed.

The birdsong commences. I can feel it coming before it starts, as if all the desert's flying creatures take one deep breath before waking the world. It always starts with a single trilling note, clear and pure, cutting through the early hush like a beam of sonic light. Then, as if on cue, a chorus of other voices joins in, each distinct yet harmonizing with the others.

I can tell them apart now. There's the melody of a curve-billed thrasher, and the song of a cactus wren soon joins in, its raspy, churring vocalizations a perfect counterpoint to the thrasher's more lilting tones. A Gambel's quail adds its unique contribution, its call a series of emphatic, nasal notes that almost sound like "Chi-CA-go, Chi-CA-go," and the gentle cooing of a white-winged dove weaves through the ensemble.

Together, they create a sound that is quintessentially Arizonan—a reflection of the beauty and resilient spirit of the Sonoran Desert. In their songs, I hear echoes of my own journey—the need to adapt, to find my voice, to carve out a place of belonging in a challenging world.

I smile, not turning, as Lori's footsteps approach. A moment later, her arms slip around my shoulders, her chin coming to rest on the crown of my head. I close my eyes and breathe in her scent, letting her presence, envelop me.

"Good morning," she murmurs, her breath tickling my ear.

"Good morning." I turn my head to capture her lips in a gentle kiss. Even now, after a year of such kisses, each and every one still feels like a gift.

"Do you know what day it is?" she asks, moving around me to sit on my lap.

"I do." I pull her close and press a kiss to her temple.

"Well, then. Happy freedom anniversary. I can't believe it's been a year already. It feels like just yesterday that I was pacing this porch, waiting for Miranda to arrive with you. I was so nervous."

I chuckle, remembering my own nerves, the way my stomach churned as the car wound its way up the long drive. "I was terrified," I confess. "I had no idea of all the good things waiting for me."

Lori cups my face and strokes her thumb over my cheek. "Do you want to celebrate this special day?"

"I do, but I'm on jam-making duty, so Tonya will be here in a few hours."

"Oh, of course," she says. "Maybe we could celebrate together later? With Tonya, Charlotte, and Miranda, if they're free?"

"I'd like that." A grin spreads across my face. "By the way, I think Tonya's got the hots for the new guy in the orchard. What's his name again?"

"You mean Peter?" Lori laughs. "That's so cute."

"Uh-huh. And he's single." I laugh along as I picture Tonya's attempts at flirting. She's certainly not the charmer she made herself out to be in prison. Instead, she's rather shy and even clumsy around men, and she has no idea what to do with herself when they compliment her. Since she joined us, Tonya's become an indispensable part of the farm, her quick wit and infectious laughter brightening even the longest days. She helps me at the market too, and although some locals joke and call us "the inmates" behind our backs, we know it's not malicious. There are still whispers, still sideways glances and awkward pauses. But it's progress, a shift in the right direction, and I can honestly say that I feel accepted in our little community of fellow farmers and market people. I take on electrical jobs whenever people ask me, but I'm more invested in the farm and love my days in the orchard with Lori and running the market stall with Tonya.

"Let's invite Peter too," Lori continues. "And our moms?"

"Sure." I raise a brow and shoot her an amused smile. "And the rest of Sedona?"

She chuckles. "Why not? And Joseph, Tom, Betty, and the dogs. Lemon would love that. We could make it easy for ourselves and light up the grill. Ask everyone to bring a bottle and I'll get groceries and do the prep while you and Tonya make jam."

"Good luck using the kitchen while Tonya's working there. She's even messier than you," I joke. Lori's so sweet. She really would have the whole town over if it would make me happy. I look at her, at the excitement dancing in her eyes, and I feel my heart swell. The idea of a big gathering, of celebrating this milestone with all the people who have become so integral to our lives...it's perfect. "Let's do it," I say. "Let's see who can make it."

The hummingbird, my tiny morning companion, hovers near the railing, then lands on the beam.

"I think it likes watching us," Lori says, lowering her voice to a whisper. "It's fascinating, right? It just sits there and stares."

"That's because you're gorgeous. Who wouldn't stare at you?"

"Oh, you charmer." Lori grins and rolls her eyes.

"I mean it," I say, drinking her in. She's wearing her favorite oversize T-shirt, a soft gray one with a faded logo from a bar in town. It's the shirt she always reaches for on lazy mornings like this. The collar is slightly stretched, revealing a peek of the tiny freckles that dust her sun-kissed skin. Her hair is a lovely mess of tangled waves, evidence of a night spent dreaming in my arms.

As she flashes me a sleepy smile, I notice a smudge of toothpaste at the corner of her mouth, a charmingly imperfect detail that makes me melt with affection. My gaze travels down to the bruise on her upper arm, a souvenir from yesterday's adventures in the orchard, and to the faint scratches on her hands from tending to our rose bushes.

With her sleep-mussed hair and her T-shirt riding up, she looks breathtakingly beautiful. Not the polished, glossy beauty I imagine from her lawyer days, but a raw, authentic kind of beauty.

I lean in, brushing a soft kiss against the corner of her mouth, tasting the faint mint of her toothpaste, and when I turn my attention back to the hummingbird, it's tilting its head, studying us like a little voyeur.

I've come to look forward to its visits, to the way it hovers expectantly, as if waiting for us to notice it. Lori thinks of it as our lucky charm.

Lemon pads onto the porch, and the hummingbird lifts off again, its wings a blur of motion. It hovers for a beat, then zips away into the orchard where it darts from blossom to blossom.

"Hello, handsome," I say, turning to Lemon.

He blinks his sleepy eyes against the bright light and lets out a huge yawn, his little pink tongue curling. He loves to sleep in, often snuggling under the covers long after Lori and I have started our day, but he also hates to miss out on any action.

Lori lets out a dramatic sigh and presses a hand to her heart. "Could you be any more adorable? Do you even know how perfect you are?"

"Oh, I think he knows. Just look at him. A microbundle of pure perfection."

With a leisurely stretch, Lemon ambles over to us, his tail wagging lazily. Lori, who's still perched on my lap, her arm draped comfortably around my shoulders, reaches out to scoop him up. He settles into her lap with a contented sigh, his head resting on his paws. I wrap my arms around both of them and feel so much love I'm about to burst.

One day, if we're so lucky, there might be four of us. When we're ready to take the next step and become parents. But for now, life is blissful and I wouldn't want it any other way.

I am not my past. I am not my worst mistake. The more I say it, the more I start to believe it. *I deserve this.*

AFTERWORD

I hope you've loved reading Songbirds of Sedona as much as I've loved writing it. If you've enjoyed this book, would you consider rating it and reviewing it? Reviews are very important to authors and I'd be really grateful!

ACKNOWLEDGMENTS

This book would not have been possible without the openness and courage of the individuals who are currently or formerly incarcerated who so generously shared their stories and experiences with me. I am deeply grateful for your willingness to speak about what are often painful memories and challenging circumstances. Your insights illuminated the harsh realities of life behind bars and the daunting obstacles faced by those re-entering society.

While you remain unnamed to protect your privacy, please know that you are the beating heart of this novel. Thank you for trusting me with your truths.

ABOUT THE AUTHOR

Lise Gold is an author of lesbian romance. Her romantic attitude, enthusiasm for travel and love for feel good stories form the heartland of her writing. Born in London to a Norwegian mother and English father, and growing up between the UK, Norway, Zambia and the Netherlands, she feels at home pretty much everywhere and has an unending curiosity for new destinations. She goes by 'write what you know' and is often found in exotic locations doing research or getting inspired for her next novel.

Working as a designer for fifteen years and singing semi-professionally, Lise has always been a creative at heart. Her novels are the result of a quest for a new passion after resigning from her design job in 2018.

When not writing from her kitchen table, Lise can be found cooking, at the gym or singing her heart out some-where, preferably country or blues. She lives in London with her dogs El Comandante and Bubba.

Sign up to her newsletter: www.lisegold.com

ALSO BY LISE GOLD

Chance Encounters

Under the pen name Madeleine Taylor

The Good Girl

Online

Masquerade

Santa's Favorite

Spanish translations by Rocío T. Fernández

Verano Francés

Vivir

Nada Más Que Azul

Luciérnagas

Solo Para Socios

Hindi translations

Zindagi

Printed in Great Britain
by Amazon

45446276R00205